Capernaum
City of Miracles

by

Thelma Sparks

Published by Kindle Direct Publishing

Cover Design by Megan Ginn
                    Sacred Studios

Copyright © 2021 by Thelma Sparks

Thelma Sparks has asserted her right under the Copyright, Design and
Patents Act, 1988, to be identified as the author of this work.

All Scripture quotations, unless otherwise indicated, are taken from the
Holy Bible, New International Version. Copyright © 1973, 1978, 1984
by International Bible Society, 1980 Edition. Used by permission of
Hodder & Stoughton Ltd. All rights reserved.

ISBN: 9798767346356

First Edition, Revision B. First Printed in England July, 2021.

To Nadya
Who never gave up hope

Acknowledgements

My grateful thanks go first of all to my husband Keith who has showed incredible patience over the many years of my writing. Thank you darling.

Nadya, the best of all friends has unceasingly encouraged me. Capernaum would be in a dusty drawer if it weren't for her. It would simply never have happened without her!

I am grateful to Kerstin who believed I could write and bought me my first computer.

Thanks also to Miriam Westendarp and Richard Hatton, both proof readers par excellence. (Did I spell that right?)

Alan Osborn, and my son Neal, both true answers to my prayers, have taken this work from a manuscript to a printed reality. It would never have happened without them either. Thanks guys!

My grateful thanks also to Jemma Evans for realizing my vague ideas and creating an outstanding painting and to Megan Ginn who turned that painting into a great book cover.

And last, but by no means least, those who have read, and constructively criticized and helped and prayed.

All of you are shareholders in this book.

I am grateful for every one of you.

Thank you!

Endorsement

It is truly my privilege to write this endorsement for Thelma's new book and to testify she is a gifted story teller.

Thelma has a wonderful grasp and understanding of the Bible and knows its Author intimately. In our church community she is our respected, prophetic friend. We are extremely blessed by her wisdom and intellect, which so often bring the prophetic insight that is required for a given situation.

I am personally grateful for her friendship, and her retentive memory that holds on to the details found in life's stories. Her dedication and love towards God have been my inspiration to seek first His kingdom.

Thelma uses all her giftings to make the context and characters of this engaging story come alive. Capernaum – City of Miracles is an absorbing and affecting fictional retelling of life in Capernaum and the extraordinary events that take place when Jesus visits the city.

I stepped into Jesus' world and fell in love with Him all over again.

This book is an absolute treat. Be blessed.

Nadya Dyett. Pastor, The Ark Community Church.

Prologue

Jacob turned a corner and found himself in the last place on earth he wanted to be. There before him was a group of men with their backs toward him; they parted briefly and in the center he saw the Rabbi who was busy turning Capernaum upside down.

'Jesus!' he muttered angrily and turned around, intending to escape the way he had come, but he had reckoned without the Rabbi's inexplicable popularity.

A whole mass of people had come up behind him into the square and pushing him forward they carried Jacob right to the front of the crowd that was forming.

Accepting the inevitable, he looked on cynically, waiting to see what amazing thing the Rabbi would pretend to do. His belligerent face caught Jesus' eye and he smiled at Jacob as though he knew him. Jacob frowned and wondered if they had met before. Every time the name Jesus was mentioned some tiny shred of memory stirred in him, but he had never bothered to tease it out. He tried not to think about the past these days. It was all too painful.

There was a sudden commotion on the right side of the square and then surprised murmuring as the crowd parted and the people drew back. Through the midst of them walked the last person Jacob expected to see. It was the Roman centurion, the man charged with keeping order in their tiny town on the northern edge of the Sea of Galilee.

This was an unusual Roman. Even the local elders appreciated his sympathetic approach to their faith, and it was rumoured he had contributed money to the repair of the synagogue. Jacob couldn't understand why. The population all hated the invading Romans, so what was it that motivated this man who had authority and power to befriend those who resented his presence? The silence in the square told its own story. No matter how generous he was, the centurion wasn't welcome here.

Jacob looked over at Jesus to see how he was responding to the sudden appearance of this despicable gentile. The centurion stopped some feet away from the Rabbi and the two men looked with interest into each other's faces. Jacob decided he hated them both equally, the Rabbi who gave false hope, pretending he could heal the sick, and the conquering soldier, imposing his hated empire's evil rule. An ugly look of disgust covered Jacob's once handsome face. He desired above all things to get away from both of them.

After a few moments the centurion spoke.

'Lord,' he said, 'my servant lies at home paralyzed and in terrible suffering.'

That caught everyone's attention, for no one had expected him to come and ask Jesus for a miracle and certainly not for a servant. Was he a Roman servant, or a Jewish servant, and why should the centurion care in any case? A servant was simply a servant, of almost no value at all, certainly not to a hardened soldier.

Jacob watched Jesus closely. He had lots of experience of the shifty look that came upon the faces of those who claimed they could cure, but who, in reality, could achieve nothing. The Rabbi was caught, whatever happened. Either he had to produce a miracle, which was impossible, or face the anger of a disappointed centurion. He expected Jesus to show fear, or to be unable to meet the centurion's gaze, but to his surprise Jesus simply nodded his head.

'I will go and heal him,' he said, almost as though it were the simplest thing in the world to do.

The crowd drew in a sharp breath. No Rabbi would go into a gentile's home! It was instant defilement! And the centurion himself seemed to understand that cultural impossibility.

'Lord,' he said, 'I do not deserve to have you come under my roof. But just say the word, and my servant will be healed. For I myself am a man under authority, with soldiers under me. I tell this one, "Go," and he goes; and that one, "Come," and he comes. I say to my servant, "Do this," and he does it.'

Jacob wasn't sure he understood exactly what this Roman was saying. He was a man under authority, and therefore he had authority. What had that got to do with his servant being healed by Jesus just speaking a word? It made no sense to him. But even if Jacob didn't fully comprehend, it seemed Jesus did.

A look of astonishment came upon the Rabbi's face and he turned to his small band of followers and said,

'I tell you the truth, I have not found anyone in Israel with such great faith. I say to you that many will come from the east and the west and will take their places at the feast with Abraham, Isaac and Jacob in the kingdom of heaven...'

Jacob couldn't bear to hear any more. How right he had been to dismiss this Rabbi from the start. Many will come from the east and the west - that meant more gentiles, didn't it? Wasn't it bad enough that Israel had been invaded by these idolatrous Romans? Were they to share their exclusive relationship with God with other appalling nations who had no morals?

He turned his back on Jesus and pushed through the crowd just as the Rabbi said to the centurion,

'Go! It will be done just as you believed it would.'

'Hah!' said Jacob under his breath. 'That servant won't be healed and anyone who thinks he will is a gullible idiot!'

Once he was out of the crowd he sat down on a wall and sank his head into his hands. At home his darling wife Rebekah was slowly fading away before his eyes. For years now she had been afflicted with an issue of blood. He had spent every penny they had on seeking a cure, but no one could help her. Now, with his business ruined, and all his hopes and dreams burnt to ashes, he could only stand by and watch as his wife's life haemorrhaged away. There was no hope, and all the doctor's failures had made his heart as hard as stone. Rebekah would die, perhaps soon, and there was no alternative but to accept that dreadful fact and, in the meantime love her and the children with everything he had.

That momentary encounter with Jesus and the centurion had stirred something deep inside him, some untapped pool of molten anger. How dare the centurion pretend to be a good man, when everything he stood for was vicious and vile? Jacob felt only untold hatred for everything the centurion stood for. And then there was Jesus, sweet, charming Jesus, offering healing when the truth was it was all a mirage; a cruel, illusory hope! He found he wanted to track Jesus down, corner him in some dark, deserted place and violently pour out on him all the years of pain, and the fearsome fury he felt that Rebekah never got any better. Anger at his own helplessness burned like fire at the very core of his being.

He staggered to his feet every shred of self-control swept away in a sudden surge of violent emotion. He hardly knew where he was. Eventually he stumbled into a deserted place behind a wall that ran alongside the road, and in his grief, he hit the wall again and again until his hands were bruised and bloodied. He didn't feel the pain.

At last, he fell exhausted onto the filthy ground, welcoming the darkness as he slipped into unconsciousness. But there was no peace for him even there. He moved convulsively as a vision of raging flames began to engulf him, then to his amazement Jesus appeared, reaching out a hand to rescue him.

The roar of the flames became so loud he was unaware of the conversation of the two men who stopped on the other side of the wall close to where he lay.

The first man spoke with great excitement in his voice.

'No really, it's a fact! The centurion's servant was healed, absolutely healed, at exactly the moment Jesus said he would be.'

The second man was obviously unconvinced.

'How do you know? I don't believe it!' he said.

'Well, because I was there.' The first man continued firmly. 'I just had to see what would happen, so when the centurion left Jesus and went striding back to his house, I went along. At a distance of course. It was much further than I thought and he was hard to keep up with, so when I got to his house he had already gone inside, but a whole crowd of his servants were standing in the road, all talking in excited voices. They were saying, "He's healed; he's up and about; it's a miracle," that kind of thing; and then this man came out into the sunshine, and they all gathered round him. One big guy started clapping him on the back and then suddenly stopped with this ludicrous look on his face, as though he had just done completely the wrong thing, but the man only laughed and gave a little jump for joy. He was so pale and thin you could see he had been terribly ill, but he just kept laughing and rejoicing and turning his face up to the sun.

Then the centurion appeared in the doorway, and he saw a group of us Jews standing watching and he said in a loud voice,

"He was healed at the very hour when Jesus promised he would be."

Everyone shouted for joy, and I did too.'

The speaker stopped for a moment, overcome by the wonder of what he had just seen. 'It was amazing.' he said, and he drew in a deep breath.

'I still think it's pretty hard to believe.' The second man's voice was full of scepticism.

'Well, I believe it.' The first man was obviously offended by his friend's lack of faith. 'You can think what you like,' he said in a louder tone, 'but I'm following Jesus,' and with that he strode off in a huff.

Somehow his last statement entered Jacob's troubled thoughts.

"I'm following Jesus." The words made their way into the experience that filled his mind, and almost despite himself he put out a bloodied hand to the elusively familiar figure of Jesus, just out of reach.

'Jacob! Jacob!' a voice called urgently.

I wonder how he knows my name, he thought, and slowly he opened his eyes, fully expecting to see Jesus bending over him. But it wasn't Jesus, it was his father Benjamin, who was placing a work-hardened palm on his forehead.

Jacob made an effort to sit up, but moaned in pain as he tried to use his hands.

Benjamin stared at them in disbelief.

'What happened to your hands?' he said.

Jacob didn't answer. The heat of the flames and the image of Jesus were slow to fade from his brain. Benjamin was not renowned for his sensitivity, but even he knew this was no time for questions.

'I will take you home,' he said, and before Jacob could pull himself together enough to protest, Benjamin picked him up like a sack of grain and carried him to his mother.

Benjamin was in shock, yet despite the fact he never found out the full details, he guessed what had happened. He was determined he and his wife Leah would keep this to themselves. Jacob's wife Rebekah must never know. They would make up some plausible story before they sent him home. An accident with a cart perhaps! Anything to keep hidden the unbearable truth that Jacob's desperation had boiled over at last.

Benjamin staggered into his house and tenderly laid Jacob down. Leah at once began to wash his wounds, speaking softly to him as she had when he was a boy, but Benjamin could only sit motionless in a chair. Suddenly, all the years of Jacob's life rushed back to him; the curious child; the gifted young man, all that potential for greatness. Broken-hearted he looked over at Jacob, a man as battered as his hands, and great sorrow gripped him.

What had become of his darling son?

Part One

Jacob

Jacob inherited his broad shoulders from his father, his long legs and tender heart from his mother, but his insatiable curiosity about God? No one could work out where that came from.

'It is a blessing,' his mother Leah declared, running her hand over her son's unruly curls. His father Benjamin, a practical man, wasn't quite so sure.

Benjamin was a prosperous merchant in Capernaum, a town built right on the shore of the Sea of Galilee. He and Leah already had two boys when Jacob was born, but this third son was special to his mother, though she could never have explained why. Perhaps it was because even when he was a toddler Leah knew there was something different about Jacob.

Every Sabbath, the family made their way through the town to the synagogue. The children were far too young to accompany their father into the men's part of the building, so Leah would usher them up the stairs into the women's gallery. The older boys would quickly become bored and restless, but not Jacob. Usually he was a lively child, never quiet for a moment, but inside the synagogue a complete change would come over him. He would sit very still on his mother's lap; his huge eyes round with wonder, fascinated by everything.

As he grew older, it was Jacob who hurried the family down the street on the Sabbath, determined they shouldn't be late. He loved this special day because going to synagogue awakened something within him: something too deep to explain. As soon as he went through the door a sense of awe came over him, as though the very air in the sacred building was heavier than it was outside, and he would gaze up above his head, half expecting to catch a glimpse of something in the extraordinary atmosphere. Of course, there was never anything there, just the bright rays of the sun pouring in the windows, lighting up the dust hanging lazily in the air. Often he sighed, for he knew something wonderful was all around him, even if he couldn't see it.

Leah would watch her son turn his face upwards and would follow his gaze, wondering what it was that captured his attention. Sometimes their eyes would meet and he would give her a radiant smile, as though they shared some special joy. To her it was a mystery, but to Jacob it was as natural as breathing to experience that indefinable sense of presence. He felt sure it must be God and everyone else could feel it too, especially his father. Jacob loved his father.

Every week he would hold onto the wooden railings of the gallery and pressing his face against them, peer down, hoping to catch a glimpse of Benjamin as he sat with the other men of the town. His favourite part was when they began to sing. Their deep voices would boom out, filling the whole building. The sound reverberated through his thin body, catching at his emotions.

Countless times, as he watched them solemnly going through the rituals, he wanted to ask if they felt it too; this strange warmth that touched him whenever he thought about God. But something held him back. He listened as his father and the other men discussed the scriptures and the Rabbi's teaching, noticing no one ever talked about how they felt. In his young mind he decided it must be a private thing; something you kept to yourself. He never spoke of it even to his mother, but he hugged the feeling to himself like his own special treasure.

From his earliest days Jacob possessed a deep longing he never spoke of, a desire to know God that seemed bigger than he was himself. Everyone came to accept his love of the synagogue, although no-one understood it. The other worshippers around him were oblivious to this small child's heart beating loudly with the wonder of God.

Benjamin was a good father, very proud of his three fine boys, and his adorable little girls. He taught the boys at home, instructing them in the scriptures, how to write, and most importantly, how to count. He knew it was an essential skill for budding businessmen.

The first two boys were easy to teach, but Jacob was a different matter. He wasn't slow in his studies, in fact he was quick-witted and clever, but he had the habit of asking difficult questions about God that made Benjamin scratch his head. Once the lad began to read the scriptures for himself it became ten times worse, plunging Benjamin into the deep waters of theology, where he was hopelessly out of his depth. Jacob asked such odd things, fixing his trusting eyes on Benjamin, obviously expecting his father to have all the answers. The poor man did his best but he was a merchant, not a scholar, and he sighed with relief when the time came for Jacob to go to school in the synagogue. Samuel, the Rabbi, was a man of deep learning and Jacob would be much better off being taught by him. Let the synagogue ruler deal with his inquisitive son!

Jacob skipped as he walked down the road with his brothers on his first day of school. He had been up an hour earlier than either of them, brushing his hair until it lay unnaturally flat on the top of his head. He wanted everything to be perfect. He loved going to synagogue on the Sabbath and now he was going to be taught there! He could hardly believe it. His heart missed a beat as he thought about it. He looked quickly at his two brothers. Were they excited too? They didn't look it, and he frowned at their glum expressions. Weren't they hungry to know God like he was? It seemed to him there was so much to learn. He looked up as the building towered above him and felt a shiver go down his back.

Synagogue! His favourite place in all the world.

In school he sat next to Jairus who was older but considerably shorter, with a serious face that lit up when he smiled. They liked each other at once, although they couldn't have been more different, the contrast between them so great others were surprised at how quickly they became friends.

Jairus was slow and steady, thinking deeply, saying little, while Jacob's mind flew from one thing to another so fast it was hard for others to keep up. Like most young boys they were uncritical of each other, laughing and arguing by turns, with Jacob talking, always talking.

Jacob loved the stories of the heroes in the scriptures, and he learnt them all by heart. He read avidly of Abraham, Isaac and Jacob, of Moses in Egypt and Joshua the son of Nun; these incredible men of God fired his imagination.

Jairus on the other hand was a solid, diligent pupil. He applied himself to every class with an unshakeable sense of duty, but his real passion was studying the law. Jacob watched in amazement as Jairus pored endlessly over every detail, memorising even the smallest thing. He couldn't understand it.

One day they strolled down to the lake, discussing the things they had been learning in class. Jacob was trying to find out why Jairus loved the law so devotedly.

'You'll be a Rabbi one day,' he teased, 'maybe even synagogue ruler'.

He saw the sudden flush on Jairus's cheeks and realised he had discovered his friend's secret ambition. He sensed Jairus's embarrassment and they walked on in silence for a while, until at last Jacob asked,

'Do you really find the law interesting - really?' It was a complete mystery to him.

'Yes,' said Jairus.

'Why?'

Jairus tried to explain it, as he had several times before.

'The law is the way we ensure we are pleasing God,' he said patiently. 'If we keep all the different aspects of the law perfectly, then God is satisfied.'

Jacob frowned. 'Yes, yes,' he said, 'of course I know all about that, and I know it's important to keep the law, but you must admit it's incredibly hard to keep it perfectly. Isn't it? Why do you suppose God made it so difficult? There must be more to it than that.'

'More to what?' asked Jairus, picking up a stone and skimming it across the water.

'Oh, I don't know; more to pleasing God. Look at all the great men in the Scriptures. Wouldn't you love to have met some of them? Or even just one of them?'

He sat down on a rock, gazing out abstractedly over the lake.

'What made them great, do you think?'

'Obedience,' said Jairus firmly, skimming another stone.

'No, no, it can't be that,' said Jacob looking up at him. 'Almost all of them had times when they weren't obedient, like Moses striking the rock when he shouldn't have. It wasn't their obedience that makes them stand out, but their relationship with God.'

Jairus sighed. 'You're not talking about that again, are you?'

'But it's really interesting Jairus, much more interesting than studying the law! They all had an encounter with God. Every experience was different of course, but they all spoke to God didn't they, and they all knew His voice and felt His presence. That must have been amazing!'

Jairus was only half listening. Although he liked Jacob, he still found him a bit strange. There were the questions he was always asking in class for instance, and then there was this conversation. How many times had they had this conversation? He had lost count, but Jacob never grew bored of it. Jairus thought it a waste of time. He looked around, wondering if they might have a chance to go fishing. He liked fishing.

Jacob was still talking.

'Abraham came to this land because God spoke to him; Jacob dreamed of the ladder into heaven; Moses saw the burning bush, and he watched God write the ten commandments. Just think what that must have been like!'

Jairus fixed his attention back on his friend and said in a very grown-up voice. 'It is sacrilegious to think about such things. You should show more reverence for the scriptures Jacob.'

Jacob snorted and gave him a really hard shove. They wrestled together on the shore, each trying to push the other's feet into the water.

'Do you think it felt like this when Jacob was wrestling with God?' Jacob asked, as they used their weight against each other.

'How would I know?' panted Jairus, and he took a step back.

'You're impossible,' he said, 'you never think about anything else.'

'But they were so amazing,' protested Jacob. 'Think about Samuel. He met God when he was just a child, and what about David, he worshipped God passionately, with dancing and singing. It can't be irreverent to think about that!'

'All I know,' said Jairus turning back towards the town, 'is they were special. God doesn't do those things today, does he?' He looked across at his friend.

'Do you know anybody who has heard God speak?' he asked.

'No,' replied Jacob sadly.

'Well until you do, I'm going to stick with the law. It's what serving God is all about. Ask anyone!'

The next day it was particularly hot in class and the boys were all struggling to concentrate as Rabbi Samuel droned on and on at the front. Everyone, that is, except Jacob. He was waiting for an opportunity to ask a question. He had gone to bed thinking about Jairus's conviction that the great men of the Bible were special, and had woken up determined to ask the Rabbi about it.

Samuel found Jacob's curiosity hard to deal with. The young boy would squirm in his seat, obviously consumed with a thought he could hardly contain, and then he would ask some challenging question that left his teacher speechless. Jacob wasn't being deliberately difficult, but he often confused Samuel, who was an old man and not much given to quick thinking. The Rabbi had never been asked such things before and he had no idea what to say. Jacob was very respectful, but stubbornly insistent. It seemed he had to have answers. Samuel began to dread the look of sparkling interest Jacob turned on him in the lessons and he wondered where these thoughts were coming from. Benjamin certainly wasn't such a deep thinker. What made his son preoccupied with God?

Samuel put down his scroll, and looked out over the class.

'Any questions?' he asked, in the manner of all teachers.

'Did God only speak to special people?' Jacob asked at once.

Jairus looked up and sighed. Jacob's constant questioning was like a piece of gravel in his sandal, a small matter perhaps, but consistently annoying.

Samuel sat and thought about this latest question. It was certainly interesting. Should he answer 'Yes' or 'No'? Obviously, the great men of the past were special, that went without saying, but had they started off that way? He found he wasn't sure. One thing he knew for certain was you couldn't fob Jacob off with a vague answer; another child perhaps, but not Jacob. He took one look at the boy's eager face and his heart sank. It was obvious the next question was already waiting, and he hadn't decided how to answer this one yet! As he struggled to frame his reply, he found Jacob's mind had already moved on.

'If they were special, then what made them special? Weren't they just shepherds and nomads and farmers?'

Samuel opened his mouth to reply, but Jacob hardly seemed to draw breath.

'Did they have faults? Well, they can't have been perfect, at least I don't think so, but if they weren't perfect then why did God choose them?'

On and on he went, in an endless stream, leaving Samuel exhausted. It was one of many days when the Rabbi felt his age.

Gradually Jacob grew dissatisfied with the answers his teacher gave him. After a while, he learnt to hold his tongue and stop asking questions in class, because they only seemed to cause problems. He wished it was as easy to make them stop going around inside his head, but they were always there, worrying at him.

Where was the God he read about in the scriptures? Why did no one ever speak about knowing God themselves? In the synagogue he was taught about a God who acted in the past, who must be honoured and respected and whose laws had to be kept exactly. But he knew there must be more than that. There just had to be more. Why were there no stories of his day; no one who talked about an intimate relationship with God; no one who claimed to speak for God as the prophets had done? He wanted God to be part of his life; a personal God who would speak to him.

Jairus longed to be synagogue ruler and he was working hard towards that end. Jacob's ambition remained locked in his heart, and he had no idea how to achieve it, or even express it. How do you get to know God, he wondered? Everyone would say it was outrageous even to think of such a thing. They all agreed with Jairus and stuck rigidly to the law. Why couldn't he do the same? Jacob bit his lip and became a model student, but he thought about it constantly. It never went away.

There was one place where Jacob could always forget his troubles: the lake. It wasn't that his preoccupation with God and the questions that surrounded him faded from his mind. It was more that down there, by the water, he could relax and simply be himself. No one was there who found his conversation strange or annoying. Often, he went alone, avoiding even Jairus's company. He loved people, but he also loved the solitude by the water. He found the fresh air exhilarating and at the same time the silence seemed to calm him down. An enigma as always.

He got up early one morning and slipping out of the house ran down the path towards the lake. His big feet sent the gravel flying and his arms flapped at his sides. He could hardly contain his excitement, though he had no clue why he was feeling this was his lucky day. Somehow, he just knew it!

When he got down to the beach he began to search along the shoreline. There had been a storm the night before and he wondered what he might pick up amongst the flotsam and jetsam. It was amazing the things he had found in the past, and despite the fact his brothers laughed and said it was all rubbish, he kept these precious things in his bedroom. He called them his lake treasures.

His head was down as he focused on the pebbly beach, turning the stones with the toe of his sandal. He looked up as the smell of rotting fish hit him. Cautiously he drew near to where a large fish, covered in flies lay amongst the stones. It was already cooking in the morning heat.

'Ugh,' he said out loud.

He walked and searched, but found nothing of interest and was about to give up when he caught sight of something flapping, just around the corner. He hesitated. Should he go and find out what it was, or should he do the sensible thing and return back to the house for breakfast? There really was no contest in his mind. His excitement had all vanished, but his insatiable curiosity remained. He would go and see what it was.

He began to whistle as his feet scrunched over the stones. He was never quite sure why he did that, but as it turned out it was a very good thing, for just beyond the corner, standing with her feet almost in the water was a young girl. It was the fringe of her skirt he had seen blowing in the wind.

She turned her head to look at him.

'Sorry if I startled you,' he said.

'That's all right. I heard your whistling. It sounded very cheery so I wasn't frightened.'

Ignoring him, she went back to gazing out over the water. Jacob stopped and looked at her with interest. He guessed she must be about seven or eight and he couldn't remember ever having seen her before. He wondered what she was doing here by the lake all alone.

'Are you meeting your friends here?' he asked.

She didn't turn her head. 'No,' she said.

He looked up at the sky. High up the clouds were scudding across it at great speed, the last remains of the storm he supposed.

'Are you watching the clouds?'

'No!' she said impatiently, and somehow, he could tell she was frowning. Intrigued he tried again, thinking there must be something significant happening on the lake.

'Is your father out fishing? Are you worried about him because of the storm?'

This time she turned her face to him, and a mischievous look came into her eyes. 'No,' she said, as though it were a game.

'Can you say anything besides, no?'

She giggled and put her hand over her mouth so he could only see her gorgeous eyes.

'No,' he said for her, and they both laughed together.

'What are you looking for out there?' he asked, waving his long arm towards the empty horizon.

'I'm not looking for anything,' she said, as she looked back at the vast expanse of water.

'So, what are you doing?' he persisted, and he sat down on the sharp stones, wondering if his height was making her feel awkward. She looked down at him, and he could see the struggle in her face.

'Could you please stop asking me all these questions?' she said politely.

Jacob felt a stab of pain. 'Sorry,' he said. 'Everyone tells me I ask too many questions.'

She was too young to realize she had hurt him. 'Yes,' she said bluntly, 'You do!'

They neither of them spoke. She went back to looking at the lake and Jacob tried to shake off the feeling of always being in the wrong. After a few moments she gave a big sigh and stepped back from the water's edge.

'Are you finished?' he asked.

'Yes,' she said. 'You've spoiled it,' and he could hear the childish catch in her voice. He leaped up at once and put his hand on her shoulder, mortified he had done the wrong thing again.

'Oh, I am so sorry,' he said. 'I didn't mean to spoil your game!'

'It isn't a game!' she said vehemently and she stamped her foot. At that point Jacob almost gave up on this strange conversation, but he decided to give it one last try. Deep inside he knew he would always be wondering what she was up to, and it would drive him mad!

'Look,' he said kindly, 'I know you don't know me, except that I am horribly curious, but I am nice; ask anyone, and if you wanted someone to talk to, about whatever it is you are doing, then I would gladly listen - anytime!' He stopped for a moment and then said in a troubled voice, 'Someone other than your family I mean, because obviously you can talk to your family, although sometimes our parents don't understand us; well, at least, mine don't understand me. Although I love them of course....' His voice trailed away uncertainly. What exactly are you talking about, he asked himself? Why was he talking like an idiot to a little girl?

'Do you know what I mean?' he asked plaintively, certain she would say no.

She looked up into his embarrassed face and simply knew she could trust him. 'If I tell you what I was doing, will you promise not to tell anyone else?'

'Of course!'

'No, you have to promise!'

'I promise,' he said solemnly. She sighed again and twisted her fingers into one another. Jacob swore to himself that no matter what she said he would never break her trust.

'We have just come to live here, and I had never seen so much water before.'

Jacob was surprised. It hadn't occurred to him there were people who lived so far away from the lake they had never even seen it.

'And you like it?' he said.

The child screwed her nose up as though that didn't describe how she felt at all. Jacob decided to keep quiet.

'When I first saw the lake, it was so huge and somehow alive it took my breath away. But I didn't know then it would look different every single day.' She stopped, as though thinking about that. 'Or at least almost every day,' she continued. 'So, I come as often as I can to see what it is doing, and it is almost always doing something! Don't you think it is full of surprises?'

Jacob, who had lived by the lake his whole life, wondered if he had ever really looked at it.

The child continued rapturously, 'I love it when Mother lets me watch the sun sink into the water; I just love it, and I love it when it is calm like today, but my very favourite is when there is a storm.'

She jumped up and down and grinned at him. 'Nothing compares to a storm, does it?'

Jacob smiled at her intensity. 'I suppose not,' he said.

'One day, just after we got here, a storm blew up. I was with my father down at the place where all the fishermen are. Honestly, it happened so fast. One minute the sky was all blue, and then there was this dark smudge on the line where the sky meets the sea, and it just got bigger and bigger, and there were flashes of lightning out over the water. I had never seen that before! Then suddenly it got cold, and I knew it was going to rain even though the sun was still shining.

I watched the fishermen hurrying to bring their boats up onto the shore, and it looked really hard work. I didn't know why they were bothering. Father explained that the storm might wreck the boats, but I still didn't see how that could happen. Anyway, black clouds raced towards us over the water and the wind began to blow so strongly I thought it might blow me away!'

'Were you frightened?'

She laughed and clapped her hands. 'No, of course not! I loved it! But the thunder got so loud I think even Father got anxious, and he made me go home. I really wanted to stay, but I had to watch the rain and the lightning from our window. Mother was afraid even inside the house! It was so exciting it gave me goose bumps. When the storm was finally over, I ran down to the lake, and oh, it was so different. I understood then about the boats. The waves were taller than me and they crashed on the shore with a loud noise and one boat had been left out on the lake, and the waves were smashing into it as though they wanted to break it all to pieces.' She banged one fist into the other as hard as she could. 'It was like it was another lake altogether, not my peaceful friend, but a dangerous stranger who I didn't know.' She stopped, the memory alive in her face. 'You understand, don't you?' she said.

Jacob blinked. Suddenly the difficulty others experienced when he asked that very same question became absolutely clear to him. Did he understand what was putting a flush on this child's cheeks and making her eyes sparkle? How could he? How could anyone really understand the thoughts in someone else's mind and what they were feeling? It was impossible.

Fortunately, she didn't wait for an answer. 'Ever since then I have been longing for another storm. Mother wouldn't let me come out last night; she said it was too wild. So, this morning I simply had to come because…'

'Because?' he prompted gently, and, forgetting completely the lesson he had only just learnt, he smugly decided he knew

22

exactly what she was going to say. She comes because she loves the lake, he thought. It was obvious. She frowned, looking into his eyes as though deciding whether she should tell him something. He smiled back at her reassuringly.

'When I look at the lake,' she said, 'it is so big and beautiful, although I never know what to expect, but it always makes me feel….' She took a deep breath. 'Close to God!' The last three words came out in a rush, and to his amazement a tear ran down her cheek.

Before Jacob could think of a suitable reply she was talking again as though once she had started, she couldn't stop.

'I know girls aren't supposed to know anything about God,' she said. 'Well, we can't even be taught in the synagogue, we have to learn at home. But I think God is like the lake - you know, huge and fascinating, and I want to know everything there is to know about him. Mother says I am too young to think about such things. But I do; I just do!'

She looked at Jacob, perhaps trying to guess how old he was.

'Are you taught in the synagogue?' she asked. He nodded his head.

She pulled a face. 'I wish I was, but I will never be allowed. Father says it isn't the right thing for a girl to want to study. But I can't help it! Anyway, that is why I come here, so I can look at the water and somehow feel how big God is.' She looked up at him wistfully. 'Do they teach you about God in the synagogue? Do you think He is big?'

He looked down into a heart as hungry as his own and realized how ungrateful he had been. It was true no one could answer his questions, but at least he was allowed to ask them!

'Yes, God is big.' he said with great assurance. 'Definitely! And you should never give up thinking about Him. I think about Him all the time, and that can't be a bad thing, can it?'

She had no time to reply.

'Rebekah!' Her mother's voice rang out in the morning air. Jacob looked around in surprise, and the little girl ran at once to her mother's side.

'Do you know what time it is? I have been looking for you everywhere.' Jocabed's anxiety was obvious.

'I am sorry Mother,' Rebekah said, and she grasped her mother's hand. Jocabed began to walk away, but Rebekah looked over her shoulder and slipping her hand out of her mother's she waved at Jacob who was still standing on the shore watching her.

'Who is that boy?' Jocabed asked.

Rebekah found she didn't know his name. 'He is my friend,' she answered and gave a little skip as her mother hurried her home.

Jacob looked after her wistfully. How could it be that he had found someone who thought like him, in a girl even younger than himself?

When he got home, he found he had missed breakfast altogether.

'Where have you been?' asked his father, who was off to the market.

'At the lake,' he replied dreamily.

Leah laughed. 'As usual,' she said. 'Did you find anything of value on the beach?'

Jacob's thoughts were far away. 'Find anything?' he repeated.

'Yes,' said Benjamin. 'Did you find anything of value on the beach?' He spoke the question slowly as though Jacob was having difficulty in understanding. Jacob's face lit up with a smile and he nodded enthusiastically.

'Oh yes!' he said.

'A treasure?' asked Leah.

'Yes, yes, a treasure!' he enthused.

Benjamin looked at his son's empty hands and shook his head. What was the boy talking about now? One thing he knew for certain, he would never understand Jacob.

Never!

Benjamin decided to take the boys to Jerusalem for Passover. He thought the experience of the big city would do all of them a lot of good; especially Jacob. Leah was worried about him and for once Benjamin agreed with her. Jacob had grown strangely quiet, almost silent, and his incessant questioning had stopped. Benjamin found to his amazement he quite missed it. Certainly, the boy was not himself. The Rabbi recommended the trip.

'It might help Jacob,' he said, walking along with his arm in Benjamin's.

'What exactly is the problem?'

'He isn't happy,' Samuel said. 'I can't answer his questions.'

Benjamin looked relieved. 'He still asks questions?'

'No,' said the Rabbi after some thought, 'actually he doesn't.' He frowned, trying to find the words to explain exactly what was bothering him. 'Jacob is a good boy Benjamin, in fact he is very good boy, a credit to you and his mother, but I am worried about his state of mind.'

'Which is what?' Benjamin was becoming exasperated. He always felt out of his depth with Jacob, and the scholarly Rabbi too. Samuel stopped and looked at him almost apologetically.

'I wish I could tell you. He is an exemplary student, he works hard; he memorises, he listens. But it isn't enough for him. That's all I can say.'

The old man looked away into the distance. 'It just isn't enough. That is why I think Jerusalem may help him. There are great teachers in the temple, you know: magnificent minds. They will be able to answer his questions. I'm sure of it.'

So, Benjamin decided to take him; it would be an expensive trip, but if it stopped Leah worrying, it would be worth it.

Jerusalem took even Benjamin's breath away. The children saw the white walls of the city, shining in the sun, vaster by far than anything they had ever seen before. Capernaum suddenly seemed small in comparison and they chattered with excitement. The crowds of people at the city gate, the noise in the streets, the wares in the market: everything made their heads spin. They held hands so as not to get lost, walking around mesmerised by a thousand sights and sounds.

For Jacob, Jerusalem was a dream come true. He was bursting with anticipation: surely here in the holy city he would see the men who were close to God? The splendour and the grandeur made him gasp, and he found himself caught up in the amazing atmosphere of the feast. He wanted to know about everything, and he talked and talked until his brothers were sick of the sound of his voice.

At last Benjamin took them to the temple. Jacob admired the great pillars on the outside, and stayed with his father as he joined the queue to buy a lamb for the sacrifice. He watched with interest as Benjamin examined with scrupulous care the lamb the merchant offered. To Jacob's surprise he rejected the first and ignoring the merchant's grumbling picked the second for himself. Jacob had never seen his father take such interest in an animal. He understood it must be without any defect, or even a blemish, but seeing the way his father ensured this perfection stirred his curiosity.

'This lamb will be sacrificed for our sins, won't it Father?'

'Yes.' Benjamin did not look up, his examination of the lamb not yet complete. Jacob looked down at him uncertainly. He loved his father, but he knew he wasn't perfect, and he didn't feel perfect either. He wondered what happened if there was too much sin for one small lamb. What if the sacrifice didn't work? What if it simply wasn't enough? He cleared his throat. He knew he mustn't ask too many questions, so he chose one carefully.

'Will we be different after the sacrifice: better I mean; or more holy, or something?' The merchant grunted his scepticism and answered before Benjamin had a chance to speak.

'These animals ensure forgiveness, but they don't work miracles on the people who buy them,' he said. He ruffled Jacob's curls with a careless hand.

'Just as well, my lad,' he said with a laugh, 'otherwise I would soon be out of business.'

Benjamin had a sour look on his face. He was a merchant too and understood the man's delight in a constant stream of customers, but still he wished the sacrifice could bring about a change in his character. There were certain things about him Leah would certainly have liked to see altered. Jacob was confused and looked from one to the other.

'But if no-one is changed, why does anyone bother?'

Benjamin looked over the boy's head at the merchant's face. The man's eyebrows were raised in surprise; another difficult question! Benjamin wasn't sure if he was glad or sorry he was being challenged again. He shook his head and began to dole out the money into the trader's hand.

'Father?' Jacob persisted.

The transaction complete Benjamin caught hold of the lamb in a firm grip. 'It's the law Jacob. This is how it has always been, since Moses. It is just the law. I can't explain it to you. Now go inside while I see to the sacrifice. There is a long line so I may be some time. You will find your brothers in there somewhere, and don't get lost!'

Jacob hung his head. Why could no-one ever give a satisfactory answer? Surely someone must know, maybe not Father, but someone! He took one last look at the lamb. How could something so innocent be of any help with his guilty conscience?

Before he climbed the steps into the temple he went to where the priest was doing the sacrificing. The man was covered in blood and the air was full of the stench of it. His nose wrinkled with distaste, but he made himself watch because he wanted to somehow grasp what was happening.

A man came forward dragging his lamb. It bleated pitifully, its wool white in the sunshine. The priest examined it even more carefully than his father had. Jacob happened to glance at the man who had brought it. He had an uneasy expression on his face and Jacob took an instant dislike to him. I wouldn't trust you in any business dealing, he thought, and the word "thief," formed itself in his mind. He felt sure the priest would refuse this man's lamb, he was so obviously not a nice person, not good like his father. But, no, the priest never looked at the man once, his whole attention fixed on the lamb.

Jacob wanted to call out, 'You can't accept his sacrifice - he doesn't deserve forgiveness!'

But the words died on his lips, for suddenly he saw it clearly. This was not about the man; whether he was good or not; sorry or not; not even if he was willing to change or not, it was only about the lamb and how pure it was. A perfect sacrifice equalled forgiveness for this man, for his father, for everyone.

He turned his eyes away from the lamb's death, unable to look upon such an unjust transaction, the innocent dying for the guilty. Yet at the same moment he felt a sudden rush of excitement inside, as though in some mysterious way understanding had come to him after all. He thought about it often afterwards.

Strangely elated he made his way into the temple and was instantly hushed to reverence by the hugeness of the building on the inside. He looked up over his head, certain he felt again the presence that was in the synagogue at home. He smiled in recognition.

Curiosity made him join the back of the group surrounding the debating Pharisees. He looked at their long flowing robes and their solemn faces and wondered what it must be like to hear the voice of the Almighty. He strained to hear their discussion, knowing they must be talking about God, but to his disappointment they were speaking of fine points of doctrine and the interpretation of the law. The sort of thing Jairus was interested in! His heart sank.

He pushed forward a little and in his youthful impatience he blurted out the question that always burned in his mind. 'Is it possible to know God'? he said.

There was a sudden silence and his eyes darted from one stern face to another. 'Like Moses; or David; or Daniel?' he continued quickly.

The man he had interrupted turned to look at him. He wore the finest robes Jacob had ever seen, but his eyes were cold and they frightened Jacob. They didn't soften at the sight of a mere boy, instead the man's lips curled in disdain.

'Of course not!' he said with crushing finality. Those around him murmured their assent. 'Only a fool would ask such a question', he sneered, and he turned his face away as though he couldn't bear the sight of such an idiot child.

Jacob, flushing to the roots of his hair, suddenly felt a strong hand grab him roughly by the shoulder. A man with an angry face yanked him from the crowd. Jacob really thought the man was going to hit him and he tried to get away. The man wouldn't let go and Jacob's best tunic was torn in the tussle.

'How dare you speak to the High Priest without permission?' the man hissed at him.

Jacob said nothing, and kept his eyes lowered.

The man shook him violently. 'Have you nothing to say for yourself? What a pity you didn't show such restraint before you interrupted the High Priest! Who are you and where do you come from?'

Jacob heard his father's strong voice calling him, and he felt the man's grip slacken slightly. Pulling away he ran as fast as he could out of the nearest doorway. He didn't want to get his father into any trouble! A heavy pulse beat in his throat and he wished with all his heart he was anywhere else in the world.

He stood behind a pillar, sobbing and sobbing, as though he really had been struck. He was a fool! The High Priest said so. There was no way to know God, no way to hear his voice. There never had been. The sound of his hopes and dreams shattering filled his ears. He was aware of nothing else.

After a time, his father found him. It took him a long while to get out of Jacob what had happened. Benjamin had never seen him so upset and he had no idea how to comfort him.

At first Jacob couldn't even speak, but Benjamin drew him down onto the temple steps and there he buried his head in his father's lap. Eventually, Jacob looked up between the sobs and Benjamin made out the muffled sound of his son's agony.

'He said we cannot know God!'

Benjamin just held him in his arms. He couldn't comprehend why such a statement had brought about this devastation, but he was wise enough to keep quiet. If only Leah was here; she would know what to say, he thought. He rubbed Jacob's back, making the soothing sounds he had always used when his children had hurt themselves. When at last Jacob could breathe properly, he picked him up and carried him back to their lodging; the other two boys trailing behind. They never could understand Jacob.

The next day Benjamin packed all their belongings and they left Jerusalem for the long journey home.

Leah was amazed to see them so soon, but her happy greeting died on her lips as she caught sight of Jacob. She turned accusing eyes on Benjamin.

'What did you do to him?' she stormed.

'It wasn't me, it was the High Priest,' he said, spreading out his arms to prove his innocence.

Leah led Jacob into the house. He had hardly spoken on the journey and had eaten less. Pale and silent, he sat while Leah fussed around him, preparing his favourite food, anxiously glancing at his face. She had never seen him look like this before.

'What happened?' she asked quietly.

His head dropped and he looked at the floor. 'I saw the High Priest.' It was little more than a whisper.

'That is a great honour,' she said.

'Yes,' he sighed, 'a very great honour.'

She sat down opposite him, wondering if he was going to tell her. When he looked up she was shocked by the pain in his eyes.

'He said we cannot know God,' his lip quivered, 'and only a fool would think we could.' The sob that escaped him almost broke her heart.

In the end she did no better than Benjamin in finding the right thing to say. She held him tightly as the grief poured out of him, angry this special child had been born with an impossible desire burning inside him. For years she had dreaded this moment, had known one day all Jacob's questioning, all his longing to know God would lead him to this place. She wanted to lash out at the High Priest for having hurt him, but in truth she wondered what else he could have said. No-one could know God. She knew it; the Rabbi knew it; everyone knew it, but perhaps it was only the High Priest who could have convinced Jacob. Surely it was better he faced the truth, however painful it was?

She kissed his hair again and again, reassuring herself he was still young, that this anguish would pass and he would forget all about it. Later she sang him a song from his childhood as she put him to bed. Jacob said nothing.

He had never felt less like a child.

Jacob was sitting by the lake when Rebekah found him.

He always believed it was purely by chance she stumbled upon him there. Later, when they were both grown up, she laughed at his naivety, but she gave no sign as she approached him that she had been to the lake many times hoping to see him. Her heart was beating with excitement when she saw that at last, he was there.

She sat next to him in silence for some time. It comforted him.

Eventually she said, 'You came home early from Jerusalem.'

'Yes,' he said.

They sat and listened to the waves lapping the shore.

'Will you tell me?' she asked softly and she turned her head so she could see his face.

He looked back at her. 'There isn't much to tell. The High Priest said I was an idiot. I expect you know that already. Everyone always knows everything in this town. They are all laughing at me, aren't they? Agreeing that I'm an idiot? I don't care!'

She had never heard him speak in such a harsh tone before. Frowning she shook her head.

'They're not laughing, and I'm not laughing.'

'Well, you should be. I asked the High Priest a stupid question and he gave me a very sensible answer. Only an idiot would have asked that question. That's what he said, and he must be right. I don't know what you are doing sitting talking to me. Don't waste your time. Go and find someone who isn't an idiot to talk to.'

She looked at him angrily. 'Don't say such horrible things! I came to tell you I will always be your friend. No matter what! And I don't care what the stupid High Priest says, so there!'

He was surprised at her intensity. 'All right, I'm sorry for being a misery, but you had better not let anyone else hear you calling the High Priest names. He is very important you know.'

'Not if he hurts one of my friends. No one is that important.'

He looked at her and some of the deadness faded from his eyes. He wondered at this strange ability she had to make him feel better.

She smiled at him, blithely setting aside the High Priest and his opinion. She leaned a little closer.

'Also,' she said, 'I want to know what you asked him.'

'Why?'

'Well, I think it must have been a very good question he didn't have the answer to, because I have discovered my parents often say "No," when what they mean is that they don't know. Your father won't tell anyone what it was and everyone is dying of curiosity.'

His face became guarded again. 'And what about you? Will you tell anyone?'

'Of course not. I know how to keep a secret!'

'Why do you want to know if you're not going to tell anyone?'

She thought about that for a moment. 'Because….'

'Yes?' he prompted.

'Because,' she said with a sly smile, 'I guessed it was a question about God, and I want to know what it was!'

'It was about God,' he answered reluctantly.

She clapped her hands gleefully. 'I knew it!' she said.

'I asked if anyone can know God.'

'And he said "No"?'

'That's right, and only an idiot would ask such a question.'

She turned to look him full in the face. 'Well, that has to be wrong, doesn't it? Because I have always wanted to know God, and you have too, and there must be lots of others like us, and maybe a High Priest can't know God, but I think we can, and we should never, ever stop trying!'

He looked at her with wonder in his eyes. 'Never stop trying?'

'Never, because I think God can't really like it that no one is his friend any more, and maybe, just maybe, he has decided we are the very ones for the job!'

'You and me?'

'And lots of others, like I said.'

'To be friends of God?'

'Yes.'

'Will you always be my friend?' he asked, and it was the first time he had smiled since he came back from Jerusalem.

'Yes!' she said, and slid her hand into his.

They looked out over the lake once more, two children determined to know God.

Levi

Levi often wondered what would have happened if his travels had taken him to Nazareth instead of Capernaum. He would sit day-dreaming, as old men will, imagining what the outcome would have been if all those years before he had turned inland instead of sticking to the shore of the Sea of Galilee.

Nazareth! So near; so very near!

Levi was a fine man. His charm and wit drew people to him, but the directness of his gaze was disconcerting, as though he was looking right inside you, searching for something. It made people uncomfortable.

He had lived his whole life in the south, just a short distance from Jerusalem and those who knew him well wondered why he did not go to live in the great city nearby. To his fellow Rabbis, his intelligence and love of the scriptures seemed wasted in a small provincial town, but Levi was content to live away from the hustle and bustle of Jerusalem's noisy streets. Although he visited the temple regularly, he was always glad to go out of the city gate and make the journey back home to where he felt he belonged. Now his children were all married; with homes close by; he and his wife Ruth lived alone. Surrounded by their many grandchildren, it seemed Levi's future was settled, mapped out before him. He would grow old in this town he had faithfully served for so many years.

He went to Jerusalem reluctantly in the spring. Ruth was sick and he wanted to stay close by her side, but she was stubbornly insistent he should attend the Passover. It seemed important to her and eventually he agreed to go, but he determined to stay for only a few days. He couldn't bear to be away from her for too long.

As he entered the city, it struck him that Jerusalem was no longer the place he had known as a young man. The influence of pagan Rome was felt on every street corner and it was gradually eroding the spiritual life of the Holy City. Jerusalem was occupied by those who worshipped other gods, and even the temple itself seemed to be in the grip of some strange malady. The Romans left the priests alone and the sacrifices went on as before, but there were few now who met at the feasts to share their understanding of the living God. Something had changed in the very center of temple life and it had become a highly political place, with the Pharisees and the Sadducees manouvering, arguing this way and that, seeking for power. It sickened him. There were still good men to be found of course, but this time more than any other he missed his old friend Simeon.

He went straight to the temple and as always, his pace slowed as he approached it. Even after all these years he never got used to the magnificence of the building or the cool peace he experienced inside. To one side he could hear the raised voices of the group surrounding the High Priest. A look of distaste came over his face and he carefully avoided walking too close. He had decided a long time ago such minute examination of the law was not for him. It was clever certainly, but empty and shallow, as unappetising as a meal without salt.

Further on he came across some old friends sitting together and with a sigh of relief, he joined them. This was his chief pleasure in any trip to Jerusalem, the opportunity to talk with like-minded men from all over Israel. Even his cares about Ruth rolled away as he joked and laughed. Slowly it dawned on him this was probably why she had sent him!

In the middle of a very interesting discussion another Rabbi rushed up, too excited to be polite.

'A young boy has just interrupted the High Priest!'

Levi was surprised. 'What did he say?' he asked.

'You should have seen his face, he was livid.'

'Not the High Priest - the boy.'

'Oh,' said the Rabbi, 'some question about whether we can know God. Very bad manners of course, but what can you expect from a Galilean? Probably the son of some ignorant fisherman, judging by his accent.'

Levi got up from his seat. 'Where is the boy now?'

'Johannes was going to chastise him for his impertinence, but his father came looking for him and the boy escaped out into the courtyard. Last we shall ever see of him I should think.'

For a moment Levi gazed at the man without seeing him, then he turned on his heel and strode off, out into the blazing sunshine of the temple courtyard.

At first, he thought he had missed them as he searched here and there, but then he came upon the pathetic scene of a large man cradling a boy's head in his lap. The child was making a terrible sound, like a wounded animal, the man silent, apparently completely at a loss.

Levi had gone to look for them on an impulse because the boy's question was so arresting. Had he not asked it himself his whole life? His curiosity had been stirred and he had wanted to meet the child. Now he was shocked to find the boy in such distress. He drew back into the shadowy darkness of the temple wall. He did not want to intrude, unsure even of what he wanted to say. As he stood watching, the boy's weeping seemed to lessen and he looked up into his father's face. Levi never forgot the forlorn expression or the huge eyes drowned in tears. He stepped forward intending to speak to them, but someone called his name and in the momentary distraction he missed his opportunity. The man must have picked the child up in his arms and carried him down the steps, for when Levi looked back again, he caught only a glimpse of the man's back as he disappeared into the shifting crowds. He hesitated just long enough to make it impossible to follow.

Perhaps it is for the best, he thought, shrugging his shoulders, but as he walked away, he felt a sinking feeling inside, as though he had missed something important.

Over the next few days, he kept a look-out for the child, but neither he nor his father ever came back to the temple. The boy's question went round and round in Levi's mind and he could not shake off the feeling of regret. He felt he understood the boy, might even have been able to help him if he had been given the chance. Levi knew the pain of carrying such a question locked up in your soul. He wished he had been able to reassure him there were many others who asked the very same question, had asked it for years - not the High Priest of course, nor any of those around him, but good men nonetheless, excellent men.

It was a minor incident and he never mentioned it to Ruth. Indeed, when he returned from Jerusalem, she was much worse and that drove everything else from his mind. It was a hard time.

Ruth died in the autumn and in the months after her death, a strange restlessness came upon him. He walked the streets where he had played as a child, greeted neighbours he had known for years, went to synagogue with grown men he had taught in school and all of it seemed dead to him. Empty. His roots were here, stretching out into everything dear and familiar. What was happening to make him uneasy? Why was the contentment he had always felt in his home town starting to slip away?

Initially, he put it down to Ruth's death. The sense of loss was painful and profound, making him feel as though part of him was missing; a huge part; the most important part. How could he go on without her? Grief swept over him in waves, but still it seemed something else was troubling him. Something hard to identify. He became impatient with himself, because it made no sense to him, but still the restlessness grew.

Every day he would walk out of town and seek his favourite place in an olive grove. It was quiet there. He would sit and think of the happy years he had spent with Ruth in this place. Was he really thinking of leaving? But why? There seemed to be no logical answer. His eyes turned often to the north. Once, years before, he had travelled through Galilee, and now half-forgotten memories of the lake ran through his mind. Why was he always thinking about it, gazing into the distance as though he half expected to see a vast sheet of water shining in the sun?

He tried to shake free of these disturbing thoughts, but as the weeks passed, he began to wonder if his future was linked in some way to the Sea of Galilee. He worked hard to put it out of his mind, but still images of the lake troubled him, working their way into his dreams. He thought often of the Galilean boy in the temple and his father. Had they somehow planted these ideas in his mind? What other explanation was there? After all, he had not thought about Galilee for years and now he thought of little else. It was a mystery.

In the end he left because he felt there was no alternative. He was compelled. The certainty there was something he needed to do, some mission that had to be completed before he settled down into old age, grew every day. He had to go to Galilee, even though he had no idea why.

When he shared his plan, his family were shocked and upset, but once he had made up his mind, nothing deterred him. He didn't try to explain because he had little hope of being understood, so he just said he wanted to travel for a while, taking the long road through Samaria to Galilee.

On the day he left he was suddenly consumed with excitement, and had to school his face not to grin as he soothed his daughter's tears. His two eldest sons were not fooled. They saw the sparkle in his eyes as he bade them farewell and they raised their eyebrows at each other. It was obvious he was off on an adventure. At his age!

The journey through Samaria was uneventful, if a little tedious. He was impatient to be in Galilee. He knew little of the geography and an unexpected thrill went through him as he came to the top of a hill and saw the lake sparkling below in the clear air. He hadn't known it was so close.

He left the road and hurried down to the shore, standing for a long time gazing over the water. He had never been more certain he was in the right place, and miraculously that feeling lessened his grief, giving him hope. A tear trickled down his face even as he laughed out loud. He was glad none of his family were there to see him. They would think he was getting soft in his old age!

When at last he turned away he realized he had made no plan of what to do when he got here. He chuckled to himself, thinking he was just like Abraham; leaving his home and everything safe, to travel to a land he knew nothing about. Now here he was, a stranger in a strange land, with no idea what to do next. The assurance Abraham had been called by God comforted him. He really hoped he had been called by God too.

He travelled from place to place, gradually making his way north along the edge of the lake. The people were hospitable and made him welcome wherever he went. He sat in the village squares, watched the children at play, worshiped in the synagogues and initially he was happy, but gradually his aimlessness began to bother him. After a few weeks, doubt began to gnaw at him, eroding the sense of destiny and purpose that had sustained him.

It came to a head as he sat outside an Inn drumming his fingers on a rough table. He looked around and one question was uppermost in his mind. What exactly was he doing here? He enjoyed Galilee's remoteness from Jerusalem, it was like stepping back in time, but he had to face the fact that he had not found what he was looking for, whatever that was!

For the first time he began to think seriously about going home. He didn't like the thought of it. He could imagine the reaction of his family when he trailed back, having achieved nothing. What a waste of time and energy they would think, even if they were too kind to say it to him; and they were right weren't they? Of course, he had never even hinted to them why he was leaving: how could he when he didn't know himself? But he knew he wouldn't be able to hide his disappointment. They would see it in his face.

He shifted uncomfortably in his chair.

'Well', he said to himself, 'we all make mistakes, but we just have to be humble enough to admit it.' How many generations of students had he taught that particular piece of wisdom? He sighed heavily, looking once more towards the north. Should he try one more town before he turned for home? Was there any point?

The inn-keeper appeared by his side carrying his meal.

Levi thanked him and asked, 'What town lies to the north?'

'Capernaum.'

Capernaum. He liked the sound of it.

'Capernaum, it is then!' he said, and thus his future was sealed.

He arrived on the day before the Sabbath, hot, weary, and more certain than ever he couldn't go on just wandering about. He was starting to feel old.

Early the next morning he made his way to the synagogue, sitting as usual amongst the local people. Most of them were fishermen, with some merchants, a blacksmith and a potter. They were good, solid folk and their rough accent amused him, so different to the cultured tones of the south. He felt at home sitting amongst them in a way he hadn't anywhere else he had visited. It surprised him. He wondered if he was supposed to come and live here and... do what? He shook his head in perplexity. He might like the people, but that didn't make Capernaum the right place for him, did it?

His gaze strayed to the women's gallery above him. A boy was seated at the front, his arms resting on the rail. All Levi could see were masses of curly hair, but something stirred in his memory and he frowned. A moment later someone spoke to the child who lifted his head to reply. Just for a moment Levi held his breath. He recognized the boy; of course he did: he was the child in the temple! He quickly scanned the room and identified the burly figure of the boy's father. His face lit up. So, he was right, it was the same boy! What incredible good fortune! If he had searched all of Israel, he could never have found him. Yet here he was.

Levi stood quite still, gazing up once more at the boy who took no notice of him at all. For all Levi's maturity he found he could still be impulsive. He made his decision in a moment. Capernaum would be his home. He still had no idea why, but what did that matter? He could never have explained it to a living soul, but he felt sure he had been led here, to this town, to this boy. It was what his journey had been about.

Levi never told anyone why he had come to live in Capernaum, but to Samuel it was an answer to prayer. The old Rabbi was almost pathetically relieved when he realized Levi was willing to teach in the school. He felt someone from the south, someone with greater learning than he had himself, was the perfect answer for his problems in class.

It was almost a year since Jacob's disastrous journey to Jerusalem and the boy seemed to have regained some of his natural good-humour. He fished with Jairus and kept to his studies, but he never asked any questions, and Samuel had been watching him with growing concern. Something inside the boy seemed to have died and Samuel knew it was beyond his abilities to help him. Now here was a new Rabbi, the perfect teacher for Jacob. A Rabbi who wouldn't be out of his depth!

After Levi's first day in the school the two men discussed each individual child at length, and Samuel left Jairus and Jacob until last.

'Jairus is a fine student,' he said proudly, 'the best I have ever taught. I have great hopes for him. He studies with such meticulous care and is a joy to teach. He was made to be a Rabbi.'

'And his friend Jacob?' said Levi.

'Ah that is a sad story. He is not the lad he once was.'

'What happened?' asked Levi.

Samuel sat in his chair and stroking his long beard he told Levi of Jacob's trip to Jerusalem. 'He seems to have got over the worst of it now, but he is not the same.'

Levi pressed Samuel for more details. Why was the boy so upset? Had he always asked such strange questions? What were his father and mother like?

After a while Samuel looked at Levi curiously.

'You seem very interested in this particular boy. Why?'

'I am interested in them both actually, Jacob and Jairus. We live in unusual days Samuel, and these two boys are growing up in the midst of them. If what you say about Jairus is true, then as he matures, he will become a man of influence, and it is a privilege to shape the life of such a man while he is still young.'

'And Jacob?'

'Yes Jacob,' he said, as though thinking out loud. 'We shall see, we shall see.'

Samuel looked at him, trying to fathom his train of thought. Then he asked the question which was niggling away at the back of his mind.

'Why do you think we live in unusual days? Everything here continues as it always has. It is peaceful here.'

Levi put his head back and shut his eyes. 'Things are not so peaceful in Jerusalem my friend,' he said.

'You have been to Jerusalem recently?'

'Yes,' said Levi and opening his eyes he looked at the other man. 'Out here in the country the effect of the Roman occupation is not felt so keenly, but there, in the city, it brings conflict on every side. Jerusalem is not a happy place.'

Samuel looked concerned. 'Is it because of the Romans then that you speak of unusual things happening?'

There was a short silence as Levi seemed to think about his reply. 'Not entirely,' he said at last, and he looked with his sharp eyes into Samuel's face. 'Many are looking for the Messiah to come and rescue the nation. Have you heard of this?'

Samuel wrung his hands together. 'I have heard rumours, but I dismissed them. Surely it isn't possible the Messiah will appear in our life-time, is it Levi?'

Levi gave a strange laugh and said, 'Not in our life-time perhaps, but then we are growing old, and who knows what may happen in the next thirty years? Roman oppression is harsh and clashes constantly with our worship of God. Caesar demands perfect obedience. It is impossible to give that and stay true to God. I do not think armed rebellion will happen immediately, but eventually it will come. Those who are growing up now may well be looking for a leader in a few years and there will be a great hunger for the Messiah then, even more than now.'

Samuel sighed. 'I can hardly bear to think of such things,' he said in a faint voice.

Levi looked at him with sympathy. 'We are far away from Jerusalem here, perhaps it is best to put such matters from your mind.'

Samuel looked at him with a sudden shrewdness. 'And is that what you will be doing? Is that why you are taking such an interest in Jairus and Jacob, because you are putting all thoughts of the Messiah from your mind?'

Levi threw back his head and laughed. 'You see more clearly than I supposed,' he said. 'Do not be concerned about them, Samuel. I promise I won't stir up armed rebellion in their hearts.'

'Then what will you do?' asked Samuel.

Levi stood and placed his hand reassuringly on the other man's shoulder.

'I shall teach them about God,' he said.

After that conversation Samuel watched Levi closely but almost at once he began to think he was worrying unnecessarily. Levi was an excellent teacher and there was nothing of a subversive nature in anything he said. If he focussed his attention more on Jairus and Jacob than on the other pupils, well it wasn't enough for anyone to remark on it, and he had a way with all the students that made them love him. Best of all he began to reawaken Jacob's curiosity about God.

One day, without any warning, Jacob asked a perceptive question that took Levi by surprise. Samuel's eyes flew to Levi's face. Would he remember all he had been told about Jacob; after all, the conversation had happened weeks before? He found he needn't have worried. Levi took the question in his stride as though nothing out of the ordinary had happened, and answered it excellently too. Samuel heaved a sigh of relief. Perhaps this new teacher was going to work out well after all.

Samuel watched with fascination as Levi drew both Jairus and Jacob into a deeper understanding of God. The older Rabbi felt humbled by the sharpness of intellect Levi displayed as he answered one question after another, all the time provoking his students to heated discussion with questions of his own. Levi taught Jairus to see beyond the letter of the law to the One who wrote it and soothed Jacob's pain until he was almost himself again. Just occasionally a look of anguish would pass across Jacob's face, and then Levi would make some comment which captured Jacob's attention and turned the moment aside. Samuel realised Levi was a man who could heal souls, as well as teach with excellence and he learnt almost as much as the boys did. Eventually he surrendered all the classes to Levi's astonishing abilities.

Jacob had never met anyone like his new teacher. The Rabbi looked at him as though he really saw him, and the things he taught were fascinating, drawing Jacob to the edge of his seat. Only slowly did he realise all the questions were coming back and he was even asking them in class again. It made him uncomfortable; he felt exposed. Something of the innocence he had once possessed was gone, and not even Levi could make it return.

After a few months Jacob felt the thing he wanted most in the world was to talk to Levi alone, away from the others, even

Jairus. He asked his father's permission, and took the uninterested grunt he received as a yes. That was the easy part. Now he had to approach Levi and ask for a private interview. After class he hung around until even Jairus gave up waiting for him. Levi was aware of the boy's embarrassed shuffling, but he took no notice. Jacob had no option but to clear his throat and say in a squeaky voice.

'Could I speak to you sir?'

Levi looked at him seriously. 'About what?'

The image of the High Priest's face sped across Jacob's mind and he hesitated as he gathered his courage together.

'I want to ask you some questions about God,' he said.

Levi's face softened. 'Of course you do,' he said, as though he had been expecting this request, and for the first time Jacob felt having questions was a natural thing.

'Come to my house tomorrow,' said Levi.

Jacob ran home so excited he could hardly speak.

The next day he combed his unruly hair with great care and put on his best tunic. It seemed to him that going to see the Rabbi was a momentous event in his life; terribly important. Levi lived alone, but a local woman came to the house to clean and wash his clothes. She let Jacob in, glancing with interest at the Rabbi's young visitor. He stood outside Levi's door, nervously pulling at his tunic and running his hand through his hair. The woman watched him curiously, wondering what such an awkward boy was doing here. He knocked at last, aware of her eyes on him. Levi called for him to enter and he opened the door and stepped inside.

He hesitated in the doorway. Levi was seated at a table spread with many scrolls. He was gazing out of the window, as though lost in some world of his own. Jacob felt his presence in the room was an intrusion, for it was full of a wonderful sense of peace and rest. He was afraid to disturb such serenity with his clumsiness and wished he could creep away unnoticed, yet he was held where he stood by an even stronger desire. He took one tentative step into the room and breathed in deeply, as though his lungs could absorb the peace which hung in the air. The intensity of it made his heart beat a little faster and he looked at Levi with wonder.

Levi turned his head and smiled. His eyes, usually so bright and piercing, had an abstracted focus, as though he had been looking at something Jacob could not see.

The invisible God, thought Jacob, and a shiver went down his spine as he clearly understood he was indeed intruding.

Levi took a moment before he spoke. 'What can I do for you Jacob?' he said.

Every question had flown out of Jacob's mind, but eventually he managed to stammer, 'I wanted to talk to you about God.'

Levi smiled broadly. 'That is the only conversation worth having,' he said. 'Although, of course, the Almighty is a very large subject, as we have been learning'.

Jacob shifted uneasily from one leg to the other. What exactly did he want to ask the Rabbi? Now it came to it he found he wasn't sure.

'Come and sit down,' suggested Levi, and Jacob moved forward, tripping over his own feet and landing in the chair with an ungainly clatter. Two bright spots of colour appeared on his cheeks, but Levi seemed unperturbed, focussing his attention on rolling up the scroll which had been open before him. There was a short silence while Jacob tried to work out what to do with his hands. Nothing annoyed his father more than fidgeting and he didn't want to annoy Levi. In the end he held them tightly together in his lap, his knuckles turning white.

He sat tongue-tied while Levi waited patiently. Jacob felt very ignorant and foolish. Would Levi laugh at his questions, or even worse dismiss him with a careless reply? An indelible image of the look on the High Priest's face lurked at the back of his mind, but he knew he had to take the risk and ask about God again. For weeks now he had been screwing up his courage as his trust of Levi grew, but now he was here it was harder than he had thought. He wished with all his heart he could be like Jairus and not care about these things; but he wasn't like Jairus; he knew he wasn't like anybody. He gulped, and at last he blurted out the first thing that came into his head.

'Do you know God?' he asked, and fixed his eyes with such intensity on the Rabbi that Levi's eyebrows flew up in surprise. Questions he was prepared for, but not something as personal as this. A sudden image of his father came into his mind. Not even in the years of his own youthful searching had he ever asked his father such a question.

'That is an unusual question,' he said, stalling for time. 'What exactly do you mean by 'know'? No man can ever really know God, for the scriptures teach us he is incomprehensible. Do you know what that means?'

Jacob nodded sadly. 'Unknowable,' he said. 'Samuel taught us that.'

He was unable to keep the disappointment out of his voice.

Levi was intrigued. 'Why did you ask me that question if you understood God's incomprehensible nature?'

Jacob gazed down at his hands, he looked much older than his eleven years and it was obvious he was deadly serious. Levi thought him a remarkable boy.

'I have thought a lot about knowing God. Why is it the scriptures teach us of so many men who talked to God, and yet now, in our day we don't seem to have any at all who do that? I mean we're still God's people, aren't we? Why doesn't he talk to us anymore? Isn't there anyone who God has given a message to, or told to do something?'

'We haven't had a prophet for four hundred years,' said Levi softly.

'Four hundred years!' repeated Jacob. 'Well, what went wrong? Did we do something terrible that made God stop talking to us? He is still our God, isn't he?'

'Yes,' said Levi, 'He is.'

'It doesn't make any sense to me.'

'Why not? Everyone else just accepts things the way they are. Why can't you?'

Jacob sat with his head lowered for a few moments, and Levi wondered what struggle was going on inside him. He was young to be troubled by such profound matters and Levi felt compassion for him.

At last Jacob looked up and all his soul was in his eyes. Levi knew the boy was about to share something he had never spoken to anyone. He was surprised by the profound sense of responsibility that came upon him as he looked into that vulnerable face.

'Don't let me fail him,' he prayed and he had never been more serious in his life.

'When I go to synagogue, I can feel God all around me.'

Levi took one swift breath, but managed to keep his utter amazement out of his face. Jacob was looking at him desperately.

Levi had no idea what to say.

At last, he said, 'Tell me all about it, Jacob, right from the beginning.'

Jacob frowned and ran his hand through his hair. Where exactly was the beginning?

'When I was small, I felt God, in the air, just like when I came into the room a little while ago. God was here. I've only ever felt that in the synagogue, and once in the temple, just before…' and his voice trailed off in distress.

Levi's thoughts jumped from one thing to another. The boy had felt God's presence in this room? In all his years of meditating he had never dared to believe what he felt was really God. How could Jacob know such an extraordinary thing? "A little child shall lead them." The scripture came into his mind from nowhere, but he had no time to consider these thoughts, for Jacob was weeping, overwhelmed it seemed by the memory of what had happened in Jerusalem.

'Jacob,' Levi said gently, 'I know what you experienced in the temple was extremely hard for you, but please, you must try and explain to me what has been going on inside you since you were a child. I promise I will listen.'

Jacob wiped his eyes.

'I told you,' he said, 'I felt God. It was so natural to me that at first, I thought everyone could feel the same thing. I was sure Mother and Father knew all about it. But it confused me that no-one ever spoke of it. In the end I decided it was a secret. Something you didn't share. The name of God is too sacred to be spoken, isn't it? I thought no-one was allowed to speak about this either. But I was filled with questions, so many questions. I didn't realise at first they were odd questions; that I was an odd person. Jairus told me that.'

Levi winced.

'I used to watch my father and the other men going through the rituals in the synagogue, and gradually I began to realise it was all about tradition and the law, and no one else felt like me. I stopped bothering people with my questions, but nothing made them go away in my mind. I just had to find out if I could get to know God for myself. That was when Father took me to Jerusalem.'

Levi put back his head and shut his eyes. The longing of his own heart was intensified beyond belief in this child. He wondered if there were others like him, spread across the nation, the generation who would follow the Messiah. He was more certain than ever he had been led here to nurture this child, to help him through the difficulties of growing up with such a burden of desire. He wondered if he was capable of caring for Jacob. A strange warmth touched him. For good or ill he was here, miles from his home and his family, believing God had given him a unique opportunity to invest in the life before him.

Getting up he went and gathered Jacob into his arms. 'I understand,' he said.

The boy sobbed on his chest as he had on his father's all those months before.

'No one understands,' Jacob said hopelessly.

Levi patted his back gently. 'Jacob,' he said, 'I don't know everything, and I will not pretend I do, but we shall go on a voyage of discovery together, you and I.'

Jacob looked at him through his tears. 'Can I ask you anything?'

Levi took a deep breath. Then he nodded.

'Anything,' he said.

Simeon

Jacob was feeling restless. Something was bothering him. In all his talks with Levi something seemed to be missing.

'Why does Levi avoid questions about the Messiah?'

'What?' asked Jairus, dragging his nose out of his studies.

'Haven't you noticed he doesn't talk about the Messiah?'

'That's nonsense,' said Jairus, 'he's taught us all about the Messiah.'

'Yes,' said Jacob grudgingly, 'but there is something else, something about the way he turns some questions aside. Sometimes I think he is going to say something really interesting about the Messiah, and then he seems to think better of it. You must have noticed!'

'You know, you are right,' said Jairus, pretending to look interested. He opened his eyes wide. 'I wonder it has never occurred to me before. It's a complete mystery! We should ask our venerable teacher what he's hiding!'

Jacob looked annoyed.

'You can laugh if you like, but I think there is something strange about it, whatever you say.'

'You know what I think Jacob? I think you have to have an unanswerable question or you're just not happy. Since Levi has been teaching us all the things you've been going on and on about for years, you are forced to create a new thing to think about. There is no mystery about the Messiah. Trust me!'

Jacob ran his hand through his hair, perplexity written all over his face. Jairus might scoff, but he just knew he was right. Levi was hiding something!

Jairus was already there, sitting quietly in Levi's room. Jairus was never late. Levi was sitting at his table, gazing out of the window, just as he had on that first day years before. Jacob slipped in quietly, glancing across at Jairus with raised eyebrows. Jairus shook his head at this silent interrogation. Neither of them had a clue as to why the Rabbi had summoned them. It was most unusual.

Levi turned and looked from one to the other of them with affection. God had given him these two sons in his old age; Jairus with his voice deepening to a bass and his dark beard beginning to show, and Jacob growing into his gangly limbs, already in love with Rebekah. Both of them were standing on the edge of manhood. His love for them almost choked him.

He cleared his throat. 'You are wondering why I have asked you to come and see me. I wanted to be the first one to tell you. I am going home'.

'But this is your home!' Jacob said instantly.

'No, I'm afraid that isn't true Jacob. My family lives in the south. You have always known that'.

'But…'

Jairus had risen to his feet and he took a pace forward. 'You are leaving Capernaum?'

'Yes, the time has come. Letters have arrived from my family, begging me to return. They need me.'

Jacob's face showed his distress. 'But I thought you would stay here forever!'

'Forever is a long time, Jacob, even for me. I have been thinking for some months that my time here was drawing to a close. You are almost grown up and my job is done. You don't need me as your teacher now.'

Jairus frowned at him. Inside he felt sick at the thought of losing Levi, but nothing he was feeling showed on his face.

'Why do you speak as though teaching us was the main reason you came to live here?'

'Because it was, Jairus, strange though it may seem to you. I was traveling through Galilee and when I reached Capernaum the two of you were the compelling reason that made me settle down and make this town my home.'

There was much about this that was beyond Jairus, and he hated mysteries. His frown deepened. 'That makes no sense. You had never met us until the first day you came to the school. How could we be the reason you stayed?'

Levi sat down and put his hands together, resting his fingers on his lips. Jacob recognized the gesture; it was what Levi did when he needed time to answer a difficult question. He flashed a look across at Jairus. Why couldn't his friend see Levi did not want to be pressed on this matter? Jairus ignored him, never taking his eyes off Levi's face. He looks just like a dog with a bone, thought Jacob.

Levi looked at Jairus speculatively. He understood Jairus well; knew he battled with inadequacy, saw beyond the closed exterior to the boiling pot of emotion beneath. It made Levi reluctant to tell him that he had seen Jacob in the temple when he was a child. Would it be the final blow to Jairus's fragile self-esteem to be told that Jacob was the reason he had stayed in Capernaum? It seemed strange that nothing ever convinced Jairus of how much his teacher loved him.

I would have stayed just for you Jairus, he thought. You will be such a strong and principled leader, someone worth investing your life in. What was it Samuel had said so long ago? "The best pupil I have ever taught."

Levi sighed. He could say the same. Jacob was extraordinary, but Jairus was a man you could build on.

'I can't explain it all to you,' he said, 'not all of it, but I do want to tell you part of what happened. I have waited for you to come to a place where you can grasp it; you and Jacob. How quickly these years have slipped away. Now I have to leave, and I cannot wait any longer even if I wanted to. You are old enough to hear what I have to say.'

He gestured towards the chairs in front of his table. 'Come, both of you and sit down. This may take a little while.'

Jacob and Jairus exchanged glances. Jacob's mind was still reeling from the fact Levi was leaving. He wanted to beg the Rabbi to stay. How could he survive without him? Jairus's heart was in turmoil too, but his face remained impassive. He sat down and gave Levi his full attention.

The old man gazed at their faces. They were not men yet, and he wondered if he was making a terrible mistake. He shut his eyes. Half the night he had worried about this moment, hoping he would know for sure what to do. Now it was upon him and he felt he had no choice. He had always been convinced God had sent him here to be their teacher, and finally they had come to this, their most important lesson. He wondered if what he was going to tell them would change their lives as profoundly as it had changed his.

He drew in a deep breath. There was much to say.

'I grew up in a town close to Jerusalem. I was full of questions, much like you Jacob, and I loved the law, much like you Jairus.' He smiled at the memory. 'I was a very passionate young man.

My father took me often to the feasts in Jerusalem and eventually I got to know an unusual man who spent most of his time in the temple. When I first met him, I suppose he must have been about the same age I am now. Which seemed very old to me! Despite his age I had never met anyone so full of excitement. He fascinated me.

'Why?' asked Jacob.

Levi paused for a moment. 'He said God had spoken to him.'

Jacob's face lit up, but Levi held up his hand to restrain him.

'Wait,' he insisted, 'or I will never be able to finish. The man's name was Simeon. There were many in the temple who did not believe him of course, even in those days, but I did, right from the start. You only had to see the light in his eyes.'

Levi fell silent, as though seeing again Simeon's face.

Jairus sat absolutely still, but Jacob was seething with impatience. What did God say? What did God say? The question ran around his brain insistently.

Levi could put the moment off no longer. He looked intently from one face to the other.

'God had told him he would see the Messiah.'

Jacob's eyes glowed. 'And you believed him?' he asked breathlessly.

'Have I not said so?'

Levi was watching Jairus's face. It was immobile, almost frozen into stillness. Shock was in his eyes.

Jacob leapt up, unable to keep still. Someone had heard God! He wanted to shout and sing, but Levi's voice cut across his rejoicing.

'Come and sit down again Jacob. There is more to tell; indeed, that was just the beginning. Year by year I visited the temple and sought Simeon out. He prayed and believed and lived always in expectation. Never once did his faith waver. For me it was an inspiration just to be around him, but the sad thing was, as he grew older and older no one took any notice of him anymore.'

'Except you!' said Jacob.

Levi nodded.

'How long did he wait?' Jairus's voice was harsh with cynicism.

Levi looked for a long time into his face.

'Thirty-five years,' he said.

Jacob's mouth fell open with shock, but Jairus leaned back in his chair, somehow deeply satisfied. 'No wonder no-one believed him!' he said.

A look of pain crossed Levi's face. 'But I believed him Jairus. I always had.'

Jairus scowled as though he had been rebuked and the tension in the room deepened. Jacob had a dozen things he wanted to ask, but something held him back. His eyes never left Levi's face as the Rabbi continued his story.

'Eight years ago, was the last time I saw him. He was sitting in the cool of the evening, dozing in a corner when I found him. His hands were thin and cold as I took them in my own, the skin like parchment. When he awoke, I knew at once something had happened. He seemed infinitely older, as though he had faded away since my last visit, but his eyes! I will never forget the look in his eyes!

"Are you well Simeon?" I asked him.

"No," he said, "I am dying," but he laughed as he said it. "It doesn't matter now Levi. I have seen him!"

I remember I sat there unable to speak. I was stupefied. I think the look on my face amused him.

"It had to happen sometime you know," he said with gentle reproof, and for the first time I wondered if I had ever truly believed him.

"What happened?" I asked.

"You know," he said, "it's strange. When God first spoke to me that I would see him, I was afraid I might miss the moment. You know, be in the wrong place at the wrong time! Such foolishness, such needless anxiety. I should have trusted God would keep his promise. And he did! They brought him in just a few weeks ago. I wish you could have been here to see him. It was the fulfilment of all my dreams."

How profoundly I wished I had been there too. To meet the Messiah. I could hardly imagine it. Like a fool I asked,

"Who brought him in?" In my mind's eye I could see them, a huge crowd of followers, absolute proof Simeon's unwavering faith had been justified.

He looked at me and it was obvious he was puzzled. "Why his parents of course," he said. "Who else? They brought him to the temple to offer the sacrifice of thanksgiving for his birth."

His eyes shone, too big for his lined face. "I held him in my arms," he said.

My mind was reeling in confusion. "He is a baby?" I stammered. I was thinking of the thousands and thousands of babies brought into the temple every year.

He just nodded his head. "I held him in my arms," he repeated, as if that memory itself held the greatest wonder.

I sat beside him desperately trying to think. In the end I had to ask some of the questions flooding through my brain. I knew they seemed full of unbelief, but I just couldn't help myself.

"How did you know it was him? Did his parents tell you? Did he seem different? What kind of people were they? Did they come from Bethlehem?"

He chuckled and laid his hand on my arm. "Levi," he said, "God told me! I have often wondered myself how I would know him, but in the end, there could be no mistake. They were just an ordinary couple, she was young; he was a good deal older. The baby looked ordinary too, just like so many others, but a light shone around them. I saw it clearly. It was the light that drew me into that part of the temple.

They were waiting in line with several other couples when I saw them. I laughed loudly, which surprised those who were standing nearby; as though that mattered! Everyone thinks I'm mad anyway. I took him from his mother and held him. God gave me words for them; not all easy words, but then think what an incredible privilege they have. They will bring up the Messiah!" His voice was full of excitement.

"Did others see the light?" I asked him. It seemed a very important question to me. For a long time, I had been resentful that the powerful men in the temple refused to believe God had spoken to Simeon. I had huge respect for his godliness and I wanted him to be vindicated before everyone. I felt he deserved it. I remember the look of deep satisfaction that came over his face.

"Oh yes," he said, "Anna the prophetess who lives in the temple like me, she saw it too, and she also spoke to them."

"But," I stammered, "what about the Pharisees and the High Priest? Did they see it? They must have seen it!"

He gave me a knowing smile. "You have met them, my boy, would you expect them to see it?"

There was nothing more for me to say. I led him out into the temple court and made him sit down so the dying rays of the sun could shine on his face.

"I will not live long now," he whispered. "I have been waiting to tell you."

He squeezed my arm as I sat by his side. I had never understood until then how much our friendship had meant to both of us. I was desolate at the thought of losing him.

"Don't grieve too much, my son," he said, although I knew he was almost too weary to speak. "Always remember, he is here. I have seen him!"

He gestured out at the vast, noisy crowd. "Somewhere, perhaps very close, he will grow up into manhood. I will not live to see him in his glory, but that does not matter. He is here! That is the only thing that matters now for any of us."

His head dropped onto his chest in the sudden sleep of old age, and I sat beside him for a long while, looking out on the crowd as he had, trying to come to terms with what he had said.'

Levi put his hand up to his face and slowly ran his fingers across his brow.

'I never saw him again,' he said.

Silence filled the room. The usually talkative Jacob sat immobile. Jairus said nothing. Levi sat for a while deep in thought and then he dragged his attention back to the boys who sat before him.

'The child Simeon spoke of is already eight years old,' he said. 'I still believe what he said was the simple truth. I believe the Messiah is here.'

Jacob could only whisper, "the Messiah," as though the words were too sacred to be uttered.

'Yes, the Messiah,' said Levi, and standing up abruptly he began to pace around the room. 'I have thought and worried and prayed about this information, this revelation, for years. It will shake the nation. Do you remember Herod killing all the baby boys in Bethlehem?'

Jacob nodded, that seemed long ago, when they were children.

'Most people think it was an act of meaningless violence, but I am not so sure. Odd rumours were flying about Jerusalem at that time; stories of Magi from the East. It is said they came looking for a new king. Herod is ruthless and would do anything to safeguard his throne. What if he discovered the Messiah had been born, and tried to kill the child? The scriptures predict the birth in Bethlehem. The massacre there is surely too much of a coincidence. It must all be connected. I am convinced God will have protected the boy. I must believe that.

But still the fact the Messiah has been born is a very dangerous piece of information. Can you imagine how many enemies he will have? More enemies than friends. He must be kept hidden, given time to grow up and reach maturity in safety. If only I could help him, but there is no way of knowing where he is! Ah the frustration of knowing too little.'

Jacob had never seen the Rabbi so animated. He felt he was listening to arguments rehearsed a thousand times; concerns that had no answer.

'Secrecy is his best protection. I came to that conclusion long ago. So, I have told no-one.'

Jairus suddenly sprang to his feet. 'But you have told us!' he cried. 'Why have you broken your long silence and laid this terrible responsibility on us? Even if we believe you, what do you expect us to do?'

Jacob looked up at him in surprise. He had never heard Jairus speak to Levi in such a way. He seemed angry, thrusting out his jaw as he faced Levi across the room. Levi pulled himself up to his full height, unused to anything but respect from his pupils. After a moment he relaxed and spoke softly, almost hesitantly,

'I am sorry you are finding this hard Jairus. You are right, I have kept this to myself for a long time; perhaps too long. I knew it would be a shock to you both. How could it be otherwise? You and Jacob will need time to think about what I have said.'

Jairus let his eyes drop and walked to the other side of the room. Levi sat down once more in his chair. He wanted to kick himself. He had said too much too soon. The relief of speaking about the Messiah at last had swept away all his good intentions of breaking the news to them gently. How exactly do you tell someone the Messiah has been born, he wondered? Apparently, it was beyond him, even with all the years he had had to plan it.

Jacob went and knelt beside him. 'Levi,' he said, 'please tell us why you have shared this with us when you have kept it secret for so long. Explain that to us.'

Jairus stood in the corner with his arms folded; shaking his head when Jacob motioned him to come closer.

Levi began to speak again more slowly. 'When the letter came from my eldest son asking me to return home, I was not surprised. I have known for months my time here was drawing to a close.'

He looked over at Jairus. 'You will become a fine man and an excellent Rabbi, maybe even synagogue ruler one day.'

When he looked at Jacob, he smiled. 'You will marry a certain young lady and become Capernaum's best merchant'.

Jacob flushed scarlet.

'These things are obvious, and I am proud of you both, proud to have been part of your life. But there is more to my being here than that. Nothing is ever by chance. From the first day Simeon told me the Messiah is growing up somewhere in Israel, I have been thinking about him.'

He looked at Jacob's face, and then at Jairus who still stood immovable.

'Don't you see it could be another twenty years before his mission begins? Too long for me; I am too old. I will not live to see him grow into a man. But with you two it is different. You are young. The day will come when you will see him revealed to Israel and then you will have the opportunity to become his disciples. What a privilege! Simeon passed this revelation on to me and I am passing it on to you. Think of it! You will see his day. You will be the ones who follow him. Doesn't that thought fill you with excitement?'

Jacob knelt on the floor unable to lift his head. A strange sensation was going through him. Was this the reason for the

awareness of God he had always experienced? Could God be
calling him to follow the Messiah in the days to come? Was this
his destiny? He remained motionless as a puddle of tears formed
beneath him on the ground.

Levi saw the hardness on Jairus's face. How well he
understood these two young men. Jacob would accept all he said
without question, but Jairus was different. His character was
such that he hated to make sudden decisions and took a long
time to come to any conclusion. To have this presented in such
a manner was almost impossible for him. Levi wondered if he
should have been introducing this subject gradually, over years.
He had thought about it often and hadn't known what to do.
How could he have shared such an important secret before the
boys were old enough to keep it successfully? Now as he saw the
resistance in Jairus he wished he could soften the effect of such a
bald revelation.

'Do you believe me?' he said at last.

Jairus's eyes narrowed. 'What do the scriptures say?'

Levi sighed. 'I have studied them for years Jairus, and I have
taught you what they say. Is it so hard to believe the Messiah has
come?'

'For me it is, although it probably won't be for Jacob!'

'I feared you would find this difficult. I wish I could have told
you before. Now I can only assure you I would stake my life on
the truth of what Simeon said. I wish you could trust me.' He
shook his head. 'Perhaps it is not my task to convince you.
Perhaps the Messiah will do that for himself. I think it will be so.
All I ask is you remember what I have said and keep it secret. If
the Messiah never appears, you can be satisfied you were right,
and put all this down to an old man's ravings, but if one day you
see him for yourself, then you will have a decision to make. I
cannot make it for you, even though I love you.'

His face softened as he looked at Jairus. 'I know you will come to understand all this in the end, even if I am not here to persuade you.'

Something in Jairus broke and crossing the room, he grasped the Rabbi's hand. 'I am sorry to be so uncertain. I want to believe you, but it seems - incredible.'

'It is incredible, especially for you who have not met Simeon. Wait Jairus. When he is grown, he will not stay hidden forever. Once he is revealed you will be certain. I know it.'

Levi sat for a moment saying nothing. He seemed to have shrunk in size, as though in sharing his secret he had somehow grown older. Jairus stood by his chair, laying aside the mystery of the Messiah, focusing only on the terrible truth that his beloved teacher was going away. His eyes filled with tears. No one noticed.

Jacob slowly got up from the ground, conflicting emotions in his heart. They would have to say good-bye to Levi; it was terrible news, yet at this last moment he had deposited something inside them which was beyond price.

The truth burned secretly within him. The Messiah is here, he thought in wonder. He is growing, playing, learning, scraping his knees. Is he quick and clever or a silent withdrawn little boy? Does he know already who he is? Does he hear God? Is he ever disobedient to his parents, or is he perfect in every way? The question filled his mind, as it would for years.

What must it be like to be the Messiah?

Micah

Micah loved business. It wasn't just the sweet contentment of having enough money, although anyone from his poor background could be excused for feeling that. No, it was something about the actual making of the money that kept him trading, even when his wife vehemently declared they had enough.

He was in Capernaum on a new venture and there was a lightness to his step and a tingling in his veins. He was going to strike a good bargain. He could just feel it.

He strolled through the market and noticed there was no stall specializing in spices and none of the spices on display were up to his excellent standard. It was hard not to rub his hands together with satisfaction, but he kept them firmly at his side. It wouldn't do to look too eager.

Benjamin's stall was in a prime position in the center of the market. Micah stopped in front of it and admired the well displayed, high quality produce. Perhaps he should take some fruit home to his adoring wife and his baby son Simon.

'Can I help you sir?' Jacob had been watching him from behind the stall.

Micah's hand hovered over some exceptional figs, but eventually he decided on the glistening dates which made even his mouth water. 'Are these dates good?' he questioned.

He hadn't intended to say that, but found he couldn't help himself. He had to strike a deal even over a few dates!

Jacob's eyebrows lifted in surprise. No one questioned the quality of his father's merchandise. At least no one in Capernaum.

'I think you will find them the best in the market. Would you like to try one?' he said. Micah nodded and selected a date carefully. Jacob noticed the rings on his hands and his fine clothes. A rich stranger was a novelty in a town full of fishermen.

'Excellent, really excellent!' said Micah. 'Your proud boast is well deserved.'

'My father sells everything of the finest,' said Jacob with a smile.

Micah looked over the produce. 'But no spices I see.'

Jacob looked at the man again, glancing down at his hands and instantly he understood. This stranger was a spice merchant and a successful one at that. Jacob called to his father who was chatting just a short distance away.

'Come and greet this gentleman Father, he is a spice merchant.'

Benjamin came over at once. 'I am pleased to meet you. Do you indeed deal in spices?'

'I do, although I am at a loss to know how your son guessed my occupation.'

Benjamin shrugged his shoulders. 'This boy is a mystery to many, although I believe he may have seen the spice stains on your hands.'

Micah looked at his fingers and laughed. 'A clue indeed, but still an unusual boy to have noticed.'

'Yes,' said Benjamin. 'Very unusual.'

The two men quickly became involved in conversation, and to Jacob's frustration he was called away to serve the many customers who lingered over the stall. After a while he was able to stand and listen as Micah offered Benjamin a business opportunity.

'I would supply you with the finest spices Capernaum has ever seen.'

Jacob's heart was beating with excitement as he waited for his father's reply.

Benjamin looked unconvinced. 'I know spices need special care to keep them fresh and aromatic. I don't have the time or the inclination to set up a different kind of business here. We are already committed to searching out the best growers and often we have to bring the produce in from the country ourselves. I cannot maintain a high standard without ceaseless hard work. A new venture? It would be hard.'

'Hard but not impossible? I would love to do business with you.'

Benjamin shrugged his shoulders. 'Why?' he said.

Micah didn't have to think about it. 'You are an excellent businessman and they are difficult to find. My guess is I could scour this whole market and not find another with your skill and expertise. I want to set up a stall here. Will you consider my offer?'

Benjamin opened his mouth, but it was Jacob who answered.

'I could do it Father!' Benjamin spun round to look at him.

'Do what?' he said, annoyed the lad had been listening.

'Run a spice stall!'

Benjamin laughed. 'As if you know anything about spices!'

'No, of course I don't, but this gentleman could teach me, and you must admit I am quick to learn!'

'Why would you want to learn?' asked Micah, who was interested in the lad's enthusiasm. Jacob shifted his weight from one foot to another and then began to speak too quickly.

'Father says I have a gift for business, but I don't just want to work for him forever. No offence Father, but I think I could do something different, and selling spices would be perfect because everyone uses them all the time. When you were talking, but I couldn't hear you, I felt what you were discussing was something to do with me; about my future. So, I think I am supposed to be the one who runs the spice stall. In fact, I am sure of it!'

He stopped and looked expectantly from one face to the other. Benjamin had the stolid, patient look he always wore when Jacob was being incomprehensible, and Micah simply looked bemused. All Jacob's excitement vanished in a moment. It was obvious neither of the men had a clue what he was talking about. Didn't anyone else ever get these strange flashes of inspiration? He felt stupid and hopelessly inexperienced. Hanging his head, he mumbled,

'I'm sorry if I interrupted your conversation. I didn't intend to be rude. I just think a spice stall would be a wonderful idea, absolutely wonderful.'

Benjamin ignored him and turned to speak to Micah. 'I will consider your proposition. Will you be returning to Capernaum soon?'

Jacob had turned away so no one could see the embarrassment on his face, but Micah was still watching him.

'I will return in two weeks,' he said. Then leaning forward, he indicated Jacob with a slight movement of his head. 'And, I would be prepared to train your son,' he said softly.

Benjamin looked at him in amazement. 'Really?' he said. 'Why?'

Micah smiled. 'All good businessmen are men of imagination'. He spoke more loudly so Jacob could hear. Jacob turned back towards them and Micah could see his face. The merchant looked into the lad's eyes and Jacob returned the stare with steady determination.

Micah nodded his head and turned his attention back to Benjamin. 'You will consider?' he queried.

Benjamin looked from the stranger to his son and back again. Jacob held his breath. At last Benjamin spoke. He fully intended to say no. After all, however much Jacob thought it was a good idea, he didn't actually want a spice stall! He knew he would have to deal with Jacob's disappointment, but business was business, and it couldn't be run on sentiment. His mind was made up. He looked the merchant straight in the eye.

'I will,' he said to his own amazement, and stood dumbfounded as sheer delight leapt into Jacob's eyes. The merchant seemed delighted too and gripped Benjamin's arm as he said farewell.

Benjamin ran a hand over his confused brow. Why had he said that? What on earth had possessed him? Why hadn't he simply said no? Should he call back the merchant and explain he had changed his mind; that he had never intended to say yes in the first place? His reputation as a man of his word made him hesitate; that and the fact he would look a complete fool! Who says yes when they mean no? Certainly no one who considers themselves a good businessman. He couldn't believe his own stupidity.

Jacob spoke into his bewilderment. 'Thank you, Father!' he said, as though Benjamin had given him the world already!

'Don't thank me,' he replied gruffly. 'I only said I will consider the proposition. Nothing is settled yet!'

'Of course!' said Jacob and there was so much excitement in his voice Benjamin had to walk away before he exploded with exasperation.

Benjamin tried to dismiss the conversation with Micah from his mind. The whole suggestion was ridiculous, and he was determined it wasn't going to happen, but to his annoyance he found the idea of a spice stall persistently buzzing around in his head. If it had been a fly, he would have swatted it.

When they got home, Jacob disappeared into the kitchen and began to question his mother about her use of spices and where she purchased them. He listened attentively to her complaints of poor quality and worse availability and the more she complained the more he smiled.

The next day at the market Jacob was mysteriously missing from behind the stall. He was gone for some time and Benjamin found he was left alone to serve the customers. As the minutes turned into hours, Benjamin became more and more annoyed, but at the same time it began to dawn on him how useful Jacob was; almost indispensable. Simple, obvious tasks just didn't get done without Jacob there, and Benjamin was surprised by how much he had come to rely on his son. Of course, he didn't express any sense of gratitude for Jacob's diligence when the lad eventually came back. Quite the reverse!

'Where exactly do you think you have been? Don't tell me you've been fishing with Jairus!'

'Really Father, as if I would on a market day. No, I have been finding out about our competition.'

'But we don't have any competition!'

'Well, not much anyway, but if we went into selling spices, I reckon we would make a magnificent profit.'

Benjamin's cheeks flushed red. 'Spices? Who said anything about us selling spices?'

Jacob's mouth dropped open. 'You did Father! You told the merchant you would consider his proposition. Well, I have been considering it! I have bought spices from everyone in the market who sells them. I must say I see what Mother means about poor quality. Some of them are not kept well at all. I have learnt a lot about the different kinds and what they do. Obviously, there is much I still don't know, but I think……'

Benjamin's frustration was obvious. 'Get behind this stall; do your job; which I have had to do in your place all morning, and get rid of any notion you have we are going to run a spice stall!'

'But…'

'No!' said Benjamin, much more loudly than he intended. Several people turned to see what was going on. Benjamin's face grew even redder. Pulling Jacob to one side he lowered his voice and said vehemently, 'Even if the man comes back, which is very unlikely, I have already decided we cannot get involved in another venture and I don't want to hear another word about it!'

Jacob's ludicrous disappointment made Benjamin angrier than ever.

Jacob was unusually silent during the evening meal.

Leah looked at him with concern. 'What is troubling you, Jacob?'

Jacob looked first at her and then at Benjamin. 'Nothing, Mother, I am all right.'

Frowning she turned to Benjamin. 'Is everything all right with you as well?'

'Perfect!' he said sullenly.

'I see,' she said.

The two older sons exchanged knowing glances. They had been out on the carts bringing the produce to market when the spice merchant had been to the stall, but with the inevitable gossip of a small town they already knew something had happened to make their father and Jacob at odds with each other. The smaller children looked on in wide-eyed wonder. Tension was unusual in their loving home.

That evening when Benjamin should have been relaxing, he found himself strangely agitated. The words "spice stall" hung in the air, like an indefinable, clinging smell that permeated his thoughts. He couldn't shake it off. The fact Jacob had gone silently to his bedroom after refusing to eat his favourite meal, did nothing to help. Benjamin squirmed in his seat by the fire as

Leah sat opposite him, her needlework in her lap, waiting for her moment.

'What is it, Benjamin?' she said.

'You won't like it,' he said gloomily.

'Tell me,' she said.

'Jacob told you about the spice merchant from Gennesaret who came to the market yesterday?'

'He didn't say where he came from, but he told me the man wanted to do business with you.'

'Not just that, he wants to train Jacob to run a spice stall in our market.'

'Jacob? How would he train him?'

'We didn't discuss it. Jacob wants to run the stall, says he 'feels' it is the right thing for him. He got very excited, of course, and now he is not speaking because I said no.'

'Why did you say no? Do you think Jacob is too young? Not capable? You would be there to help him, wouldn't you?'

'Yes, I would be there, but he is young, much too young. Maybe in another year or two! This is just the wrong time.'

'I heard you only last Sabbath boasting about what a head for business Jacob has. You said he takes after you!'

Benjamin laughed ruefully. 'Oh, that is true enough, but I left out the part where I have to keep a constant watch on him or he will give away produce from the stall to those who are needy, and he often gives away the money I pay him to beggars on the road. The boy is incorrigibly generous.'

Leah tried to keep the satisfied smile off her face, but Benjamin was not fooled. 'I know,' he said, 'he takes after you too!'

He got up to put a log on the fire and Leah watched him fondly. Beneath his gruff exterior was a kind, generous man, perhaps more generous than she and Jacob put together.

'Why did you think I wouldn't like the idea of Jacob running a stall? I think he could do it, and you know very well that when he gets these feelings he is very often proved right. In fact, you are coming to rely on his judgement aren't you, despite his youth? What do you really think?'

'I think there is always something going on around Jacob I can't fathom. It's as if he was born into the wrong time, or the wrong family or something and I definitely don't know how to be a good father to him. Either he is full of questions or he is full of feelings and I'm not the right man to help him with either. I told the merchant Jacob is a mystery and that is what he is to me; a complete mystery!'

'Oh Benjamin, you are a good father to him. You will find a way through into the right thing for him. I know you will!'

'I think that's the trouble! I think I do know the right thing. Everything tells me I should refuse this offer and let Jacob continue with me in the market. He went off to discover about spices today and that made it very clear to me how much I would miss him if he were to go away.'

Leah's needlework dropped into her lap. 'Go away?' she said faintly.

'The merchant would need to take him to his home town to teach him the trade. It wouldn't be for long, but yes, he would have to go away.'

'Gennesaret?' she said, trying hard to adjust to this new idea.

The town was further west along the edge of the lake; not far, but Leah had never been outside of Capernaum. A more pressing concern made her stretch out her hand to Benjamin.

'Can you trust this man?' she asked anxiously.

'How do I know?' he replied impatiently. 'I have only just met him! Jacob doesn't see any of the difficulties, but I have to weigh them all up. Can I spare him while he is learning the trade?

After today I very much doubt it! Then there is the expense of setting up a new stall in the market, and splitting my time between the two, at least at first until Jacob is on his feet. And I will have to work out an arrangement with this merchant of how the profits will be divided. There is so much to consider!'

Leah looked at him with troubled eyes. 'But it sounds as though you have already decided to let him go! Surely you are against the idea? Aren't you?'

Benjamin looked harassed. 'I thought I was. I still am; except there is this thought or feeling or something going around inside me.'

Leah brushed away a tear. 'You are starting to sound like Jacob!'

'I know! And I have been trying to resist it; truly I have, but somehow, I get the impression Jacob is supposed to run this stall. I can't shake off the certainty that if I don't let him go it would be a mistake.'

Leah smiled at him. 'Perhaps you are the right father for him after all.'

Benjamin wrapped his arms around her. 'I hope so!' he said.

Some weeks later Micah was standing at the end of his display of spices in the market at Genneseret, some distance from where Jacob was serving the customers. Jacob was watching Micah with interest because he was talking to a thin man with an eager look on his face. Jacob shifted slightly so he could watch the expression in the man's eyes as he talked animatedly to Micah. Jacob guessed the man was talking business, and just at that moment Micah seemed to become aware of Jacob's scrutiny and glanced across at his young apprentice. Jacob frowned at him and gave a tiny shake of his head before giving his full attention to a demanding customer.

It was over in a moment, but still Micah was intrigued by that brief interaction. He brought the matter up when he and Jacob were sitting together over their evening meal. Micah's wife was putting their young son Simon to bed, and the two men were alone.

'The man I was talking to in the market today…'

Jacob's lip curled with disdain. 'Do you do business with him?'

'Not yet, and I gather you would advise against it.'

Jacob put his knife down and looked at Micah searchingly. 'I don't think you trust him any more than I do.'

'And how exactly would you know that?'

'I have observed you with people you trust; you have a way of standing much closer to them, and you laugh more. With him you kept your distance, and your hand was on your purse throughout the conversation.'

For a moment Micah was taken aback, but then he leaned forward and clapped Jacob on the shoulder.

'Very good!' he said appreciatively. Jacob was gratified by the compliment.

'Do you suspect him of unfair dealing?' he asked.

'I suspect him of anything underhand he feels he can get away with, but that is not the point.'

Jacob looked up again from his meal. 'Well, if you don't intend to have anything to do with him, what is the point?'

Micah looked across the table. 'The point is it took me many years to learn how to be a good judge of character. You don't acquire that skill overnight, and it is vital to know who you can trust, especially when you are dealing with men who come from distant lands.'

'But you are good at that now, aren't you?'

Micah nodded his head. 'Now? Yes! But unfortunately, in the past I have made some shocking mistakes and many of them were hard to recover from!' He sighed as he looked at Jacob. 'I tell you,' he said, 'experience may be a good teacher, but it can be an expensive one too. In this business you can make a lot of money very quickly or lose it just as easily. You have to have your wits about you. When I meet someone new, like that trader, I call on all my skill to deal with them. I look at their eyes, and how they hold themselves, and what they do with their hands. Just as you observed me today!'

'What was it that made you suspicious?'

Micah scratched his head. 'I can't tell you. Eventually I think you come to a place where you know certain people aren't to be trusted and you couldn't even explain why.'

'That's it!' said Jacob with satisfaction. 'I have never been able to explain that feeling to Father. He is so straight-forward and trustworthy himself he just can't see when someone is trying to cheat him.'

'But you can?'

'Yes, as you said, you just know. At first Father wouldn't listen to me, because I was young, I suppose, but now he does.'

'Why?'

'Because I get it right really often, and ....' Jacob stopped in mid-sentence and looked embarrassed.

'And he doesn't like to be proved wrong!'

Jacob shrugged his shoulders and grinned.

'There is still something I want to know.' Micah said.

'What?' said Jacob, through another mouthful of excellent food.

'I have had to learn this skill, but you say you just feel it. How?'

Micah was surprised by the anxiety which sprang into Jacob's eyes. 'You don't want to tell me?' he asked gently. Now Jacob looked trapped. Micah wondered at the extraordinary range of emotion Jacob could display on his face. It must surely be a huge disadvantage when striking a bargain. There was a short silence while as far as Micah could see Jacob was screwing up his courage. What was it his father had said about him? "This boy is a mystery."

Micah smiled at the memory, for he found he was already exceedingly fond of this mystery from Capernaum.

At last Jacob spoke. 'For as long as I can remember I have had this feeling inside, this longing to know God.'

Micah struggled to keep his amazement hidden. All or nothing with this young man apparently. When he had asked Jacob to explain his ability to read people, he hadn't expected to be plunged immediately into such deep waters. A longing to know God? How exactly was he supposed to respond to such a statement? Fortunately, Jacob didn't appear to need any response. The lad ploughed straight on, explaining about going to Jerusalem and then how Levi had come to their town and what a wonderful teacher he was.

'He helped you with this feeling you have?' Micah thought it a really stupid question, but he had never heard anyone speak of such things before and he had no idea what to say.

Jacob didn't seem to notice his awkwardness. 'Yes, he has helped me very much. He helps me to feel normal, even if no one else feels these things quite like I do. It is horrible when even your family don't see what to you is obvious. I have never been able to explain to Father that somehow, and I honestly don't know how, I just know things!'

'About whether people are to be trusted, you mean?' Micah was trying hard to keep up.

Jacob nodded. 'But not just that. Other things too. I often know whether Father should get involved with someone, and it has nothing to do with whether they are honest or not. Like you!'

'Thank you!' Micah said sarcastically, but Jacob didn't notice.

'Before you came to Capernaum, I had known for weeks I was supposed to run my own stall. I couldn't see how it was going to happen, but the plans for it were right there in my mind. Then, when you appeared at Father's stall, I just knew that......'

Micah looked into the innocent young face before him. 'You knew that...?' he prompted.

Jacob took a deep breath. 'That God had sent you!'

To Jacob's surprise Micah roared with laughter. Then he leaned forward and gripped the arm of the lad who sat mortified before him.

'I'm sorry, please forgive me! I didn't mean to laugh. It's just I have never been the answer to someone's prayers before!'

Jacob sighed. 'I don't expect you to understand. No one else does! It is the same feeling I have about God. There is something inside and I have learned to trust it. That is how I know things. All sorts of different things! I think it will make me a good businessman. Don't you?'

Micah wondered what on earth he was supposed to say, and then he reflected he wasn't required to be this extraordinary young man's teacher, or at least only in matters of business.

'I think it will make you a very good businessman, as long as it is infallible,' he said briskly, 'but in the meantime we have to work on you learning to keep your emotions off your face.'

'My face?' queried Jacob.

'Yes,' said Micah. 'You have to perfect the art of not letting everyone know what you are thinking! That face of yours is so expressive. Now look at my face. Can you tell what I am thinking?'

'No,' said Jacob uncertainly. He felt it was some kind of test and he was concerned about failing.

'Good!' said Micah.

'What were you thinking about?' Jacob asked, ever curious.

'That's my business, and I want it to stay that way. You don't want anyone to know what is going on in your mind. It has to be your secret. Whether you are delighted or disappointed your expression must remain the same, because people will take advantage of you if they can. You can't always avoid dealing with crafty people, so you must remain scrupulously honest, but hard to read. Do you understand?'

Jacob nodded.

'Excellent! I am going to teach you how to strike a great bargain. With that skill, and those feelings of yours, you should do very well!'

Jacob's face lit up, radiating sheer delight Micah had faith in him. Micah shook his head. Had he taken on an impossible task?

The Carpenter

When Jacob got back from Gennesaret his plan was to set up his stall immediately. Micah had told him to get everything prepared and then he would come and bring the first stock with him. Jacob was excited and plunged into the work with enthusiasm, but Benjamin had other ideas.

'We're off to Nazareth,' he said.

Jacob was surprised. 'Why?' he asked.

Benjamin looked at him speculatively. The lad had only been away a few weeks, but he seemed different; more confident. Somehow Benjamin felt it was important to stamp his seal of ownership on this new venture. He couldn't have Jacob and Micah planning things behind his back; after all the stall would be his, the investment his, the risk his.

'I want to visit your uncle Ebenezer. He runs a stall much like mine, but I hear there is a spice stall in Nazareth, and he will introduce me to the man who runs it. I need advice on what would be a fair price for the spices. Your uncle is a shrewd businessman and will help to ensure I am not cheated by your new friend.'

Jacob was appalled. 'Micah would not cheat you!'

Benjamin pulled a face. 'Perhaps not,' he said. 'But I want to make sure! After all he does come from the other side of the lake!'

Jacob laughed out loud. 'Oh Father, you can't be suspicious of people just because they don't come from Capernaum; and besides you know you can trust my judgment. Micah is a good, fair man. I have been working for him for weeks, and I should know. Is it really necessary to go? I want to get on with building the stall!'

Benjamin was obdurate. 'Yes, it is necessary, and you are coming with me, so don't even bother to argue.'

Jacob sighed. He didn't want to leave Capernaum again, not even for a short trip inland to Nazareth. He had counted every step as he came back home, desperate for the chance to catch a glimpse of Rebekah. His longing to be near her had been the only problem during his weeks away, and now he was to be dragged off again and he hadn't even seen her! He knew better than to try and persuade his father when he was in this stubborn mood so he gave in as gracefully as he could.

To his surprise he enjoyed the journey. He and Benjamin had much to talk about, the new town, its market and the things he had learnt about the spice trade. Benjamin listened, and found a new respect for his son. The lad was talking a lot of sense and he wondered how such a short trip away could have made such a difference. He paid particular attention to everything Jacob had to say about Micah and his business. While Jacob had been gone Benjamin had been having serious second thoughts about getting involved with this stranger, but Jacob's astute observations reassured him. Perhaps Micah was to be trusted after all.

They both enjoyed their time with Ebenezer. He was a large, flamboyant character who dwarfed even Benjamin, and Jacob felt he had never laughed so much in his life.

The first morning in Nazareth they visited the spice stall, and as they approached it Benjamin asked Ebenezer, 'What kind of man is this merchant?'

Ebenezer seemed to think about his answer. 'He is doing well,' he said.

'And obviously he is trustworthy?' Benjamin wasn't really asking a question, more making a statement. Ebenezer smiled broadly and looked from Benjamin back to Jacob. They had come within sight of the stall.

'What do you think Jacob?' Ebenezer asked. 'Do you think he is trustworthy?'

The lad looked at the merchant who was coming over to greet them.

'Definitely not!' Jacob said without hesitation.

'You amaze me!' said Ebenezer as he walked forward to embrace the man. Benjamin was deeply embarrassed, but there was no opportunity to remonstrate with Jacob for insulting a complete stranger. The stall holder was eager to show them all his wares and ignoring Jacob, he began to engage Benjamin in conversation. Benjamin found the man charming, and fully intended to let Jacob know how wrong he was, but when he looked around for his son, he saw things had gone from bad to worse.

Jacob was looking over everything in a critical way, obviously unimpressed and he was actually shaking his head with disapproval. Benjamin quickly moved to his side and when the owner's attention was distracted by a customer, he gave Jacob a sharp kick. Jacob, who had just been about to comment on the poor quality of the merchandise, rubbed his ankle indignantly.

'What was that for?' he asked.

'One word out of you and I shall kick you much harder,' said Benjamin fiercely.

Ebenezer stepped forward interposing his large body between the two of them and the market trader. Jacob looked confused, but Benjamin was grateful. He could see Ebenezer's shoulders shaking as he covered the obvious awkwardness with loud conversation. He was grateful Ebenezer was his friend as well as his brother. There was a sudden rush of people around the stall and Benjamin gratefully took the opportunity to stand back and watch the customers.

Jacob quickly joined him. 'You see the money that is changing hands?' he enthused. 'And this is not even a good spice stall!'

'Quiet!' hissed Benjamin, annoyed at his son's continued tactlessness.

'We will make a lot of money, honestly we will! Just look at the merchant's clothes.' Jacob's voice was still too loud, despite the fact he was whispering.

'I said be quiet!' Benjamin insisted, unaware his own voice was increasing in volume. Ebenezer looked over at them with his eyebrows raised in a comical way. It was obvious he could hear every word. Jacob tried not to laugh and wondered what life would have been like with Ebenezer as a father. He thought he had never met two such different brothers. His uncle strode over and stood behind them, draping his arms across their shoulders.

'You two have remarkably loud voices!' he observed jovially. Benjamin and Jacob looked at each other ruefully. Ebenezer's tone became much more serious and he spoke almost in a whisper, so only they could hear.

'Now listen to me! Watch, but don't speak. There will be plenty of time to discuss everything later. Learn all you can from this man, because his situation is much like your own. Observe what you think works well and what you would do differently. What do you think of his position in the market; the way he speaks to his customers; the way he handles his goods? Where do you think he could improve? Oh, and when it comes to money - don't believe a thing he tells you!'

Jacob twisted round to look at him. 'So, you don't trust him either?'

Ebenezer shrugged his shoulders and gave Jacob the most innocent look the lad had ever seen. Benjamin shut his eyes as though in pain. He knew his son! Jacob would be intolerable now he had been proved right. Absolutely intolerable.

They left Nazareth the next day and Ebenezer accompanied them to the outskirts of the town. He drew Benjamin aside and engaged him in a low-voiced conversation which excluded Jacob completely. They had stopped at the entrance to a carpenter's workshop and Jacob wandered over to watch a young lad putting the finishing touches to a stool. Jacob loved to watch people and he was fascinated by the tender touch the boy gave the wood. It was almost as though he were caressing it.

'Do you enjoy your work?' he asked.

The boy looked up and gave him a radiant smile. 'I do,' he said.

'You have made a fine job of this stool.'

'My father and I make beautiful things,' he said, and there was no trace of boasting or arrogance in his voice.

Jacob picked up the stool and examined it. He found he too was running his hand over the wood, somehow feeling its quality through his fingertips. He had never had that experience before. He looked back at the boy who was watching him with interest. Their eyes met, and Jacob had the strangest sense there was some connection between them, some affinity he could not identify.

'What is your name?' he asked.

'Jesus,' the boy replied.

'Well Jesus,' he said, 'I have to build a market stall, and my father is unlikely to employ as good a workman as you or your father.' He looked over and saw Benjamin and Ebenezer were now in conversation with the carpenter.

'Do you think in such a short space of time; while our relatives are talking; you could teach me how to handle the tools of your trade? I am afraid I have much to learn.'

Jesus nodded, grinning with delight, and in a moment the two of them were bending over a piece of wood, laughing at Jacob's poor attempts at carpentry.

Ebenezer introduced Benjamin to Joseph. 'I feel you two have much in common,' he said. 'I have been telling Benjamin you also have an unusual son.' Benjamin blustered, 'Well I wouldn't say Jacob is unusual.'

'Yes, you would,' said Ebenezer, 'you've been saying it for years! Now tell Joseph about your trip to Jerusalem and what happened to Jacob there.' Benjamin frowned, but in the end, when he began to speak of Jacob's childhood and what happened in the temple, he found it was a great relief to talk about it, even to a stranger. To his surprise Joseph seemed to understand completely.

'We took Jesus to the Passover last year,' he said with sympathy. 'A large group of relatives and friends went, which was nearly our undoing! You know how much confusion there is and I thought he was with his mother, and she thought he was with me!'

Benjamin looked at him in surprise. 'You lost him?'

Joseph shuddered as though the horror of it had never left him. 'We had travelled a whole day before we even missed him. Then when we began to search in earnest, we realized we had left him behind. Mary was beside herself, as well she might be. I had to be strong and reassure her everything would be all right, but inside I could hardly bear it. You know what Jerusalem is like at Passover, it's full of strange people from strange lands, and of course there are Roman soldiers everywhere. Anything could have happened to him!'

Now it was Benjamin's turn to feel sympathy. 'How long did it take to find him?'

Joseph shook his head at the memory. 'Three days,' he said.

Benjamin's mouth dropped open. 'Three days?' he repeated.

'The worst three days of my life. We searched all the places we had been in, and many we hadn't. We were at our wits' end. Then Mary suggested we look in the temple. It was a piece of inspiration! There he was, not anxious or fretting, not even feeling lost, just sitting amongst the teachers of the law, listening and asking them questions; as though he belonged there!'

Benjamin was indignant. 'What punishment did you give him? Any son of mine who gave his mother so much worry would have known my wrath, I can tell you.'

Joseph looked at him in perplexity.

'Punishment? I don't think that even occurred to us. We were just delighted to have found him. To lose any child would have been a disaster, but Jesus? That was much worse. How could we have forgiven ourselves?'

Benjamin tried to grasp this. 'It was worse because?'

Joseph seemed flustered, as though he had said too much.

'That doesn't matter. I shouldn't have mentioned it. Let's just say finding him was the best thing that has ever happened to me. His mother remonstrated with him of course, because we had been beside ourselves with worry, but he gave her an answer that left us with nothing to say.'

Benjamin looked at Joseph, a deep frown between his eyes.

'What answer could he possibly have given that would excuse such irresponsible behaviour?' he said.

Joseph smiled gently at him. 'I can't really explain it to you. The truth is I still don't think we fully comprehend his answer ourselves.'

'But you accepted it?'

'Yes.'

'Why?'

'That is inexplicable too. Perhaps you have to know Jesus. He is a remarkable boy. It is simply our privilege to be bringing him up!'

Benjamin looked at him, feeling completely confused. Privilege? It was a privilege to bring up a boy who deliberately gets lost? What exactly was this carpenter talking about? He rubbed his hand over his brow. Somehow this conversation reminded him of the strange complexities of the questions Jacob used to ask him, and now, as then, he found he had a headache.

Ebenezer felt sorry for his brother. Benjamin's expression of complete incomprehension begged for some explanation, but Ebenezer found he had none to offer. Everyone in Nazareth had grown accustomed to the mystery surrounding Jesus. The boy was beloved of all, but different in some indefinable way. Certainly not like his brothers and sisters who were ordinary, every-day children. What marked Jesus out from everyone else? Ebenezer hadn't a clue!

'As I said, you both have unusual sons,' was all he could find to say.

He put his arm reassuringly around Benjamin's shoulder, 'but similar don't you think?'

Benjamin looked over at the young lad who was talking to Jacob. Even he could see that in some way they were alike. But why? Was this boy consumed with questions about God as Jacob had been? Is that what made them seem akin?

Jesus laughed at something Jacob was doing and Benjamin turned back to Joseph.

'You say Jesus had been in the temple all the time, talking to the teachers there?'

'That is certainly where we found him.'

'My Jacob only managed one question and they completely demolished him. They gave no thought to his youth or inexperience, they just crushed his young heart mercilessly. When I thought about it afterwards, I was very angry. How did Jesus fare so much better, especially as you weren't even there?'

Joseph's pride in his son was obvious. 'It would take a lot to demolish Jesus. He is peaceful, even in stressful situations, and wise, way beyond his years.'

'I'll testify to that,' said Ebenezer, 'he is an outstanding boy. I've never met the like of him. He will become someone great when he grows up. You mark my words!'

Benjamin thought of how he had always been uncomfortable with who Jacob was. He certainly wasn't proud like Joseph. How often had he silently wished this son could be more like him? Now Ebenezer said Jacob and Jesus were alike, and that Jesus was going to be someone great. Was Jacob going to be someone great too, and he had just never seen it?

He looked suspiciously at Ebenezer, and sure enough his brother was wearing that innocent expression again. Benjamin recognized that look from their childhood. It meant Ebenezer was up to something. Only gradually did he begin to realise what it was. This was why Ebenezer had stopped here, at the carpenter's shop, to teach him the thing which was obvious to everyone else. Everyone that is, except him!

Jacob was special.

Slowly the truth dawned on him. It was a privilege to raise this son. Not a trial, but a privilege. Leah had been trying to tell him this for years. Why had he never seen it? He could almost feel this new concept changing the way he thought; a special child, a privilege!

He gazed in wonder at his son. Had he ever seen him before? Jacob was a fine young man; faithful; honest, hard-working, but more than all this, he had been born with something extraordinary on the inside of him, something that marked him out as different. Why had he never considered that a good thing?

The three men stood for a while in silence, then with a sigh Benjamin turned to Joseph, one last question uppermost in his mind.

'Ebenezer thinks Jesus will be someone great one day, Joseph. Is that how you see him? Do you think Ebenezer is right?'

Joseph's face lit up and he smiled. 'Undoubtedly!' he said.

'And who does he get that from?' asked Ebenezer, slapping Joseph on the back.

A strange, almost secret look, passed across Joseph's face. 'From his father,' he said softly, and he moved away to where Jesus was teaching Jacob how to use a saw.

Jacob picked up the stool as Benjamin approached.

'Can we buy this stool, Father?'

'What on earth for? We don't need another stool at home.'

'I want to buy it. It is superbly made by this young man and his father and I would like to own it. Customers could sit on it while they choose from the finest spices in the district. Now don't you think that is a great idea?'

Benjamin laid aside the new thoughts about his son. This was a practical matter and he was good at practical things. He didn't want a stool; perhaps he didn't even want a spice stall, but he was learning that as far as Jacob was concerned, his negative answers didn't seem to matter. Still in his mind the unspoken answer was no. In the meantime, Joseph laid his hand on Jesus' shoulder.

'I agree it is a great piece of work, but I can take no credit. Jesus made this all by himself,' he said.

Jacob frowned for a moment. 'I must have misunderstood,' he said. 'Anyway, that simply makes me more convinced I want to own it, as a reminder of my lesson.'

Benjamin examined the stool. He was impressed despite himself.

'You must be very proud to have such a skilled son. He will be a fine carpenter when he is older.'

Jesus looked up at his father in a troubled way, but Joseph spoke without hesitation.

'He would indeed make a fine carpenter, but somehow I do not think that is the future God has for him!'

Benjamin frowned. Surely the boy would one day take over the carpenter's shop? It was tradition. Benjamin had never given any thought to Jacob doing anything except working for him. He looked from Jesus to Jacob, sensing Ebenezer was right: these two were similar in some way beyond his understanding. Jacob had always made him feel there was something unspoken, something he wasn't grasping. Now Jesus was just the same!

He sighed resignedly and drew out his purse to pay for the stool. It somehow comforted him to see Joseph's grip tighten on Jesus' shoulder. He recognised that piece of silent communication. Joseph was restraining Jesus from giving the stool away, just as he had to keep a constant check on Jacob's generosity. Certainly, Jacob and Jesus were alike in many ways!

He looked into Joseph's face and found he wished they lived closer. He felt Joseph had much to teach him.

'I hope you have found this a worth-while trip,' Ebenezer said as they wandered to the edge of the town.

Benjamin laughed. 'You are a rogue Ebenezer, but you have a good heart. I am grateful for everything you have taught us. Especially this last lesson, which may be the most crucial of all.'

Ebenezer smiled.

Jacob opened his mouth, but Benjamin put up a hand to hold back the inevitable question.

'Don't ask,' he said firmly. 'Just say good-bye to your uncle and let us get on the road, and don't speak to me for a while. I have something to think about.'

Ebenezer watching them until they were out of sight, nodding his head with satisfaction.

'Good,' he muttered to himself. 'Very good indeed,' and then he strode off, already making a plan of how to improve the life of someone else.

Rebekah

It seemed to Jacob he had been away forever when he finally got back from Nazareth. He talked incessantly to Leah about Micah and his spices, and Ebenezer and the crooked merchant in Nazareth and woven into it all were the plans he and Benjamin had made for their stall. It made her head whirl, but she listened delightedly, happy to have him home again.

One day Jacob was talking to her about how Micah had been teaching him to hide his feelings. Jacob was quite offended when she began to laugh, but Leah, planting a kiss on the top of his head, said nothing. For her there was one area at least where there could be no mistaking how he felt. She had always known.

Rebekah, his childhood friend, was now separated from him by the strict rules of their culture, but Leah had been watching the direction of his eyes. Her heart went out to him as he became awkward and embarrassed whenever Rebekah was close by. It was obvious to her, as it had been to Levi; Jacob's choice was made. When he was a boy, she wondered if this was simply a childish infatuation, but Jacob's passion had never wavered. Now as he returned from his two trips away, she saw he was leaving childhood behind. Choosing her moment carefully she spoke to Benjamin.

'Rebekah is the one,' she said.

Benjamin scowled and shook his head. He was having to revise his view of Jacob in all sorts of ways and the thought of marriage was just another added complication. One of his older sons wasn't married yet and he had no thought of choosing a bride for Jacob. Benjamin could foresee a great future for him. The other boys had never shown his aptitude for business and choosing the right wife for him was of critical importance. This matter could not be left to a woman's intuition, not even Leah's.

His loving wife recognized the stubborn set of his jaw and said no more. She was content to have introduced the idea to him. She knew he would come round eventually. It just needed time.

But to Jacob there was no time. The impetuosity of youth overwhelmed him and the insurmountable problem of persuading his father to let him marry made him feel he was about to explode. Now the matter of the spice stall was settled his thoughts inevitably had turned to Rebekah. Being away from her for so long had been absolute torture and he knew without a doubt he wanted to marry her, and soon. Yet his father could be so unreasonable! He had said yes to the spice stall, but Jacob just knew he would never say yes to marriage as well. How could Jacob explain he had loved Rebekah his whole life, had adored her even when they were children, and that his feelings for her were growing, not fading away? His father would never be persuaded by talk of emotions. The only thing he cared about was business!

Jacob had never spoken of Rebekah, not even to Jairus, but instinctively he knew he could trust his mother. He could always tell her anything. Still, he kept his desperation to himself until one day he could stand it no longer and he suddenly blurted it all out to her when they were alone in the kitchen. To his amazement she seemed unsurprised, only laying a reassuring hand on his shoulder and smiling up at him.

'I know Jacob. I know. You must be patient. God will not allow Rebekah to marry another if she is destined for you. I have spoken to your father about this already. Don't be anxious'

Jacob couldn't sit still. He walked about, pulling at first one hand and then the other.

'Father knows already? Did he say I was too young? Did he say he'd think about it? What did he say? No, don't tell me what he said. I know he refused!'

She looked at him with compassion. 'Be patient Jacob. I am certain something will happen to persuade him this is the right thing for you.'

'Patient!' Jacob muttered the word under his breath. He did not want to be patient, he wanted Rebekah, and how exactly was he supposed to express that to his mother? His cheeks flaming red he stomped out of the room.

Jacob said nothing more, but Leah watched him with concern. Beneath his quiet exterior she knew he was bubbling with impatience. She wondered whether she should speak to Benjamin again, and how long it would be before Jacob took the matter into his own hands.

Benjamin and Jacob were working long hours setting up the spice stall. Even Jacob had been surprised at the amount of hard work it took to set up one stall while trading on another. Benjamin could hardly stifle the "I told you so," which sprang to his lips several times a day, although he couldn't complain about Jacob's commitment. The boy worked as though something inside was driving him and creating the stall was his only outlet. Benjamin scratched his head, but eventually it all became clear, even to him.

It was early morning, and they were standing beside the house when a group of three girls appeared in the distance, walking up the road which passed their home. Benjamin was not known for his sensitivity, yet even he could feel the sudden tension in Jacob as the girls came closer. He shielded his eyes against the rising sun and recognized Rebekah walking towards them with two of her younger sisters.

As they drew near the house the other girls glanced quickly in Jacob's direction, giggling and whispering to each other, but Rebekah kept her head bowed and did not look up until she had passed them by. That impressed Benjamin, for it showed modesty and a maturity beyond her years. In contrast the look on Jacob's face exasperated him. Never had he seen such a look of disappointment and frustrated longing. Why couldn't the boy follow Rebekah's example and school his features, as Micah had tried to teach him? But no, Jacob still wore his heart on his sleeve, just like his mother. Benjamin sucked his teeth with annoyance. Such things were better left to parents; it definitely was not for the children to decide. He looked back at the girls, just in time to see Rebekah turn her head, unable it seemed to hold her resolve right to the end.

Benjamin was never quite sure what happened next; one moment Jacob was standing beside him, and the next there was a scuffle and a terrific thump as his gangly son fell backwards over the low wall that surrounded the house. Benjamin looked down, blinking in surprise. Behind him he could hear Rebekah's exclamation of dismay and the spontaneous laughter of the other girls as Jacob disappeared from their sight. Only his feet remained visible, absurdly sticking up over the wall. The girls laughed all the way down the road as they pulled Rebekah away, while Benjamin looked down with fond amusement at the red face of his embarrassed son. Why had he never noticed before how big Jacob's feet were?

'Slay you with one glance of her eyes, did she?' he chuckled indulgently.

Jacob lay on the ground with his eyes closed, so covered with confusion he was hardly aware of what his father had said. He had hit the back of his head very hard on the ground and little images of Rebekah's face were going round and round inside it.

Slowly he got up, gingerly rubbing the huge lump that was already appearing.

'I fell over the wall somehow,' he mumbled.

Benjamin studied him for a moment. 'How old are you?'

Jacob was surprised and opened his mouth to answer when Benjamin snorted and said,

'It doesn't matter. I suppose your mother is right. As usual!'

'About what?' asked Jacob still trying to stop his head spinning, but Benjamin said no more. He simply went into the house and filled it to the rafters with the sound of uproarious laughter.

Jacob stood, peering up the road, trying to catch a glimpse of Rebekah as she disappeared from view. What must she think of him? Falling over a wall like some idiot! What a fool he must have looked. Kicking himself he went and doused his head in a bucket of cool water from the well. He wandered around for the rest of the day with a sore head, bruised pride, and desperation in his heart.

Fine husband I would make, he thought to himself cursing his clumsiness, but little did he know Rebekah was thinking exactly the same thing. The other girls teased her mercilessly, but she was wise enough to keep her own counsel. No one heard as she whispered to her pillow, 'Please let him ask for me,' and no one heard her rapturous sighs just at the thought of it.

That night Jacob lay in bed with every fiber of his being focused on Rebekah; his heart in agony. He needed Rebekah, could not live without her! He thought about the happy years of their childhood, how no one else had even remotely understood him. Now he was not allowed even to speak to her and she had grown more beautiful while he was away, which only made things worse. What if she wasn't interested in him anymore? What if she had changed and wanted someone more handsome or charming? How could she even consider a clumsy dolt like him?

His face screwed up with the memory of the morning. He hadn't been able to believe his luck when she came into view. Perhaps he would have been able to hold his emotions in check if she hadn't turned and looked at him. But she had! She had looked at him! He had wanted to run up the road and speak to her, reach out a hand and touch her. Oh, what a terrible breach of custom that would have been! Unforgivable. It was then he had taken a step back in an attempt to curb his own impetuosity. That was when he had fallen over the wall. He couldn't explain that to his father, could he? Benjamin would have been furious! He tossed restlessly from side to side, unable to sleep despite the long hours of strenuous work.

'Rebekah,' he whispered into the night air, wondering if she was awake too in her father's house. Could she hear his heart beating for her, longing to marry her?

Sometimes he thought she noticed him when he caught a glimpse of her in the market. Did she remember their childhood, their promise to be friends forever? Did she remember? Today as she turned back to look at him hope had leapt up inside him. He was certain he had seen a softness in her eyes, a tenderness which matched his own. His face was wreathed in smiles as he thought of it. A moment later he turned over fretfully. Why had he made such a fool of himself? Right at the wrong moment. She would never consider him now. Who wanted to marry the town idiot? Rebekah was another reason why he was determined to make a success of the spice stall. He had to have something to offer her, more than just being his father's apprentice in the business. Would her family consent to her marrying a man without land? It seemed unlikely.

The bed creaked with his constant movement, the pillow a stone. Sleep completely eluded him. He lay on his back picturing her beautiful face; his heart beating hard in his chest. Then he turned over again, tormented by the thought everyone else must see how lovely she was, how perfect. Someone else would claim her while his father delayed. He was sure of it.

After a while he began to pray.

'Oh God of my Fathers, please give me Rebekah for my wife.' How many times had he prayed this prayer? A hundred? A thousand? He thought of what he could give to God. Devotion? Offerings? A life-time of worship? All of these belonged to Him anyway; they were His by right.

'Levi has taught me you are merciful and kind, even to the poor. I have nothing to offer you. Please be generous to me, and hear my prayer. I know it is much to ask, but if you grant my request and give me Rebekah, I will be grateful forever. I promise.'

As he prayed, he suddenly felt God had drawn close to him. He remembered this feeling from his childhood in the synagogue, but now it was much stronger, and it was right here in his room! He lay on his back, unsure how to respond, or what to say. All his life he had wanted to know if God still spoke to men. Was this his time to find out? He wondered if God had come to wrestle with him as he had with his namesake long ago. A thrill of fear went through him. What would happen next? The silence in the room seemed to intensify, even the sound of his brother's breathing disappearing, swallowed up in a quiet which held him motionless. He was sure he felt a breath upon his cheek, but his eyes straining into the darkness could see nothing.

'You will marry Rebekah.'

His ears heard no voice, yet the power of the words sounded in his head with startling clarity. He knew without doubt it was true, and the certainty of it rippled through his whole being, like a pebble dropped into a pool, causing waves that reached out, touching everything. It wasn't just a thought, or a figment of his imagination. It was God and he knew it.

In a moment it was gone. The room was back to normal, his father snoring loudly in the next room, everything exactly as before. But Jacob was not the same. Deep inside, a seed of faith had been planted and as he lay, hardly daring to breathe, it grew and grew until he thought he would burst with it. He wanted to leap out of bed and shake his brother awake to tell him. Trembling, he restrained himself, stuffing his head under the cover to muffle his sudden laughter, hugging himself with sheer ecstatic joy. Eventually he drifted off to sleep with a smile on his face, and the image of a wedding filling his dreams.

When he awoke the next morning, he bounced out of bed with so much enthusiasm his brother groaned in protest.

'What's up with you?' he grumbled. Jacob didn't reply. Who would believe him?

All week he grinned his way through his work, and his mother watched him, trying to fathom what had happened. Benjamin grunted when she tried to discuss it with him. So, the boy was happy. So what? Perhaps the fall had knocked some sense into his head at last. At least he had given up moping around all day, sighing like a girl. Leah got Jacob on his own and did her best to draw it out of him, but he was unusually reluctant to speak. He turned her questions aside, only smiling secretly. It was all very mysterious.

Jacob spent the next few days in an odd euphoric state. He sang and laughed and teased his young sisters until everyone, even Benjamin, agreed with Leah. Something had happened, but what?

'He has spoken to Rebekah,' his brother mocked, only half joking, but the usually placid Jacob denied it so fiercely his brother was amazed. His whole family were at a loss to explain it and Jacob remained tight-lipped. Time alone was a rare commodity in their crowded lives, so Jacob would lie awake at night, waiting for his brother's steady breathing and the stillness which meant the whole household was asleep. Then he would slip silently from his bed and kneeling on the floor pour out the worship and thanksgiving which had consumed him all day. He didn't seem to need much sleep, losing track of time in the welcome privacy of darkness. In those precious hours he could never be sure what filled his heart more, the fact that now he knew for certain he was going to marry Rebekah, or the unutterable wonder that God had spoken to him personally. The God of Abraham and Isaac and Jacob, the one true invisible God had spoken to him; given him a promise. For Jacob it was the fulfilment of a desire too lofty even to articulate. He knew he would never speak of it to a soul. It belonged only to him.

He didn't experience anything more on those nights he spent alone with God. One sacred encounter was more than he had any right to expect anyway, but he gave himself fully to worshipping God and expressing the gratitude he had promised. As the sky grew brighter, he would return to his bed, capturing one hour of sleep; then rise as refreshed as if he had been dreaming the night away.

Leah watched him carefully. By day he was a joy to be around, but in the mornings something indefinable was on his face. Perhaps only a mother would have seen the changes as night by night her son was transformed from a gawky youth into a man. His eyes held some depth with which she was unfamiliar, she who knew his every thought; and he carried his height and his broad shoulders with a strength and ease she had never seen before. He smiled down at her and she marvelled that her little boy was gone forever. She grew to respect him as a man in those days.

The change in him convinced Leah he needed to be married. Urgency began to boil through her blood, and that meant trouble for Benjamin. She gave him no rest and began to pressure him in the time honored way of women.

'Rebekah is beautiful and hard-working,' nagged Leah in her husband's ear. 'You must act quickly.'

'Yes, yes,' said Benjamin, feeling stubborn. 'I can see they will marry, but not yet! They are still too young, and we have plenty of time. Besides I cannot have Jacob distracted until our new venture is established. No, the spice stall comes first, then later he can begin to think about marriage.'

'And what if another asks for her and her father agrees. Would you break both their hearts? Don't delay,' she pleaded picking up his hand and placing it on her cheek. 'After all, did you not receive your heart's desire when you were young?' She turned on him the look which always melted his heart.

Benjamin's eyes softened and at last he capitulated, not just because she begged him, but because he saw something new in Jacob. The boy was different these days, more mature, and he didn't look at him any more with those pitiful eyes. In the last week he had seen it was possible for Jacob to become a full partner in the business. Perhaps this son was old enough to be married after all.

Micah came to the wedding with his family. He had been amazed at how quickly his latest venture here in Capernaum was turning a profit and he was delighted to be invited to Jacob's wedding. Even though they were strangers they quickly felt swept up in the love and rejoicing that surrounded the happy couple. Jacob was the most besotted bridegroom anyone had ever seen, and Rebekah was radiant, shining with joy.

A girl called Abigail was there too, sitting amongst the women, enjoying every moment. She was the same age as Rebekah and had always watched her with admiration. Rebekah was so self-assured and confident. Abigail was a more quiet, gentle person, with grown up sisters and brothers who were married already, and younger siblings too. It was a big family. She couldn't imagine what it must feel like to be getting married and her eyes strayed around the room wondering if anyone would ever take an interest in her. Jacob was so obviously in love with Rebekah. Would anyone ever want to marry her? She knew her parents would arrange a good match for her, but who, watching this bride and groom, would not wish for the same sparkling excitement? She lowered her eyes and gave herself a lecture on being content with what God provided.

What was it her mother had said? "Love will grow after you are married."

She certainly hoped it was true, since surely no one was likely to fall in love with someone as uninteresting as she was! She lifted her head, putting away all thoughts of romance and found she was looking straight at Jairus. He, like Jacob, had left his child-hood behind and grown into a young man, already commanding respect in the community. Abigail had never really noticed him before, but now her heart mysteriously skipped a beat, and a slight flush touched her cheeks. She looked across at him in surprise. What was there about this young man that had caught her attention? Why was it, as she was sitting wondering if anyone would notice her, suddenly she had noticed him? Was he the one for her? Was this how Rebekah had known about Jacob? Her mind was flooded with questions.

Don't be silly, she told herself impatiently, and looked away; but to her amazement she found although she knew it wasn't sensible to look at Jairus, the temptation was hard to resist. She sneaked one more glance, and then wished she hadn't, for just that glimpse made her heart beat wildly.

Stop this at once, she commanded herself, but found she was looking up again in his direction. He had moved away and her eyes scanned the room desperately until she found him. The relief she felt because he hadn't left was almost comical.

Her mother spoke to her and she was glad to be distracted, but she was a sensible girl, far too sensible to believe nothing had happened. As the dancing began, she allowed herself to watch Jairus. He wasn't tall, or strikingly handsome like Jacob, but there was something about him that held her attention. Her heart still refused to behave itself and return to normal. It was very confusing.

No one falls in love with someone they have known their whole life, not in a moment, and certainly not someone with a calm and peaceful character like hers. That's what she told herself repeatedly after the wedding, but she still found herself smiling whenever she thought of him and others noticed an indefinable change in her too. She seemed more confident than before. In her own quiet way, she treasured that moment and never forgot it. It was as though God had shared a secret with her and though at times she felt she might have imagined it, she never really doubted.

Jairus was totally unaware of Abigail at the wedding. He was part of the celebrations, of course, yet still he had a strange ache in his heart. He knew nothing could ever be the same in his friendship with Jacob. Change was inevitable he told himself, but it had all happened so swiftly. Jacob had gone away to the other side of the lake and come back completely different. Suddenly the strange, intense friend of his childhood had become a man and was getting married!

As he watched, an unexpected feeling of loneliness swept over him. He was going to miss Jacob.

He stood stroking his new beard, smiling at Benjamin taking the credit as though it was all his idea, but underneath feeling a pang of grief for his own father who had died when he was a child. He envied Jacob his close family. His thoughts strayed to when Jacob had told him he was going to be married. Jacob had finally confessed he had known for years he would marry Rebekah. Jairus had been stunned. Here was Jacob, younger than him, declaring he was in love! The very thought of it terrified Jairus. How were you supposed to know you were in love anyway? What if the girl you chose didn't like you? He knew he wasn't popular like Jacob. All the girls had wanted to marry him! Who would want to marry someone who couldn't express how he was feeling? He cursed his stupid nature. Why couldn't he be more like Jacob? The whole world of emotions was like a mystery to him.

Jacob was having no trouble expressing his emotions. He was grinning from ear to ear and Jairus tried to imagine what it would be like to be the center of attention at his own wedding. He moved uncomfortably at the thought of it. He was never any good at being relaxed in a social gathering and though he was soon caught up in the dancing, rejoicing with Jacob, he moved away when he could.

Jacob's shouts of joy followed him as he made his way home.

'Thou shalt not covet,' he murmured to himself; 'not even your best friend's nature, or his happiness.'

He wondered if it had ever been possible to keep the law perfectly, and deep inside he sighed.

Rebekah opened the door to her parent's house and unconsciously breathed in the familiar smell of home. All her life this had been a safe place for her and just being there recaptured the joys of childhood. Her mother was baking, her hands covered in flour and smudges on her face. Rebekah relaxed at the sight of her. Mother always made everything all right.

'Rebekah, I was just thinking about you, what are you doing here? Is Jacob with you?'

'No, he has gone off fishing with Jairus,'

Rebekah sat down and watched Jocabed making the bread. Now she was married this was her duty. Why did her efforts never taste quite as good as mother's?

Jocabed pulled a face. 'Jairus! He is such a solemn young man. A strange choice of friend for your Jacob. What do you make of him? Does he come and visit Jacob often?'

'Yes, he does. He came and had a meal with us last week, our first guest, and I fussed about the food for hours. As I opened the door he swept in like some ancient patriarch in his long robes. I can hardly believe he is only slightly older than Jacob, he carries such an air of authority. I found myself imagining him with a long grey beard and a lined face. I think they would really suit him.'

Jocabed laughed, 'Be careful Rebekah, they say he is going to be synagogue ruler one day.'

'Oh, I know,' said Rebekah, 'and he will probably be a very good one, but he seems too young to be learned and wise and he is so different from my loving Jacob.' She frowned as she thought about that. 'It is very perplexing', she mused, 'because they are exact opposites.'

Jocabed nodded. 'In looks you mean?' she said.

'Yes, but not just that. Jacob is quick-witted and clever. He says there is something inside him that tells him when to take a risk, and that is what makes him a good businessman. Can you imagine Jairus taking a risk? I can't. Very slow and steady, that's Jairus. Jacob says he needs time to consider every eventuality before he makes a decision.'

'You make him sound boring.'

'Not boring exactly, just cold and distant. Pity the poor woman who marries him! I can't imagine him ever expressing his feelings. I'm not sure he has any feelings!'

'Your Jacob probably has enough for both of them.'

Rebekah sighed rapturously. 'Yes, you can always tell what is going on inside Jacob. It is amazing how much he can convey with a single look, but I shouldn't think anyone will ever be able to tell what Jairus is thinking!' '"Jairus has schooled his countenance to holy impassivity," that's what Jacob says.'

Jocabed wondered how quickly she was going to tire of the words "Jacob says," in her daughter's conversation. She finished the baking as they talked and laughed about the wedding, but she sensed there was something behind this visit and as she stood washing her hands a happy thought occurred to her.

'Shall I brush your hair?' she said.

Rebekah's eyes lit up. 'Would you? Jacob does try, but he hasn't your skill.'

Jocabed gave a quiet chuckle - as if a man would know what to do! Rebekah removed her veil and pulled out the pins from her hair. It fell in glossy heaps about her shoulders, black as a raven's wing. Her mother stood behind her and picking it up in handfuls she began to smooth it out.

'Solomon could have been speaking of you when he wrote the Song of Songs,' she said.

'Your hair is like a flock of goats descending from Mount Gilead,' Rebekah quoted. Then she giggled. 'I can't imagine the Shunnamite maiden thought it was a compliment to be likened to a flock of smelly goats!'

'Rebekah!' said her mother, 'You know he was talking about their curly, black coats.'

'I know, Jacob quotes it thinking it is romantic, but I always have to stop myself laughing. Goats indeed! Besides, sometimes I wish I had straighter hair. It's hard work trying to tame it. I don't have your skill either Mother, and it is very unruly these days.'

'Your hair is beautiful Rebekah, as well you know, don't tell me Jacob doesn't quote the rest of the Song to you!'

Rebekah's voice took on a dreamy quality, '"Your hair is like royal tapestry; the king is held captive by its tresses." Yes, he quotes that too, and other things.' Her voice faltered uncertainly. 'I love him very much Mother.'

'That is as it should be.'

Jocabed unconsciously stopped brushing as she thought about Jacob. She had watched him as he grew up and wondered about him. There was something about this lad, something she couldn't define. All the mothers wanted him for their daughter, not just because he came from a fine family, but because he captured all their hearts with his gorgeous eyes and glorious smile. But her daughter had won him, and now Rebekah was living with this man who was somehow different from all the rest. Not just different from Jairus, but different from everyone around him. Jocabed was very fond of Jacob, but she wondered what kind of a husband he would be to Rebekah. She began again the long steady strokes and Rebekah closed her eyes and felt the years slip away. When she was a child, this had been one of her favourite occupations, sitting as her mother brushed her hair, talking about their lives, looking into the future.

Jocabed was the first to break the silence, speaking of some trivial matter. An unspoken question lay between her and her daughter and she didn't want to be the first to broach the subject. Rebekah would speak when she was ready.

After a time Jocabed realized Rebekah was weeping. Her hand grew still as she tried to decide what to say.

'Is everything all right Rebekah? Is Jacob kind?'

'He is wonderful Mother, kinder than I could have imagined. It isn't that.'

There was a silence until finally Rebekah said in a small voice.

'Last night my cries of pain woke him up.'

'Ah,' said Jocabed. 'Was it very bad?'

'I suppose it must have been. I would never have let a sound escape me if I had been awake, but in my sleep…'

Jocabed stroked her daughter's hair gently with her hand. 'I know darling,' she said. How many times had she risen from her bed in a vain attempt to ease her daughter's monthly agony?

'He wanted to comfort me; to hold me in his arms.' Rebekah's voice caught on a sob. 'But of course, the law would not allow him to touch me while I have my period. He didn't know what to do, and I didn't know how to reassure him. In the end I told him what the doctor said.'

'That a baby might cure you?'

'Yes, a baby. It has to be true doesn't it? Some of the others have told me how things have changed for them once they have a child. It will be the same for me won't it, Mother? It has to be the same for me!'

'Of course, darling,' she said, but a nagging doubt plagued her. Would Rebekah be healed so simply? She prayed it would be so.

Abigail and Jairus

Six months passed and Rebekah was already beginning to feel a weight of anxiety descending on her. Where was her longed-for child? A strong relationship had begun to grow between her and Abigail and she shared her secret concerns with her. They had been friends before, but now Rebekah was married, Abigail could often be found in their home. Rebekah grew to trust Abigail's quiet goodness and was commenting on it to Jacob when he said something which really shocked her.

'Yes, she is lovely,' he said, 'and perfect for Jairus.'

Rebekah looked at him with her mouth open. 'What do you mean?' she said.

'You know,' he said, 'Abigail and Jairus! She's in love with him, isn't she? Although of course he doesn't have a clue. I was wondering whether I should mention her to him; just casually. Do you think it's a good idea?'

Rebekah was stunned. 'What are you talking about? Abigail isn't in love with Jairus! The whole idea is preposterous!'

Jacob looked with surprise into her indignant face. 'But I thought it was obvious, and you knew all about it and that is why Abigail spends so much time here.'

'To see Jairus?' she fumed.

Jacob could see this conversation was going from bad to worse. 'Not just Jairus, I know she loves you too, but you must have noticed how self-conscious she is when he is here.'

Rebekah tossed her head. 'Well, everyone is self-conscious around Jairus, except you of course.'

There was an awkward silence.

'I didn't mean to offend you,' Jacob offered tentatively.

Rebekah laughed and sat down on his lap wrapping her arms around him.

'I'm not offended, I'm just shocked. Do you really think she's in love with him? She has never said a word, not one single word, and she must surely have told me something. I am her best friend!'

'Did you say anything to anyone about me, as madly in love with me as you have always been?'

Rebekah punched him gently.

'You know I didn't, and you didn't tell Jairus about me either, did you?'

'Not one single word!'

'Oh Jacob, what if it is true? They could get married and we could all be really close.'

'Do you think I should speak to Jairus?'

'No, don't you dare! I have to find out if you are right first.'

Jacob squeezed her gently. 'Of course I am right. I am a highly skilled observer of people. It's my job!'

'Oh really!' Rebekah looked him straight in the eyes. 'And what do your keen observational skills tell you about your wife?'

'Well, that's easy. Anyone on the street could tell you that!'

'Which is?'

'That you absolutely adore your husband.'

She ran her hand lovingly through his hair and sighed. 'True, quite true,' she said.

He looked beyond the laughter into the sadness he saw growing in her eyes. What could he possibly say to comfort her? There was nothing to say.

'He adores you too,' he said, and then he kissed her.

The next time Abigail was in their home Rebekah watched her closely. That first visit she thought Jacob was imagining the whole thing. She deliberately mentioned Jairus several times and Abigail showed no reaction at all.

'You are completely mistaken.' she told Jacob with great satisfaction.

'We'll see,' he said.

The next day Abigail came to visit them again. She was sitting quietly sewing with her back to the window, so she was unaware of Jacob's sudden and unexpected appearance behind her. He peeked in the window and Rebekah took one look at the mischievous grin on his face and frowned. What is he up to now, she thought? Jacob gave one swift glance at Abigail and then disappeared, obviously heading round to the door. Rebekah looked puzzled, and Abigail, noticing her expression, turned around just as Jairus's face replaced Jacob's at the window.

Abigail and Jairus stared at each other, face to face. Jairus looked hopelessly embarrassed, and nodding his head to her and Rebekah he moved away at once. Two male voices could be heard in heated conversation outside the door. Rebekah and Abigail strained to hear what was being said, but the voices were too muffled. Then there was the sound of someone walking away. When the door opened at last, only Jacob came through it.

'Jairus, um, had to be somewhere else.' he said airily. Rebekah glared at him. He gave her a sweet, innocent smile, worthy of his Uncle Ebenezer, and turning to his guest said,

'How are you today Abigail?'

Both he and Rebekah looked at Abigail, but they could not see her expression for she had lowered her head, apparently focussing intently on her stitching. She didn't speak. Rebekah's eyes rested on her husband's smug face. The look in them did not bode well for Jacob. Wisely he began to move towards the door.

'Uh, I think perhaps I need to be somewhere else too,' he said; and moments later he was gone.

Rebekah got up and pulled her chair closer to Abigail's. She watched as Abigail furiously plied her needle as though her life depended on it. No needle woman herself, even she could see the stitches were uneven and misplaced, not at all like the rest of Abigail's exquisite workmanship.

'Abigail,' she said tentatively. Slowly Abigail looked up. Rebekah hadn't been sure exactly how her friend would be feeling, but she certainly didn't expect the look of red-faced anger Abigail turned on her.

'Did Jacob do that on purpose?' Abigail's voice was shaking.

Rebekah couldn't lie. 'Yes, I rather think he did.'

'How dare he? Did he do it to humiliate me?'

Rebekah looked appalled. 'No, no!' she cried. 'Jacob would never do such a thing, he is far too kind.'

'Kind?'

'Yes, foolish perhaps, but kind and caring.'

Abigail got up and walked away from the window. 'So why did he arrange for me to see Jairus like that?'

'He felt convinced you had feelings for Jairus, and I told him he was imagining it, but I think he thought if he brought Jairus into the house and the two of you were here together, then I would see he was right. I honestly don't think he intended Jairus to look in the window. That was just unfortunate!'

'Unfortunate!' said Abigail in a stricken voice as she sat down on a chair and dropped her head into her hands.

'Oh Abigail, I am so sorry. Jacob and I really do love you, and we would never do anything to hurt you. Please forgive us.'

Abigail sat, not speaking, for what seemed to Rebekah like an eternity.

Eventually Abigail looked up and her face was now unusually pale. She was still fighting to control her emotions. Rebekah was unaware of the two bright spots of colour on her own cheeks, and the pleading look in her eyes. Abigail's anger drained away and her tender heart went out to her friend. Getting up she embraced her.

'I am sorry too.' she said. 'I never get angry. It was just such a shock.'

Unexpectedly there was a gentle knock on the door. Abigail moved quickly to the other side of the room and turned her back on the door as Rebekah went to open it.

'Oh, Jairus, it's you,' Rebekah said in a loud voice.

Behind her there was the sound of smashing pottery, and a horrified gasp. Jairus looked through the door in time to see Abigail kneeling on the floor, picking up the shattered remains of Rebekah's favourite dish. He looked into Rebekah's face with perplexity, but before he had time to speak Rebekah said,

'Jacob is not here. Try the market!' and she shut the door with a firmness bordering on rudeness.

Abigail knelt on the floor with fragments of broken pottery in her hand. 'What did he want?' she asked anxiously.

'I didn't ask him!' Rebekah replied, chuckling to herself.

Abigail was mortified. 'It isn't funny Rebekah! Quite apart from anything else I have smashed your dish. I don't even know why I picked it up, and then you said his name and it just slipped out of my fingers. I feel so stupid. What is the matter with me today? I will buy you another one! I promise!'

'As if I care about that. What I do care about though is Jacob is absolutely right. I may be finding it hard to believe, but I do know exactly what is the matter with you, and so do you. It's

Jairus!' She tried very hard to keep the incredulity out of her voice. Abigail's eyes darted from one side of the room to the other. Rebekah felt she was looking for a way of escape.

'I never meant to let anyone know.' Abigail whispered. 'I haven't even told Mother! It is just this strange feeling I can't shake off.'

'What feeling?'

Abigail gave her a harassed look, but in the end the need to share with someone overcame her deep-seated reserve. Taking a breath, she said, 'That we are supposed to be married!'

Her voice was so forlorn it made Rebekah laugh. 'Well really Abigail,' she said, 'That may be a somewhat surprising feeling, but it isn't the end of the world!'

'That's easy for you to say,' Abigail declared indignantly. 'You are married to the man you love, but the man I love doesn't even know I exist'!

Rebekah blinked. This was the second time in one day Abigail had expressed a strong emotion. It was most surprising.

'Even if that is true,' she said, 'which I strongly doubt, it is only because he is the most insensitive man I have ever met! It is blindingly obvious you are perfect for him. Why hasn't this occurred to me before? I will do something about it!' she said with her usual determination.

'No, no!' said Abigail in horror. 'You must not say anything to anyone. Promise me!' Rebekah sighed. Visions of becoming a successful matchmaker slowly faded from her mind.

'I can't promise,' she said truthfully. 'Tell me how long you have been feeling like this.'

Abigail sat down again. 'Since your wedding.'

Rebekah's curiosity was piqued. 'What happened?' she said.

Abigail looked up at her. 'Did you always know Jacob was the one for you?'

'Yes! Right from when we were children.'

'Well, I looked at Jairus at your wedding and I just knew.' She frowned as she tried to describe her feelings. 'It took me by surprise, just like when you are outside in the pitch dark and the moon suddenly leaps up into the sky, surrounding you with soft light.' She paused for a moment. 'Yes,' she said. 'It was like that - illuminating!'

Rebekah looked at her in wonder. 'You really do love him!'

Abigail laughed at her. 'No one could be your friend for long without realising how you feel about Jairus, but despite what you think, I have formed a different opinion!'

Rebekah laughed too. 'Good for you Abigail. There is much more to you than I thought.'

Abigail pulled a face. 'Why thank you!' she said.

Rebekah frowned. 'Have I offended you?' she asked.

'No, I know it is hard to get to know me. You and Jacob are really open people, but you mustn't make the mistake of thinking those who keep their thoughts to themselves simply don't have any.'

Rebekah sat down next to her. 'No, I won't make that mistake again. I know you probably wish I hadn't found out your secret, but I think it is a very good thing, and I am going to prove to you I am a trustworthy confidant.'

'And not tell anyone?' Abigail queried hopefully.

Rebekah smiled, 'I told you, I can't promise, but I do promise not to do anything you wouldn't like.'

Abigail sighed. 'I have no confidence at all in you knowing what I wouldn't like,' she said.

Rebekah reached out and squeezed Abigail's hands. 'Trust me,' she said reassuringly.

Abigail looked into her friend's face.

'As if I have a choice,' she said.

Jairus stared blankly at the door Rebekah had just closed in his face. He was lost in a swirling mass of unfamiliar emotions. What had just happened to him when he looked into Abigail's eyes? Why had he felt compelled to come back to the house? Was he really longing for just one more glance at her beautiful face? Why had he never noticed her before? He felt tossed about, just as he did when he was out in a small boat and the wind began to make the waves slosh over the side.

An acquaintance passed and called out, 'Hello Jairus!' The man was wondering why Jairus was standing outside Jacob's door. Jairus came to himself and wondered the very same thing. What exactly was he doing? I need Jacob, he thought. He will understand all this; although it wasn't clear to him what "all this," was.

No one ever saw Jairus hurry, but he did make it to Jacob's stall incredibly quickly. He flopped down on Jacob's stool and wiped his sweating brow with the edge of his robe. Jacob thought he looked positively distracted.

'Are you all right Jairus?' he queried.

'Yes! No! Yes of course!' Jairus looked at him with desperate eyes. 'Why do you ask?' he said.

Jacob looked at him more closely. 'Because you somehow don't seem your usual, calm self!'

A woman came and stood next to Jairus, examining the spices.

'Good day,' she said. Jairus got up at once to offer her the stool. Smiling, she shook her head and began to purchase first one spice, then another. Jacob was busy for several minutes, as business seemed unusually good. When he was free for a moment he looked over to where Jairus had been, but another customer was sitting on the stool. He cast his eye quickly over the market, but there was no sign of Jairus.

'Now where has he gone?' he muttered, but the steady stream of customers continued and drove his friend completely from his mind.

At the end of the day, when he had packed all the spices away, and was tallying up the takings, he found himself inexplicably reluctant to go home. The scene with Abigail came strongly back to him, and he was certain Rebekah would have something to say about it. As he picked up the unusually heavy bag of money, he suddenly felt he was being watched. He looked around, holding the money close to his chest with both hands, but it was only Jairus standing near-by.

'Did you think I had come to steal your great wealth?' he joked.

'Yes,' Jacob said. 'Where did you disappear to, earlier? I thought you wanted to talk.'

Jairus nodded. 'I did, but I quickly came to the conclusion the market is no place for private conversation, so I went somewhere quiet to think.'

Jacob slung his bag over his shoulder and the money jingled inside.

Jairus looked at the bag.

'Did Abigail make this bag for you?'

Jacob shook his head. 'Not Abigail. It was Rebekah's mother.'

'Oh,' said Jairus, and it seemed he was disappointed. Jacob opened his mouth to ask the inevitable question, but thought better of it. He knew his friend well, and decided to wait for Jairus to speak. They walked slowly towards Jacob's house, but the silence seemed endless. Jacob did his best to wait patiently. When at last they were in his street he said,

'Well, Jairus, are you going to tell me what is going on?'

'No! This morning I would have, but I have had time to reflect and I think I will keep it to myself for a while.'

Jacob faked annoyance. 'You don't mean to tell me you have built up an air of mystery around whatever it is, and now you are going to just leave me to guess?'

'Yes, that is exactly what I am going to do!'

'But Jairus you can't,' he said indignantly. 'You know me! I shall be consumed with curiosity, and you are never a mystery, which makes whatever it is all the more interesting! You can't seriously expect me to act as though nothing has happened! Not that I know exactly what has happened.' He looked at Jairus with a twinkle in his eye.

'You could give me a clue!' he said hopefully.

Jairus stopped walking and looked straight into Jacob's eyes. 'Don't joke Jacob,' he said seriously.

Jacob had never seen such a look on his friend's face before. His own smile faded, replaced by a solemn expression matching that of Jairus. 'My apologies; of course I will wait. And if you chose to tell me I shall be honoured by your confidence.'

Jairus laughed despite himself. 'Will you indeed? Honoured by my confidence? When did you turn into someone with a mature attitude like that?'

By now they had stopped outside Jacob's door.

'I will have you know I am a married man, and a full partner in my father's business, and above all, the best friend of the man who will shortly be synagogue ruler. Surely all of that commands respect!'

He expected his friend to laugh, but instead Jairus was gazing at the door with an odd expression on his face. Jacob turned to look at it too, and at that instant it opened, and Abigail came out. She was surprised to see Jairus standing there and somehow missed her footing. Jairus moved faster than Jacob had ever seen him and catching her by the arm he held her steady. For the second time that day the two were unexpectedly face to face.

Jacob dragged his eyes away from the look on Jairus's face, looked fleetingly at Abigail who was covered with confusion, and finally gazed knowingly at Rebekah who had appeared in the doorway. Everything was clear to him; what Jairus was trying not to tell him; what Abigail was trying to hide. Everything. His eyes sparkling with triumph, he laughed out loud, but neither Jairus nor Abigail noticed. In fact, Rebekah wondered if the pair of them would notice anyone else ever again.

Rebekah and Jacob were thrilled Jairus and Abigail had so obviously fallen in love. Yet despite Rebekah's confident assertion she would 'do something' about it, in reality this proved almost impossible. Jacob assured her Jairus had made it perfectly clear he would not discuss the subject, but she was not so easily put off. On several occasions she tried to draw the taciturn Jairus into conversation on the subject of marriage. Every attempt ended up in awkward, embarrassing silence, and eventually she gave up, even more frustrated with Jairus than before.

Abigail was confused and disappointed. She had been sure from the moment on the steps of Rebekah's house that Jairus had suddenly become interested in her, but then he said nothing and avoided her if he could. At first Rebekah reassured her he would ask her parents eventually, but as the weeks passed Abigail began to give up hope. Rebekah was mystified by his silence and found it harder and harder to encourage Abigail to wait patiently. The only conclusion they could come to was his feelings must have changed towards her.

'Perhaps it was all wishful thinking on my part!' Abigail said mournfully.

Rebekah pulled a face. 'He doesn't deserve you!' she said.

Abigail sighed. 'He might think I don't deserve him.'

Rebekah stamped her foot. 'Absolute nonsense!' she said.

These were difficult times for her. Abigail was deeply unhappy and month after month she herself was pierced with pain. She and Abigail hardly spoke of the disappointments they carried, but often they would simply hug each other; there was no need for words. Inexplicably Jairus became the focus of Rebekah's anguish. She held her anger behind a tight-lipped silence, but even insensitive Jairus knew there was something wrong. He began to avoid the house, painfully aware he wasn't Rebekah's favourite person. Poor Jacob was at a loss. Jairus could not or would not speak to him, and Rebekah was seething. He had no idea what to do.

One day Jairus appeared unexpectedly at the market. Jacob was pleased to see him.

'Are you well Jairus?' Jacob greeted him.

Jairus nodded. Jacob wondered if he was going to stop talking altogether. It was all very odd. He tried again. 'Can I do something for you?'

Jairus cleared his throat. 'I came to say I am going to Jerusalem to the Feast of Tabernacles.'

Jacob's face lit up. 'Oh, how wonderful. I have heard it is the most joyful celebration on earth. They say unless you have heard the rejoicing at the feast, you have never really experienced rejoicing. I would love to come, but I really cannot leave Rebekah or the stall.' He looked into Jairus's face and the joy faded from his own. He wondered who this stranger was in front of him. Jairus's expression made it perfectly clear. Jacob was not invited.

'I am going a few days early, so I am leaving tomorrow. I thought I would let you know.' Just for a moment the old Jairus appeared in his eyes, pleading with Jacob. Jacob came out from behind the stall and hugged him. He felt like a solid lump of wood.

'Be blessed my friend,' Jacob said, and slapped Jairus on the back as though nothing was wrong. Jairus nodded his head again and walked away. Jacob felt genuine concern for him. What was going on?

Later when he talked to Rebekah, he said, 'I can't fathom what is happening to him. Ever since he became interested in Abigail, he has become even more withdrawn than usual. What can possibly be wrong with him?'

Rebekah shrugged her shoulders. 'He has always seemed strange to me, but he shouldn't be breaking Abigail's heart like this. That I find hard to forgive!'

'Maybe he will be helped by attending the feast.'

'Helped by Tabernacles; with all that dancing and singing? It doesn't sound like the right place for Jairus even when he is in a good mood. Don't pin your hopes on that! If he isn't at least a bit more normal by the time he comes home I am going to insist you speak to him. He can't go on like this!'

'No,' said Jacob. 'I agree.' He frowned as he thought about his conversation with Jairus. 'Why wouldn't he want me to go with him?'

'Because you would expect him to talk to you! Why do you think he is going early? It's because he doesn't want to be in a crowd. Jairus wants to travel alone.'

Jacob shook his head. Surely no one would prefer to be by themselves when they could be in the congenial group which went year by year to the celebration of the harvest? Everyone assured him it was a wonderful social event.

The next morning, he happened to catch sight of Jairus as he left Capernaum. He lifted his hand in greeting, intending to call out and bid Jairus a safe journey, but something in the set of his friend's shoulders made him hesitate. His hand dropped to his side, and he stood silent. He knew Rebekah was right. Jairus had separated himself from everyone on purpose; some dark isolation had enveloped him and there was no way to reach him.

Jacob turned away wondering what was going on inside his best friend.

Jairus arrived in Jerusalem and was immediately swept up in the excitement as the whole city prepared for the feast. The noisy activity and raucous laughter didn't suit his mood at all. He found a simple lodging and getting up early the next morning he left the city as soon as he could. He trudged along the dusty road, heading slowly in the direction of Levi's village.

He told himself he hadn't really planned to come here, but the innate honesty of his character wouldn't let him lie to himself. As he sought directions to the Rabbi's house, he faced the truth. He had travelled from Capernaum, not to attend Tabernacles, but to visit the only father he had ever known.

He hesitated before he knocked. What if Levi were away from home, or this was an inconvenient moment, or worse still he would be an unwelcome visitor?

'Don't be ridiculous!' he muttered and rapped loudly on the door before he could change his mind.

Levi of course was delighted to see him, offering hospitality and the warmest of welcomes. Something inside Jairus relaxed. He sat opposite his old teacher, who appeared completely unchanged, and an unfamiliar feeling of being at home swept over him. He hadn't realised how much he had missed Levi, and just the sight of him made him smile.

They spoke of many things, of life in Capernaum, the journey to Jerusalem, the feast and its significance, the influence of Rome. Levi watched the pinched look around Jairus's mouth slowly soften, but still there was a frown behind his eyes. Levi waited his time.

'How is Jacob?' he asked. The frown on Jairus's brow deepened.

'Married as you prophesied; running his own spice stall; very happy.'

'And you?'

'Yes, I am well. I love my life in the synagogue and may well be synagogue ruler one day, which you also prophesied as I recall.'

Levi fixed his eyes on Jairus's face. 'And are you happy?'

Jairus had almost forgotten how Levi's eyes could look into your soul. He knew there was no escape. He might be able to shut Jacob out, but not Levi, and anyway, this was why he had come wasn't it? To sit once more with someone he trusted completely and tell the truth at last.

'No.' he said, and he dropped his head into his hands.

Levi reached out and touched him with compassion. He gave Jairus a moment and then he asked, 'Why my son? What has happened to cause you this anguish?'

Slowly at first Jairus began to tell him, about his own longing to be married and the fateful day when he had come face to face with Abigail. Levi frowned with the effort of remembering.

'I remember Rebekah of course, but I don't recall a girl called Abigail.'

Jairus's face lit up at the thought of her. 'She was still a child when you were with us, but now she has grown into the most beautiful woman. She is not lively like Rebekah, but quiet and serene. She is so peaceful.'

He paused and Levi said,

'And you love her!'

Jairus nodded, and the love he had for Abigail shone out of his face for one fleeting moment, and then was gone. A look of despair took its place.

Levi was at a loss. 'Come Jairus, you have to explain this to me. You love her, and yet you haven't asked for her. Why not?'

Jairus began to wring his hands. Levi had never seen him do that before and frowned at this sign of deep agitation. It was not like Jairus at all. He was determined not to prompt a reply, so he waited, positive Jairus needed to express what was going on inside him. When Jairus did speak he took Levi by surprise.

'When you were our teacher, I always knew Jacob was your favourite.'

Levi wanted to reply but Jairus held up his hand.

'No please, let me speak. I didn't blame you. Jacob is everything, isn't he; kind, handsome, quick-witted, interesting? Everyone loves Jacob.' He sighed deeply. 'Do you know how many people have told me how wonderful Jacob is and how completely different I am from him? As if I don't know! Anyway, I could cope with that, or at least I thought I could, until he got married. Rebekah had loved him for years, and he had loved her. I couldn't believe I had never known! It made me feel I didn't know him at all. And there he was at the wedding, deliriously happy, and there I was, dependable, boring Jairus, standing alone. I could see I wouldn't even have Jacob anymore; not really. The way they looked at each other, it was obvious. He was Rebekah's now. Things had changed and I had just got to make the best of it.

So, I made a decision; a vow. I swore to myself I would never put myself through the pain of risking rejection. I would remain single and be everyone's favourite bachelor. You know, the highly respected, slightly aloof religious leader, and I was content with that. It was safe anyway.

After the wedding I didn't see much of Jacob. Rebekah doesn't really like me, so I would go and visit them now again, but not often. Jacob is busy, very busy and I have my work. I've got used to being lonely. And then, one day I saw Abigail, as I told you, and my whole world fell apart in a moment.'

Levi wasn't quite sure where to begin. 'Did you tell Jacob?' he asked.

'No, it was my first impulse, but I had time to think better of it. I have hardly spoken to anyone since.'

'But why Jairus? Why haven't you asked Abigail's parents if you can marry her?'

Jairus stood up and spoke almost fiercely. 'Would you if you were me? She will say "No" won't she? And how am I supposed to live with such a rejection? Everyone would know and pity me. My reputation would never recover. Of course, they would all understand her refusal and laugh at me for having the stupidity to ask her. Better by far not to take the risk. Yes, better by far!'

Levi looked at him in amazement. 'Never mind what everyone else would think; that is irrelevant. What do you think? How do you feel about living the rest of your life not knowing whether she might have said yes?'

Jairus spat out one word. 'Tormented,' he said.

Levi stood and clasped him firmly by the shoulder. 'Tell me Jairus, do you believe your destiny is to be synagogue ruler, that indeed you were born for that very purpose?'

Jairus was surprised by the question. Hesitantly he replied, 'Yes, I do.'

'And Jacob is not supposed to be fulfilling that role in Capernaum?'

Jairus shook his head at such a ludicrous thought. 'Certainly not!' he said with absolute conviction.

'But why not?' Levi probed. 'He is everything isn't he? Why not synagogue ruler?'

'Because….'

'Because?' prompted Levi.

'Because God has another purpose for him!' Jairus said, running his hand across his brow.

'And his destiny is more important than yours?'

'No,' said Jairus firmly, somehow feeling cornered. His great love and respect for his work in the synagogue made him want to defend it. It wasn't inferior to anything God might call Jacob to do. How could it be? He looked at Levi with a troubled expression.

'What are you trying to say?' he asked.

Levi's heart was filled with compassion. 'What I am trying to say is you have lived your whole life under the shadow of a lie. You have always believed you were nothing, but it just isn't true Jairus. In fact, nothing could be further from the truth.'

The old man sat down and gazed out of the window, reaching back into his memory. 'Sit here beside me,' he said, and he waited for Jairus to sit down. 'I have things to say which should have been said long ago.'

He reached out and laid his hand on Jairus's arm. 'You always felt I came to Capernaum because of Jacob, didn't you?'

Jairus nodded.

'Well, that is true. I came to the synagogue and recognised Jacob from his trip to the temple, and that is what decided me to stay.'

Pain crossed Jairus's face.

Levi's grip tightened on his arm. 'Listen to me,' the Rabbi said urgently, and Jairus responded, recognising his teacher's voice from his childhood.

'When I began to teach you both, Samuel told me what an incredible student you were and I quickly came to realise he was right. Every teacher hopes for a pupil who loves the scriptures as much as you do. How can I convince you I have always loved you as much as I loved Jacob? More perhaps. The truth is, if I had a favourite, it was you. Don't look shocked. How many hours have we spent together studying and memorising the sacred scrolls? Did you think I was wasting my time? I had never had such a diligent student as you. You were like a gift. I have always seen such greatness in you, and I counted it a joy and privilege to be your teacher. If Jacob had not been part of the school, still I would have stayed; for you! Why has something prevented you from believing this?'

Jairus looked at him with wonder. Countless memories flooded back to him of Levi's patient mentoring. The Rabbi had invested so much in him. Why had he never seen it for the faithful care it so obviously was?

One last shred of self-doubt clung to him. He tried to close his lips, but the words slipped out from between them.

'You're not just saying this to comfort me?' It sounded pathetic even to him.

Levi threw up his hands. 'In all our years have I ever lied to you?'

Shamefaced, Jairus shook his head. 'I apologise,' he said. 'It is hard for me to believe what you are saying.'

Levi grabbed his hands in a surprisingly firm grip. 'I am not offended Jairus my son. I should have told you before. My only excuse is I thought it was obvious! Now I realise you don't see yourself very clearly at all. You are much respected and much loved and the sooner you recognise it the better. You are not the same as Jacob, indeed nor is anyone else! But no one else is like you either. I have always believed God put you two together for a reason; to complement each other. You cannot and must not build your life on this strange belief that because you are not exactly like him you have no value.'

Levi looked at Jairus with great affection. 'How I wish you had talked to me about this years ago. So much needless pain and for

131

so long! I knew you struggled with jealousy, but I had no idea it had warped your own sense of worth as badly as this.'

Jairus drew his hands away and rising went to the other side of the room. 'Jealousy?' he queried. It was his turn to be offended.

Levi didn't back down. 'What would you call it?' he said. 'Realism!'

'Nonsense,' said Levi. 'You are an intelligent man and you know I am speaking the truth. Let go of these feelings left over from childhood. Believe me when I say they have no substance except in your imagination. You have to throw this lie off your thinking just as you would if it were an unclean thing. Which it is! Don't let it defile you. Be ruthless with it, every thought, every attitude. You are a man of great worth with much to offer. Why is it you can believe God has created you to rule the synagogue, but you cannot believe he created you to be the perfect husband for Abigail?'

Jairus looked at him with panic in his eyes. 'What if she says no!'

'If that happens you will just have to cope with it and ask again if you are certain. Ruth refused me the first time I asked her.'

Jairus laughed uncertainly. 'Are you joking?' he said.

'Is that a matter to joke about? She said she wasn't worthy of me. Absolute nonsense of course, but women can get strange ideas sometimes. She accepted the second time.'

Jairus blinked, surprised the Rabbi had shared such an intimate detail of his life; he sighed as some deep insecurity dropped from his shoulders. He was a grown man, not a child, and Levi saw him as such.

Levi spoke to him strongly, 'You go home and take the risk. Frankly you are being a bit of a coward. Courage, Jairus, courage! You have to trust God! He was well able to send me to Capernaum and what a blessing it was to me. Don't you believe he can provide the perfect wife for you? Go home and rejoice in God's great love for you.'

Jairus knew he was right. He laughed, and said, 'Rejoicing? You must be mistaking me for Jacob!'

'No, I am not! You have hidden depths to you Jairus and it wouldn't surprise me if this young lady is just the one to draw them out.'

Jairus lifted his head up high. 'I am honoured to have been your student and I pray I may be a credit to you. I don't think either Jacob or I ever expressed our thanks to you for all your love and patience. No one could have wished for a better teacher than you. Thank you, my father, not just for then, but for now.'

He knelt down beside Levi's chair and bowed his head.

Levi stretched out his hands and spoke a blessing over him, father to son. Jairus was never the same.

He went back to Jerusalem, packed his bag and walked out of the city against the flow of pilgrims coming to the feast. They were all dusty but excited, and Jairus watched their faces, alight with anticipation. Anticipation was written all over his countenance too, as he thought of Abigail and his absolute determination to ask for her in marriage. He faced the fact there was no guarantee she would accept him, and fear that he had mistaken the look she had given him on Jacob's steps darkened his face again and again as he trudged home. Conflicting emotions raged through him, sometimes hopeful, sometimes fearful, just like any man preparing to ask the most important question of the woman he adores.

More than once he declared to the empty road, 'It feels like jumping off a cliff!' But Levi's words rang in his ears. He was determined not to be a coward. On his journey he thought often about his precious teacher. He had never respected anyone the way he respected him. The man's integrity and goodness had been a powerful example to Jairus, and he had always tried to emulate them.

Perhaps there was no one else in the world who could have challenged the dark thread which had run through his character for years. No one else whose love and reassurance could convince him he really did have worth, indeed had always had worth.

He saw for the first time that comparing himself with Jacob, or indeed anyone else, was a huge mistake. He thought of all the times his sense of inadequacy had made him unbelievably awkward in social situations. He realised how often he had mistaken people's reactions to him, misunderstood what they were actually saying. It was as though light had flooded into a darkened room and suddenly the strange, incomprehensible shapes he had stubbed his toes on had become clearly defined, normal pieces of furniture. He thought of the many who respected his opinion, the countless invitations he so consistently refused, the open-heartedness of his community, and for the first time he recognised what his mother had asserted for years.

'People like you Jairus!' She had declared it repeatedly, but he had never believed her.

Rebekah came into his mind. He saw clearly how he had been unspeakably cold and reserved around her. He realised it was because he was afraid of rejection, afraid the most important person in Jacob's life would dislike him; just as he felt he deserved! He shook his head, almost unable to cope with the flood of self-revelation pouring through him.

'I am going to be different!' he declared into the still, hot air, and laughing he did a little jig of joy, almost as though he had been to the feast after all. He didn't know then that in the days ahead the darkness of self-hatred would at times resurface to torment him, but for now its power over his thinking was broken, and he was grateful.

Jairus almost ran the last mile home to Capernaum. His mother was shocked to see him, hot and dishevelled, days before he was expected.

'What has happened Jairus? Are you well?'

Jairus didn't reply, but turned on her a shining face she hardly recognised. She was completely unable to read him at all.

'Jairus?' she queried uncertainly.

Laughing he kissed her cheek. 'I have to go out,' he said, 'it's very important.'

He stripped off his travel cloak and looked down at his clothes. Swiftly he poured some oil on his beard, and straightened out his robe.

'Do I look presentable?'

'Presentable to who?'

His eyes glowed. 'Never mind,' he said as he made for the door. He turned back in the doorway and smiled at her.

'You were right Mother, about me I mean. Thank you.'

Without a single clue as to what he was talking about she raised her hand to wave goodbye.

'You're welcome,' she said.

Abigail's father was so amazed when Jairus asked for permission to marry her that his mouth simply hung open. All the normal formalities deserted him and he asked rather stupidly,

'Abigail?'

Jairus thought he would never forget that look. It somehow eased the crippling nervousness he was trying his best to conceal. Hope and fear swept over him by turns.

When her parents presented the proposal to Abigail her mother watched her closely. Abigail was an obedient girl and Mary wanted to be sure this unexpected proposal wasn't distasteful to her. She thought it important Abigail didn't accept out of duty, no matter how excited her father was. To Mary the radiant delight which lit up Abigail's face was an absolute mystery, and the fact she didn't seem to need any time to consider.

Her ecstatic, 'Yes! Of course, yes!' was so out of character it demanded an explanation. Abigail saw the amazement on her mother's face and did her best to school her response to meek acquiescence, but Mary wasn't fooled. Abigail was able to keep the smile off her face, but nothing could stop her eyes sparkling with joy.

As soon as they were alone, Mary said, 'Abigail, has Jairus already spoken to you?'

Abigail hotly denied any such impropriety. 'No Mother! Of course not!'

'Then why is it I get the feeling you knew Jairus was going to ask to marry you?'

Abigail sighed. 'I didn't know Mother. I just hoped.'

Mary frowned. 'Hoped?' she queried.

'Yes,' Abigail said, 'hoped and prayed and dreamed and gave up hope.'

Then she grabbed her mother's hands and twirled her around, her face blossoming once more into a radiant smile.

'But now you see, dreams really do come true!'

Mary laughed in wonderment and took Abigail into her arms.

'I'm delighted for you,' she said. Abigail laughed too and Mary held her close, never having seen her daughter this happy before.

All that day and the next Abigail beamed at everyone, as though a lamp had been lit inside her. Mary was amazed.

Abigail told her all about Rebekah's wedding and meeting Jairus on the steps. For Mary it was like a glimpse into the secret world Abigail had always kept hidden. From that time on Abigail shared much more openly and gradually Mary came to the conclusion that for all the years of her growing up, she hadn't really known her daughter at all.

Jairus decided not to go to the market. He didn't want to see Jacob in a public place, but he had reckoned without the amazing speed of gossip in a small town. Jacob knew he was back, he even knew he had been to Abigail's house, although the lady who leant confidentially over the market stall to share that information with him hadn't guessed the significance of the visit. She looked at Jacob with her head on one side, trying to gauge his reaction to this interesting circumstance. For once Jacob managed to give nothing away, only conveying the genuine surprise he was feeling.

As soon as he could he escaped from the market and met Jairus on his way home. Jairus ran towards him and embraced him. Jacob was delighted, but stunned. Had Jairus forgotten the stiff formality of their last meeting? When eventually Jairus released him, Jacob was able to look into his face. 'What happened?' he said.

Jairus beamed at him. 'Now that would be telling.' he said, and his eyes were full of an excitement Jacob had never seen before.

'All right you imposter,' Jacob said. 'What have you done with my friend Jairus? He went off to Tabernacles with some heavy burden on his soul, and you have come back in his place. And I don't recognise you at all!'

'I don't recognise me either. I didn't go to Tabernacles. I went to see Levi.'

'What! Without me?' Jacob was indignant.

'Yes, without you,' Jairus chuckled, and slipping his arm into Jacob's began to steer him down towards the lake. They walked in silence for a while. Jacob was consumed with curiosity, but something made him hold back the hundred questions he was waiting to ask. When Jairus did speak it was the last thing Jacob had expected to hear.

'I'm sorry Jacob,' he said.

Jacob stopped walking and turned to look at his friend. Jairus had many fine qualities, but apologising wasn't one of them. Jacob had learnt when he was young an apology was the best way out of the many difficult situations he found himself in when he spoke without thinking. Jairus seldom spoke out of turn and always aimed at doing the right thing. Apologies weren't part of his daily life and didn't come easily to him. Jacob wondered how he was supposed to respond.

'Are you apologising for not taking me to Levi?' he asked light-heartedly.

'Yes that, and so many other things.'

Jacob scratched his head. They had walked along the edge of the lake until they were quite alone.

'Jairus what has happened? You went away like a stranger and now you have come back joyful and apologetic, which is wonderful, but odd! Tell me everything.'

'Levi told me some hard, but truthful things. He made me see myself differently. He told me I had always been jealous of you.'

Jacob's mouth was open, but Jairus didn't draw breath. 'No, let me finish,' he said. 'He really loves us you know, Jacob. I don't think I ever understood that before. When he told us he had stayed in Capernaum because of us, he really meant it. I always thought he stayed because of you, because you went to the temple and you always asked such a constant stream of questions, but he genuinely settled in Capernaum because of us, and I was part of that, although I never knew. He made me see I needn't be ashamed to be myself. I don't have to be you. I can be me, and that is more than enough!'

Jacob's mouth was opening and shutting like a fish. Jairus laughed. He had never seen his friend lost for words, and he guessed it wasn't because he didn't have anything to say, but because he didn't know where to start. Just to make Jacob's discomfiture complete he said, quite casually,

'Oh, and by the way, I've asked for Abigail.'

Jacob looked as if he was about to explode. He gave a great shout and then jumped up and down before hugging Jairus mercilessly.

'We must go and tell Rebekah!' he said.

Jairus nodded his head. 'I owe her an apology too.'

Jacob frowned. 'Rebekah?' he queried.

'Yes, Rebekah, and almost everyone.'

'Well, I don't think Rebekah will be expecting an apology, but Abigail might.'

Jairus turned on him swiftly. 'Abigail?' he said mortified. 'What have I done to hurt Abigail?'

'Um,' Jacob sought for the right words. 'Kept her waiting for months until she gave up hope?'

Jacob thought it was almost comical how suddenly he could read what was happening inside Jairus - comical and illuminating.

'Oh, of course!' Jairus said, and it was clear such a thought had never occurred to him before. He looked horrified. 'What an idiot I have been!'

'Yes,' said Jacob helpfully. 'But if she has accepted you then I suppose it must be all right now. I can't say I really understand what has happened to you Jairus, and if you return to normal then this may well be the only conversation we shall ever have about whatever it is. You have to explain it to me. You just must!' Then as an afterthought he said, 'Are you going to return to normal?'

It appeared Jairus wasn't listening. 'Do you think she will forgive me?' he said anxiously.

'Rebekah?' said Jacob.

'No!' said Jairus. 'Abigail!'

Jacob shook his head. 'I was joking Jairus. Of course Abigail will forgive you. And Rebekah will too, eventually.'

'I thought you said Rebekah wouldn't be expecting an apology.'

'Ah! So, you were paying attention after all.'

'Always, my friend, always. More than you have ever known.'

As they walked back to the town Jairus did as Jacob asked. He told him all about Levi, and the feast, and the proposal, and even what was going on inside him before he left. Jacob was delighted. Jairus reminded him of a dried up river bed when the rain suddenly comes; nothing; then everything at once. Words gushed out of this taciturn man in a seemingly endless stream, where once there had been only silence. Jacob listened and grinned and hardly got a word in edgeways, which suited him. He rejoiced in watching Jairus's animated face.

He stopped where the path turned in among the houses. He looked around and seeing no one he interrupted his friend. There was one question he felt he had to ask.

Lowering his voice, he said, 'did Levi talk about the Messiah?'

Jairus shook his head. 'No, and I was grateful. He knows I have serious doubts about that. I always have. He may have talked to you if you were there, but he said nothing to me. It is a forlorn hope Jacob, no matter what Levi believes. No Messiah is coming; not in our life-time.'

Jacob looked distressed. 'But you must believe the Messiah will come eventually. Why not now?'

Jairus shrugged his shoulders. 'Eventually, yes of course, the scriptures declare it, but he will be a King of the house of David, not some obscure child growing up who knows where!' He waved his hand dismissively.

Jacob was reluctant to let go of his dream.

'But you know many believe he will come and deliver us from the Romans and make us a great nation again.'

Jairus nodded and pulled at his beard. 'Yes, many do believe that. It is sad really,' he said.

'But Levi…..'

'Yes, Levi! I respect him now more than ever, but I cannot believe he is right about this. I have thought about it often. He was persuaded by the testimony of a very old man. I know he was completely convinced, but I am not. I cannot afford to believe in such a tenuous hope.' He looked into Jacob's face. 'Can we lay this subject aside Jacob? You know we cannot agree on it and I don't want to argue on this day. As I said, Levi didn't mention it. Let's talk about something more joyful. I am getting married! Let's go and tell Rebekah!'

Jacob wanted to say more, but he saw the wisdom of letting the subject go. He clapped Jairus on the shoulder.

'Do you seriously think we will get to Rebekah before Abigail does?'

Jairus's face lit up. 'Do you think she might be there?'

'Patience, Jairus!' he said. Jairus turned a mock angry face to him.

'I can't believe you of all people would counsel me to be patient!'

Jacob shrugged his shoulders and they laughed together like the old friends they were as they hurried up the road.

Marriage

For Jacob and Rebekah, the only thing overshadowing the happiness of Jairus and Abigail's wedding was that Rebekah was still not pregnant. Their families had been looking at them expectantly for a year now, waiting for news, and although Jacob shrugged it off with a light laugh, Rebekah could not. She saw the frown behind her mother's eyes and her heart sank. She could guess what Jocabed was thinking.

As anxiety began to take hold of her, night after night she tossed in her bed, unable to sleep. During the day there were always things to occupy her mind, but in the darkness, fear began to torment her, fear that something was wrong inside her, something which meant she would never give Jacob a child. Every month she hoped and prayed, waiting almost with bated breath, but always the familiar pain would sweep over her. Disappointment began to haunt her.

Jacob poured out his heart to Jairus. 'The waiting is very hard,' he said.

Jairus nodded, trying his best to understand. He thought about his own life. He was married now, so happy he could hardly express it. Abigail truly loved him and his whole life was changed. His confidence was growing every day, and he felt mature; a man at last. It seemed strange to him that it was at this moment in his life Jacob was turning to him for help. At last, the mysterious world of love was opening up to him and here he was, almost immediately, called upon to be a support to his friend. A sudden thought flew across his mind. When he finished his training, he would be a Rabbi. Would many people come to him and share their problems? He wondered if he would have anything useful to say. He cleared his throat.

'Um, do you want to talk to me about it?'

Jacob didn't notice his awkwardness he was too caught up in his own thoughts. 'Rebekah thinks I am disappointed by the fact she isn't pregnant yet.'

Jairus began to feel his way into this unknown territory.

'And that's not true?' he ventured.

'Well of course I am disappointed, a little at least, but the real problem is Rebekah's disappointment. Month after month it is the same; she tries not to let herself get excited, and then she is devastated when… Oh well, you know Jairus don't you?'

Jairus flushed, 'Yes, yes,' he said. 'I know.'

Jacob sighed. 'I love her so much, but I can't help her. It makes me feel completely useless. I've always dreamt of making lots of money and then building a house for Rebekah.' He hesitated, 'and our family.'

'You are certainly achieving the "making money" part.'

'Oh, money! That's easy! God has blessed me with that; but how will we cope if we can't have children? Rebekah doesn't believe me when I tell her I only care about her, but it is true! She is my life Jairus, my whole life!' He dropped his head and began to weep. 'I never let her see me crying, not about this anyway. Please Jairus you must pray for us. Pray for us every day. My darling Rebekah!'

Jairus placed his hand on Jacob's shoulder. He wondered how he would respond in such a situation. Not with tears he thought, unaware they were already sliding down his cheeks. He prayed without being aware of that either.

'Give them a child,' he murmured, 'Please give them a child.'

Time seemed to slow down for Jacob and Rebekah as their lives settled into a steady routine. Everything which should have brought them joy seemed meaningless as they were caught up in a cycle of waiting. The shame of childlessness hung over them like a dark cloud. Rebekah heard the whispers in the streets as she passed, and she grew to hate the frozen smile which was all she could manage as she admired the new-born babies of family and friends. Abigail and Jocabed comforted her as best they could, but the laughter died out of her eyes and her sunny nature seemed gone forever.

Benjamin had given Jacob the spice stall as his wedding present. It was flourishing and he buried himself in his work as he began to travel all over the district, widening the scope of his business. Benjamin was very proud of him and boasted to anyone who would listen how he had trained Jacob. The stall rivalled any other in the market. Everyone loved and admired Jacob, and it seemed everything he touched turned to gold, except this one thing. He tried to fill the emptiness of Rebekah's life with plans for a new house, but it was like a game they began to play, pretending to each other that building a new home would somehow help. They both knew it wouldn't. The weariness of fruitless waiting was crushing them both.

Rebekah was at the new house when Jacob arrived unexpectedly.

He looked around, pleased with the building's progress. He had chosen the site carefully, close enough to the main street to be convenient, but set back a little up an alleyway so there was privacy too.

He put his arm around Rebekah and squeezed her gently. 'You really do like it sweetheart?' he said.

Rebekah looked up into his eager face. Not even these long months of disappointment had erased his endless enthusiasm, but there was a wariness behind his smile, a caution in his tone. Where had her light-hearted Jacob gone?

She smiled up at him reassuringly. 'It's lovely Jacob,' she said, 'just lovely.'

He squeezed her again and turned to leave. 'And, by the way,' he said, 'Jairus and Abigail have invited us to their home tomorrow. We will be their first guests.'

She nodded. 'I know,' she said.

Jacob pulled a face. 'You women; you always know everything.'

'Of course,' she said.

'Hm!' he said, pulling the door closed behind him.

After he was gone, she wandered around the empty rooms thinking about Jairus. He had been their first guest too, but he was a different man back then. Jacob had told her about Jairus going to see Levi, but still the change in his character seemed inexplicable. Was Levi a miracle worker? What had he said that had so completely revolutionised Jacob's friend? For one thing Jairus had come and apologised to her. She thought she might never get over that, and then he had finally married Abigail, after all those months of waiting. She had come to wonder if she had had anything to do with the delay. In her worst moments she feared their childlessness and her shrewish behaviour had put Jairus off marriage. She could never express such concerns to Jacob of course. He would be appalled. Yet still it was hard to throw off these negative thoughts. Everything inside her recoiled as another hideous question filled her mind. Did Jacob wish he had married someone else?

She stood looking into the room they planned would one day be a child's bedroom. Or would it? Did Jacob regret not marrying someone who could fill his house with the sound of childish laughter? He had built her this new house, an expression of his growing wealth. She knew she should be pleased for it was beautiful, even with a well of its own, but there was no escaping the reality that surrounded her.

She walked back into the living room. She could see herself here, cooking, mending, waiting always for Jacob to return from work to give her life some meaning. She could not deceive herself, knowing that even when it was filled with furniture it would be empty, hollow, echoing with the absence of children. Always it would mock her barrenness and failure. What use was a brand-new house without new life to fill it to overflowing? What use was anything money could buy? She gazed out of the window and up the alleyway. Jairus was married at last. She was glad for him; truly glad. Abigail was a darling, and their wedding had been as full of rejoicing as her own. She sighed as she remembered her boundless optimism. She had been sure the future would be full of unspeakable happiness for her and Jacob.

She looked around the house once more. 'God grant Abigail and Jairus are happy and blessed,' she prayed out loud, 'and their home is full of children.'

It was the first prayer she had prayed here. 'Children are a blessing from the Lord,' she quoted wistfully, and then she pulled the door shut gently behind her.

She walked wearily home, bearing an invisible burden.

Rebekah felt numb when Abigail drew her aside only four months after the wedding. She was pregnant already. Abigail held her in her arms knowing how difficult this news must be, but Rebekah didn't cry. There were no tears left. Pain was etched into Jacob's face when Rebekah told him, but she was adamant.

'We will rejoice with them,' she declared firmly, 'and we will not begrudge them a single moment of their joy.'

Yet despite her determination to put her own feelings aside, as she watched them a stab of regret went through her again and again. Almost unconsciously she would turn her face away. What would she not sacrifice to give to Jacob the sense of pride which simply oozed out of Jairus? But she could not.

Abigail miscarried two weeks later. Rebekah rushed to her and discovered the fountain of her tears was not empty after all. They sobbed together inconsolably. Rebekah couldn't be sure if she cried for Abigail or for herself, but once begun, the tears would not stop and the two women clung to each other, each sympathising with the agony of the other.

It was just the beginning. Rebekah could not conceive and Abigail lost every baby in the first twelve weeks. They came to accept the inevitability of it all, the way those around them were careful about what they said, the unasked questions, the looks of sympathy. It was particularly hard for Jairus. His new-found freedom and enjoyment of life survived the first miscarriage and then the second, but gradually he became more and more withdrawn, even from Abigail. Jairus was lost in his pain and Jacob in his. The two men drew apart while their wives drew closer together. Suffering affects people differently. They all did their best to survive.

Two years after Jairus and Abigail's wedding, Rebekah realised five weeks had elapsed and there was no sign of her period or the pain which always accompanied it. She didn't dare to hope at first and determined to say nothing, not even to Jacob, although she was certain he knew. As first one day and then another passed, she could feel him watching her, but she was willing him not to say anything in case it broke the spell of hope gradually settling over her.

Early one morning she slipped from her bed without waking him. She wasn't quite sure why she was getting up so early, but there was an urgency about it.

I just need some fresh air, she said to herself and quietly felt her way to the door. She was standing outside, breathing in the last coolness of the night, when a flood of nausea suddenly hit her. She had never felt so ill, but she didn't care, for joy was flooding through her, instantly sweeping away all the years of disgrace.

Later, hugging her secret to herself, she quietly pushed open the door intending to go back to bed unnoticed. Instead, she walked straight into her husband's waiting arms. He put his hands on her shoulders and looked intently into her ashen face before lifting his face to heaven and giving a huge shout of delight. Picking her up he swung her around as though she were a child and then deposited her gently on the ground as she chided him, laughing, 'Be careful Jacob!'

She never forgot it, the whooshing sound in her head, the rush of excitement in her veins, the look in his eyes as he gazed at her with such tenderness. 'Ah Rebekah,' he sighed, and she felt her life as his wife had truly begun at last.

Rebekah promised to stay in the house and rest all day. Jacob insisted on it. She in turn insisted he went to work as usual.

'If you don't go, everyone will want to know what is wrong, and I don't intend to tell anyone about the baby for weeks and weeks.'

She could see he didn't understand, but she didn't feel safe yet, not after enduring so many heart-breaking disappointments with Abigail and Jairus who now said nothing to anyone. They had grown to find the sympathy of those with children almost too much to bear. Rebekah felt saying nothing for a while would somehow protect her baby, although she wasn't sure how. She placed her hands onto her stomach, willing everything to be all right, realising she was never going to feel safe until the baby was actually cradled in her arms. She wondered if all pregnant women felt as insecure as she did, and as emotional.

Eventually she pushed Jacob out of the door, with strict instructions to tell no one and to "take that look off your face," but then she found herself restlessly moving from room to room. Years of blighted dreams came rising inexorably to the surface of her emotions. She felt she would burst if she didn't get out of the house and into the air.

Rebekah thought it was still quite early in the morning and she hoped to stroll for a while without meeting anyone, but she had seriously misjudged the time. Almost in a daze she wandered down the alleyway and out into the main street. She gazed around her in bewilderment, marvelling that everything could look so different and yet be exactly the same. The whole world seemed to be alive with something delightful she dimly remembered from her childhood. Surely the sun had never shone with such glory as it did today, and every child was not as sweet as suddenly they appeared to her.

Looking around she realised Abigail was standing amongst a group of women just ahead of her. She was torn between the desire to see her and the sudden compulsion to turn and walk away. The pulse in her throat began to beat hard, making a strange sound inside her head, threatening to deafen her. A second later and it was all too late, for Abigail saw her and came over at once. Rebekah found she was beginning to shake and Abigail frowned with concern, obviously thinking she was unwell. Rebekah, fearing her friend would make a fuss that drew attention to her, reached out and grabbed her arm, pulling her aside.

Abigail looked at her with surprise. 'Are you ill?' she asked.

Rebekah laughed a little unsteadily. Any minute now, she thought, and bent down a little, trying to maintain control of her queasy stomach.

Abigail had seen the blood drain from her face and held onto her arm to support her. 'Rebekah what is it?' she asked urgently.

Rebekah looked up and shook her head slightly. 'Not here!' she whispered looking past Abigail at the other women who were beginning to wonder what was going on. A light of sudden comprehension dawned in Abigail.

'Rebekah are you…?'

Rebekah flushed to the roots of her hair, too honest to lie, too confused to dissemble, she simply nodded. 'I haven't even told Mother yet,' she whispered urgently.

Looking up into Abigail's face she suddenly gave a terrific gulp as though she were going to burst into tears. Abigail used her own body to shield her from the curious stares of the others.

'I'll help you home,' she said decidedly.

Rebekah nodded again, leaning on her thankfully. She began to wonder if she could carry a baby at all. After all, this was just the beginning and already it was too much for her.

They walked in silence. Rebekah felt mortified Abigail had found out in this unfortunate way. She should never have gone out into the street in the first place. She should have chosen her moment to tell Abigail, when Jairus was there. It should have been something the four of them shared together, in private, where the inevitable joy and pain could have been expressed with safety. What a fool she was: a stupid tactless fool! She sneaked a look at her friend's face and saw Abigail's eyes were brimming over with tears.

Rebekah's steps faltered and she began to sob. 'Oh Abigail, I'm so sorry, so very sorry! You shouldn't have found out like this. Please forgive me.'

Abigail stopped walking and looked at her in amazement. They were standing in the alleyway which led to Rebekah's house.

'What are you talking about?' Abigail asked. 'Are you worried because I am weeping? Jairus and I have prayed every day God would grant you a child. How could you doubt I would be delighted? Don't you pray every day for us too?' Rebekah nodded dumbly.

'Then you must understand. God has granted our prayer for you first, but I am still certain our day will come. This gives me hope. I rejoice with you Rebekah, just as you would rejoice with me.' She hugged Rebekah, who rested her head on her shoulder thankfully.

Rebekah sighed, challenged by Abigail's goodness. She knew, whatever Abigail thought, her own response would not have been so sweet. And Jairus, she thought: what about him? There was no time for more as with a loud clatter Jacob came hurtling down the alleyway from their home. His face was a picture of concern.

'What are you doing out here in the heat?' he asked anxiously. 'I thought you were going to stay in the house today.'

'I am not ill.' Rebekah replied, although Abigail thought she certainly looked it.

Jacob looked at the tears on Abigail's cheeks as she smiled at him gently.

'Congratulations,' she said, and Jacob's look of anxiety vanished for a moment.

'Thank you Abigail,' he said. She wondered how anyone could express such joy and sympathy at the same time. Jairus said Jacob wore his heart on his face. How right he was.

Abigail stood watching as Jacob gently led his wife back up the alley to their home. She used her veil to wipe her tears, and then she moved swiftly up the street.

When Jacob got Rebekah back to the house, he made her sit quietly in a chair. He fussed about her, getting a cushion for her back and drawing fresh water from the well. She watched him fondly and was about to speak when she looked up in surprise at the sound of hurrying feet just outside the door.

'Who can that be?' she wondered, when the door flew open and Jairus rushed through it, almost falling into the room in his haste. He came over at once and touched her shoulder, although he seemed unable to speak, and then he hugged Jacob until she feared he would break her husband in half. They all wept, Jairus unashamedly, and as Rebekah brushed the tears away, she suddenly knew how much this seemingly unemotional man cared for them both. She gave thanks from the bottom of her heart for his friendship.

As the months went by Rebekah knew how much her growing waistline gave pain to Abigail. There was no disguising it, even though Abigail did her best.

'One day,' Rebekah encouraged her. 'Just look how long we had to wait.'

'Yes of course,' said Abigail, and forced a smile.

A week before the baby was born the four of them were together and Jairus was being very loud and pompous. He was synagogue ruler now, a man of great importance, or so he said. Rebekah thought his nonsense was covering a broken heart, but she couldn't say anything.

'You should be like the prophets of old and begin to speak for God,' said Jacob, entering into the banter. He honestly thought this would provoke Jairus into the familiar arguments of their childhood, but instead Jairus went to the centre of the room and struck a pose.

'You will have a son,' he boomed prophetically. There was a shocked silence. No-one had ever seen Jairus anything but serious about matters touching God. Jacob blinked and standing up he went towards his friend. To everyone's amazement Jairus gave him one anguished look and then fled from the room. Abigail called after him, and then without a word she followed, leaving Rebekah and Jacob looking at each other in dismay.

'Oh Jacob,' said Rebekah, 'poor Jairus!'

Jacob nodded, looking quite as anguished as Jairus had. 'No one will ever know what he is going through,' he said quietly. 'He will be furious with himself for having caused such a scene. Poor Jairus indeed. I have failed him of late, too caught up in my own affairs to be there when he most needed me. I should have been more aware of him, should have persuaded him to talk to me!' He shook his head sadly. 'After this, he will keep his feelings in check, imposing new standards of self-control on himself. He takes being a good example very seriously. I fear for him. We must pray all the more for them to have a child.'

Rebekah got up and hugged Jacob. It was so like him to take the blame upon himself. If anyone understood Abigail and Jairus, surely it was them. They must be able to help!

The next day Jairus appeared at Rebekah's door, looking solemn and with a strange deadness in his eyes. Rebekah invited him in and he stood in the centre of the room, looking so bereft that Rebekah's heart went out to him.

'I have come to apologise for my outburst yesterday evening.' Her hands moved towards him and then returned to her sides.

'There is nothing to forgive,' she said earnestly. 'Jairus, I....'

He held up his hand. 'My behaviour was inappropriate, especially for a man in my position. I was betrayed into unseemly jesting. It won't happen again. I have seen Jacob and apologised to him, and I hope, with your permission we can forget all about it.'

Rebekah was paralysed by his formal manner. For months Jairus had grown more distant, but now he seemed unreachable. She put a hand over her mouth and nodded, incapable of any other response.

'Thank you,' he said and turning on his heel he left. Neither Rebekah nor Jacob saw him again during that last, long week.

Jocabed boasted her daughter behaved as though she had had a dozen children already and the birth was easy, which somehow made up for the long wait for this precious child.

'At least he is having the good sense to come swiftly at the end,' Rebekah said between contractions and with one more push the baby was born.

'What is he like?' Rebekah asked anxiously. 'Is he perfect?'

'Not exactly,' said her mother, bringing the baby and placing it in her arms. 'He's a girl,' she said; and then laughed indulgently at the total shock on her daughter's face.

When eventually Jacob was allowed to hold that tiny bundle, he felt he was the clumsiest man in the whole world. He genuinely believed he might break her, so fragile did she seem to him. It was as though no one had ever had a child before. She was a wonder to him from the start and she won his heart simply by wrapping her tiny fingers around his own. As he gazed down at her he experienced no twinge of regret she wasn't a boy, for wasn't she the most beautiful baby in all the world?

Rebekah agreed wholeheartedly and named her Sarah, meaning princess. She was the joy and delight of their hearts.

Jairus and Abigail came to see them of course. At first Jacob thought Jairus wouldn't hold Sarah, but after Abigail had cradled her in her arms, cooing over her softly, Jairus came and took the baby from her. He stood looking down at her for a long time. 'A girl,' he said, almost with awe in his voice.

'Yes,' said Jacob,

Jairus looked up at him. 'Let this be a lesson to you! God doesn't speak to people today, not even synagogue rulers!'

Rebekah drew in a quick breath, but Jacob only went and put his arm around his friend, chuckling softly.

Rebekah loved Sarah extravagantly, enjoying every moment as though all the years of disappointment had simply intensified the wonder of having her own child. Jacob would watch as she caressed Sarah's tiny fingers or kissed her perfect little toes. His heart felt as though it would burst with joy, yet at the back of his mind was a niggling worry. Rebekah was already praying for the next child to come. Jacob sighed. Could she not be content with their darling Sarah? But Rebekah was adamant, she must have a son. The need drove her.

The months passed swiftly with Sarah growing into a lively toddler. Abigail and Jairus loved her almost as much as her parents, but their own disappointment continued as before. The two women hardly talked about their desire for a child anymore; each coping with the pain in a different way. Abigail gave herself to beautiful weaving and embroidery, while Rebekah focused her whole life on encouraging Jacob in his business and of course caring for her spotless home.

Nothing is impossible, Rebekah would repeat to herself as her painful periods continued. The promised cure from having a child had never materialised. Instead, her monthly cycles grew shorter and shorter, with less and less chance of conception. Each month she lived in hope, reassuring herself that after all she had conceived Sarah hadn't she? Having her made the waiting easier to bear.

In the spring of the second year, she became sure. She was pregnant again. She danced Jacob around in her excitement. Maybe this time a son! They couldn't bring themselves to tell Jairus and Abigail and they agonised over this, their only sadness, but in the end, it turned out to be easy.

Abigail came to see Rebekah one day, holding a beautiful baby shawl. Rebekah looked at it, and then swiftly at Abigail. Who could have told her?

'You are pregnant, aren't you?' Abigail asked. The colour fled from Rebekah's face.

'It's all right,' said Abigail, 'Sarah told me!'

'But Sarah doesn't know!' said Rebekah, indignant.

'You cannot keep a secret from children,' said Abigail softly. 'She came to sit on my knee and patted my stomach, asking me if there was a baby inside. I guessed the rest.'

'What can I say Abigail? We wanted to tell you, but….'

It seemed Abigail hardly heard her, she was looking down at the soft material of the shawl she held in her hands. At last, she spoke,

'Don't you want to know what I answered her?'

A hush came over the room. Rebekah sat perfectly still.

'I told her there was, a baby inside me I mean. I have been waiting for a chance to tell you too!'

When Jacob came home his first thought was how Rebekah was feeling.

'Are you tired my darling?' he asked, for she was sitting in a chair looking out of the window, a piece of material carefully folded in her lap. He watched as with the lightest of touches she moved her fingers over it, almost caressing it.

'Has Abigail been to see you?' he asked gently. He knew she had been dreading this conversation. Rebekah nodded her head and lifted the soft material to her cheek.

'Was she very upset?'

Rebekah sighed. 'No,' she said, 'she was deliriously happy.'

Jacob frowned. 'But...' he said, as Rebekah finally turned towards him.

He looked at the glow on her face and comprehension dawned instantly.

'No!' he cried.

'Yes!' she said, and getting up she threw herself into his arms.

Jairus swore he heard Jacob's shout of joy all the way up the road at the synagogue.

Jacob was sure they were both having a boy, although Jairus warned him not to make rash pronouncements. But Jacob was certain, at least about Rebekah and he would place his hand on her stomach, teaching Sarah to speak to her brother. Sarah giggled with delight, while Rebekah laughed at their foolishness, praying always that Jacob was right.

This pregnancy was so different from her first Rebekah could hardly believe the contrast. With Sarah she had been horribly sick and at night she had hardly slept, so she had been constantly exhausted. Day after day she had dragged her unwieldy body around the house, telling herself the baby would be worth all the back-ache and discomfort, which of course she was. With this second baby Rebekah felt wonderful, her skin glowed and she was never sick. In fact, she had never felt so well. Jacob had watched her anxiously through every day she carried Sarah, treating her like a fine piece of pottery that required careful handling. This time he was different too, somehow shedding the anxiety of the first pregnancy as though it had never been. Rebekah silently rejoiced to hear the sound of his boyish laughter and a great peace come upon her. She was filled with happiness as at last her family began to form around her. They waited for the baby eagerly, greedy for the joy awaiting them, convinced now all their troubles were over.

The day the pains started Rebekah felt nothing but heady excitement. Giving birth to Sarah had certainly been hard work, but she didn't fear the confinement as everyone told her second babies were easier. She was unprepared for what was to come. Hour upon hour the contractions bore down upon her, and as exhaustion stripped her courage away, she began to realise something was wrong. Jocabed used every art she knew to help her, but as night began to fall the pain intensified, and even Rebekah, so used to agony, could not hold back her cries of distress. In the brief respites between the spasms her mother would mop her brow and speak calm encouragement to her, but then another pain would hit her, searing through her with such violence she wasn't sure she could bear it. But there was no choice; she had to bear it.

All through the next day the pain continued, Rebekah so exhausted she completely lost track of time. In the dim lamplight she became aware of the frightened looks of the women gathered around her and she began to wonder if she was going to die and the baby with her. Somewhere, in the haze of pain, an image of Jacob came into her mind. She saw him alone with Sarah, grieving for her, grieving for his lost son.

She called out breathlessly, 'Tell Jacob I'm sorry.'

Jocabed's face became grim and set, but the other women tried to soothe Rebekah, speaking reassuringly to her all would be well. Poor Rebekah, her self-control shattered by fear and blinding agony, wanted to scream at their stupidity. She was dying, didn't they know that? Wasn't it obvious to all of them? She opened her mouth to speak when her mother gripped her hand firmly.

'I am here Rebekah,' Jocabed said, and all Rebekah's anger disappeared in a moment. She lay back on the pillow fixing her eyes on the dear, familiar face. Mother won't let me die, she thought, will she?

Another hour went by with Rebekah growing weaker and weaker. The women's faces began to swim in the lamplight and she became so lost in the pain it didn't seem to matter whether she lived to see the morning. Jocabed watched with deepening concern and at last she sent Jacob out into the darkness to find the best midwife in the town and drag her from her bed.

When the midwife arrived, even Jocabed drew back respectfully, but it was obvious this woman was unimpressed with having been disturbed in the middle of the night. Everything appeared hazy to Rebekah, but still she could see that the woman's face looked bad-tempered as she bent over her. It seemed the midwife was unconvinced this confinement was worthy of her attention. Her expert hands explored Rebekah's body, just as another pain exploded through it. Rebekah gave a gasp as her back arched and suddenly the midwife began to bark out orders.

'Save the baby!' Rebekah whispered as the woman came close beside her.

'Hm!' said the midwife scornfully, 'I shall save you both!'

She was as good as her word.

Rebekah hovered somewhere between the world of pain and the soft comfort of unconsciousness that beckoned to her. The midwife worked tirelessly, and then, like a miracle, as the morning light streamed into the room, Rebekah heard the first weak cry. Her beloved son. She lay back on the pillow, barely conscious, but as the midwife put the baby in her arms, Jocabed's grey face somehow came into focus bending over her. With the last of her strength Rebekah smiled at her.

'He's worth it,' she whispered, and her mother's hand trembled with weariness as she caressed the baby's head.

'Every baby is worth it,' she said.

They called him Benjamin after Jacob's father.

Abigail and Jairus had Hannah a month after Benjamin was born. The birth was a typical first delivery, long and difficult, but Abigail made light of it. The two couples practically lived in each other's houses, and Sarah seemed to think both tiny babies belonged to her. She could be very possessive, even when Jairus held Hannah.

'My baby,' she would say and they all laughed.

Jacob declared it was obvious Benjamin and Hannah were meant for each other, as they had been born in the same year, after so much waiting. Rebekah wasn't sure he was joking. Abigail at least took it seriously.

'He means it you know. He would love us all to be one family,' she said to Jairus. Rebekah looked over at the Rabbi's straight face, wondering if he didn't approve.

'We'll see,' he said and shrugged his shoulders. She looked up at Jacob who was standing beside her. His face was full of laughter as he looked at his friend. Rebekah glanced back at Jairus. Why could she never work out what Jairus was thinking? Was he teasing her? A second later she caught his mischievous smile, and sighed with relief. Jacob punched him playfully as he passed him.

'Show some respect for your synagogue ruler,' Jairus said severely, but not even Rebekah was fooled that time.

The weeks passed and gradually Rebekah established her new routine. Two children: she could hardly believe it; but something was wrong and Jacob became really concerned about her health. He was adamant he didn't want her to have another child until she was completely better. Rebekah laughed at his anxieties, excited at the prospect of being pregnant again. She reassured him she wasn't afraid, not even after such a difficult birth, but he only shook his head. Another six months went by and the pain came back worse than before. Rebekah was trying to ignore it and the flow of blood that remained longer and grew heavier and heavier. Shrugging it off she still hoped to become pregnant. She could not face the truth.

One year after Benjamin's birth her period began and just went on and on. She refused to worry. It couldn't go on forever, could it? It would stop eventually. She made up her mind to continue life as normal, but week after week passed and fear began to stir within her. What was wrong? Would this affliction never leave her? In the still hours of the night when it was hard to control her thoughts, she would lie awake with her heart pounding. She felt weak and sick, the truth hammering constantly through her mind. The issue of blood was continuous. Their chance of another baby was gone.

Rebekah forbade Jacob to share with anyone and she was deaf to his insistence she should go to the doctor. She determined to live life as though nothing was wrong, and for a while she even refused to acknowledge to herself just how sick she was becoming. In some strange way she believed if she ignored her illness, never thought of it or spoke of it, then miraculously it would disappear. It was a forlorn hope.

As her health deteriorated it became more and more important to her Jacob shouldn't know that slowly, imperceptibly her

162

strength was ebbing away. She continued with her chores, at least when Jacob was close enough to see. She hid her weariness and the shaking of her hands, somehow managing to care for the house and the children. At night she would gratefully collapse on her mattress and try to stifle the fear that washed over her. What if she could not rise in the morning? What if this bed became the place where she lived out her future and this bedroom a prison with no escape? What if? What if? She would weep silently, brushing the tears away with trembling fingers lest Jacob should sense her distress. In the end only sheer exhaustion calmed her, sweeping the tormenting thoughts away into troubled sleep.

Jacob was busy building the business, and he was often away, so for a while she managed to hide the true state of her health from him. But she could never fool Jacob for long and one day when she thought he had left the house to go to market, he secretly returned. Rebekah had no idea he was at the window as she slowly made her way to the well. She sank down upon its edge as though the journey from the house had been a score of weary miles. Jacob watched as she slowly let down the bucket before the daily nightmare of drawing up the heavy load of water. The children played around her and she was shamed by the impatience she felt at their noisiness. She was thinking about the past as the bucket fell out of sight into the blackness far below, remembering how simple fetching the water had been. Like so many other things it had been an unconsidered expenditure of her boundless energy. She used to sing as she drew up the sparkling liquid from the depths below, and play games with Sarah, splashing her and chasing her around the well.

Now the drawing of the water was always the first task of her day when Jacob was gone. She had to do it first, while she still had the strength to pull the heavy rope. She would not give up and admit defeat, confessing to Jacob it was too hard for her, not with this job, not with any job.

She leant over the edge of the well, putting forth every ounce of her strength in a vain attempt to lift the bucket. The well swam before her and a pulse pounded in her throat. Tears of frustration ran down her face as gasping for breath she gathered herself together for another attempt. It had never been as bad as this. She steeled herself to try harder. When it was half way up, her strength gave out and she had to let it go, the rope burning her hands as it slipped from her grasp.

She didn't hear Jacob as he came up quietly behind her. She only became aware of him as he gently picked her up and carried her back towards the house. He shouldn't have touched her of course, because it would make him unclean, but he didn't seem to care, and she had no energy left to protest. Exhausted she leant her head on his broad shoulder and tried to work out what the strange muffled sound was which seemed to accompany them. Only slowly did she realise it was the sound of her own weeping. Jacob spoke soothingly to her, but she sobbed inconsolably, her determination to live a normal life melting away forever.

After the incident at the well it seemed pointless to pretend anymore and Rebekah shared everything with Abigail. It all came out in a jumbled rush, and although initially Abigail looked relieved at finding out at last what was wrong, yet as Rebekah spoke a deep trouble came into her eyes. She held Rebekah tightly in her arms and comforted her as best she could, but when she left the house, she hesitated in the alley resting her hand on the wall. A terrible sense of foreboding was settling over her. This news changed everything and well she knew it.

At first Rebekah hardly noticed Jairus had stopped coming to see them. Abigail still came with Hannah, but Rebekah could feel an unspoken tension underlying their conversations. She didn't mention it to Jacob as she puzzled over what was wrong. Gradually even Abigail's visits became more infrequent until eventually Rebekah knew she had to speak to her. How could she let their friendship fade away as though it had never been? Her only course was to confront the problem, for she loved Abigail too much to lose her.

That was the day when Abigail came alone. It was unusual to see her without Hannah, but it was the look on her face which frightened Rebekah.

'Abigail, what's wrong?' she cried. Abigail didn't answer, but stopped in the doorway, tears pouring down her face.

Rebekah stood frozen to the spot with Benjamin in her arms, trying to understand what was happening. Had someone died? What could possibly be the matter? She made a move towards her, but Abigail shook her head and put out a hand to stop her. Rebekah stood immobile, quite bewildered.

At last Abigail said, 'I am sorry Rebecca, so sorry, but I couldn't bear not to tell you myself.'

'Tell me what?'

'I cannot come to see you anymore. I am so sorry!'

Abigail looked at her imploringly, as though willing Rebekah to understand, then without another word she left.

When Jacob came home, he found Rebekah sitting stupefied in a chair.

'What happened?' he demanded anxiously.

'Abigail came and said she couldn't come and see me anymore.' She turned on him a blank, uncomprehending stare. 'What does she mean Jacob?'

At first Jacob's face turned deathly pale, but moments later his cheeks grew livid red. Rebekah was more confused than ever. She had never seen Jacob's eyes blaze with fury before. He looked as though he was going to murder someone. It was frightening.

'It's Jairus,' he said through clenched teeth and wrenching open the door he flung himself out of the house.

Jarius was in his study at the synagogue when Jacob found him, the room once occupied by Levi years before. Neither of them thought of Levi.

Jairus stood up as Jacob stormed into the room. He braced himself, knowing Jacob would be angry, but nothing could have prepared him for the ashen whiteness of Jacob's face or the fire in his eyes. His closest friend looked at him with loathing and Jairus recoiled in shock. He held out his hand, but Jacob ignored it, speaking in a cold, rigidly controlled voice Jairus had never heard before.

'Well, our illustrious synagogue ruler, the pride of Capernaum, I hear your wife Abigail has recently visited mine, to graciously inform her you have forbidden your family ever to visit our home again. So caring of you!'

Two spots of fire burned on Jairus's cheeks as he tried to swallow the lump which had mysteriously appeared in his throat.

'Jacob, try to understand, I have been struggling with this decision for weeks....'

Jacob watched him with narrowed eyes. It was the first time he had ever noticed that Jairus's jet-black beard bobbed up and down as he spoke. He had the insane desire to tear it out with his bare hands and stuff it down Jairus's throat. His fingers curled into fists at the satisfying thought of it.

'You don't have to explain anything to me, dear friend,' he said, and the bitterness in his voice turned Jairus's face as white as parchment.

'I understand you fully. I have always understood you. Rebekah is unclean, isn't she? And you, our beloved spiritual leader cannot take the risk of being made unclean by some accidental touch she may place on you or your family. It is the law isn't it, the cold, hard tenets of the law? The love of your life!'

'I should have told you myself,' Jairus murmured.

'And why exactly didn't you? Were you afraid I might strike you?' Jacob's eyes glittered so strangely Jairus was almost afraid to look at him. 'I still might you know! I might even murder you!'

Jacob lunged forward, but hit himself on the corner of the table. Jairus instinctively reached out to him, but Jacob drew back and fell into a chair.

'Don't touch me!' he hissed. He dropped his head into his hands and Jairus, unable to see his face, could hear the anguish in his voice.

'How could you Jairus? Does Rebekah not have enough to bear? Must you reject her in her hour of need and strip away even her friendship with Abigail? And the children! What about the children?'

Jairus hung his head but said nothing.

Jacob looked up at him in the wonder of disbelief. Slowly it dawned on him how much he despised this man and his slavish adherence to the law. He got to his feet. Only one thing surprised him now. How could they ever have been friends? He felt again the heady power of anger, and with it came a hatred both passionate and deadly cold. His voice was harsh with it.

'None of that matters, does it? Nothing but your precious position in the synagogue. Well, go ahead Jairus, you keep yourself pure. It must after all be the most important thing. The thing God requires. Or at least so you have always told me! As for me, I don't want to serve a God whose dictates cause such heartache. Some might think the law a hard master, but I'm sure you don't feel that way. You love it don't you?' His eyes fell on the parchments Jairus had been reading.

'What a pity you don't have the ten commandments here in your keeping; your beloved law! One might almost say you belong together. They are carved in stone too, aren't they?'

Jairus tried to speak, but no words came.

Jacob could no longer bear to look at him and turned away. With his hand on the door, he looked back over his shoulder. He ignored the look on Jairus's face. He had forgotten what mercy felt like.

'Don't worry Jairus,' he said, 'you will never have to take the risk of being defiled in my home. When the issue of blood ceases and Rebekah is well again, don't trouble to come to my door. You simply won't be welcome. Ever. Do give my regards to Abigail. I am sure none of this is her idea. How could it be? She loves us, doesn't she?'

The words pierced Jairus like arrows. The door slammed and Jacob was gone.

Jairus turned and sank into his chair banging his head on the desk again and again. No one was near to hear his pitiful groans as his heart seemed torn from his chest. His best friend was already far away.

After Jacob stormed out, Rebekah sat thinking for a long time. Jairus! Of course! What a fool she had been! She had let their friendship blind her to the one overruling factor in Jairus's life.

168

He was the ruler of the synagogue, the local upholder of the law, and there was no way he could have anything to do with an unclean woman. Not even if she was the wife of his oldest friend. Slowly she realised she had been lying to herself, hoping the issue of blood would one day miraculously go away. But Jairus had faced the truth. Jairus the realist.

For the first time the full implications of her illness came home to her; who she was, and how people would see her from now on - not just Jairus, but everyone. When she left the house, she would have to cry out "unclean, unclean," to allow people to get out of the way and avoid touching her. The deep humiliation of it brought a sour taste to her mouth, even before she spoke the word for the first time.

After a while she stopped crying. She knew there was no escape. It must all be borne, every bitter consequence and without complaint, for Jacob's sake and for the children. It was the only way.

When Jacob came back, he looked long and searchingly into her face and she returned his gaze without flinching.

'What happened?' she asked.

'I told him some things I thought it was important for him to hear.'

She saw his hands were still shaking. 'It is no good being angry Jacob. You must forgive Jairus; you must!'

Jacob flung himself down in a chair. 'Forgive him! I'd like to strangle him!'

Rebekah reached out a hand in her distress, but withdrew it again quickly, grateful Jacob hadn't seen the gesture. 'But I have great sympathy for him Jacob, he is caught in a terrible dilemma. You may not agree with his decision, but you must see it is costing him everything to make it.' Her heart was touched with pity. 'Poor Jairus!' she said.

He only snorted angrily, 'Poor Jairus!'

She hardly recognised his voice. What was happening to them? It seemed her gentle Jacob was gone without trace. Was everything in their life going to be ruined by this sickness? Rebekah struggled to control the aching sobs which threatened to overwhelm her.

At last, she said quietly, 'I am going to forgive him, and you must forgive him too Jacob, or bitterness will make your heart grow cold.'

'I have told him that even when everything returns to normal, he will not be welcome in my house, and I promise you I meant every word. You may forgive him, but I never shall. I never want his name mentioned again. I will forget he ever existed and I suggest you do the same.'

'Forget he ever existed? But what about when you see him in synagogue?'

Rebekah recoiled at his cynical smile.

'Yes,' he said, 'that will be interesting, won't it? He is separating himself from us, pretending you do not exist my darling. Well, I can do the same. In fact, I have this strange feeling I shall do much better at it than he can.'

He nodded his head, as though with some deep satisfaction. 'Yes,' he said, 'Jairus thinks he knows me, thinks I will forgive and forget, but he is going to discover there is a side to me he has never seen. I will shut him out of my life as though he were unclean. Let's see how he likes it!'

He got up and walked away and Rebekah sat staring out of the window, seeing nothing, horrified by the look in his eyes.

Jacob never talked to her about the subject again, so Rebekah never knew what had passed between him and Jairus. Perhaps it was better not to know. The friendship was finished and Jacob kept his word, never speaking Jairus's name again. He was like a stranger. It seemed to Rebekah she had lost not only Jairus and Abigail, but Jacob as well. Her life lay in ruins around her and there was no way to rebuild it. The future became a fearful thing.

Jacob insisted Rebekah went to the doctor of course, and when this old friend shook his head, Jacob simply moved on to another and then another. The new doctors prescribed treatments which didn't work and willingly took his money. Even he came to distrust their smooth reassurances and the shifty look in their eyes. Rebekah tried to reason with him, begging him to stop throwing his money away.

'I have known for years there is something wrong inside me. Accept it Jacob, there is no cure.' But he could not accept it, would not accept it, his determination fuelled by anger and frustration. Stubbornly he refused to give up hope. He threw off the pity everyone offered as though it might weaken his resolve and ferociously pursued a cure, as though his life depended on it.

With each attempt more expensive than the last, gradually his business began to fail as their money drained away. Eventually only his original spice-stall in Capernaum was left, but even that was not flourishing as it once had. The supply of spices from Micah was beginning to become unreliable, and Jacob felt a trip to Genneseret to see his old friend was the best thing to do. He knew something must be wrong. Yet this was an added worry, for how could he leave Rebekah? In the end the decision was made for him, the supply suddenly stopped, and a message came from Simon, Micah's son. It was written in the beautiful hand of an educated man.

"I am sorry to have to tell you that my father has been ill and died unexpectedly yesterday. I know this will be a great shock to you. I think it unlikely I will continue with my father's business. My whole world has changed and I cannot see a way forward yet.

Please do not concern yourself with any money you may owe my father. I know he would wish me to thank you for your integrity and friendship over the years. He often spoke of the time you came to stay with us, and your many visits since. I do not know what else to say. Please pray for me. Simon."

Jacob stood with the scroll in his hand for a long time. He knew it was the end of the spice-stall. He went at once to see Benjamin.

'Micah is dead,' he said woodenly.

'What!' Benjamin was shocked.

'His son has no heart for the spice trade. He will not step into his father's shoes.'

Jacob's face showed no emotion. 'I will sell off the spices and we will close the stall,' he said.

Benjamin looked at him with concern. 'You will come and work for me,' he said firmly.

'No,' said Jacob, 'I will hire myself out, someone will want me.'

'Don't be ridiculous,' said Benjamin. 'I want you! You are the best business man I know. You cannot go and work for someone else!'

Jacob shook his head. 'I know there are already too many mouths being fed by your business Father. I will not add my family to those of my brothers. I will find an employer. Micah's son has forgiven me any money I owe. I suppose Micah has left him a large inheritance and he will probably never have to work again. I have one last thing to do with the money from the spice-stall. One last journey. Will you come with a cart when I break the stall down?'

Benjamin didn't know how to respond to the deadness in Jacob's voice. 'Of course,' he replied. There seemed nothing else to say.

A few weeks later Benjamin came to the market with an empty cart and slowly he and Jacob demolished the stall, as once they had built it, what seemed a life-time before. Jacob said nothing as they worked side by side, but when the last piece of wood was thrown into the cart the two men stood together and looked at the spice-stained ground. Micah's face stood out clearly in Jacob's memory. Grief over the loss of his friend threatened to overwhelm him, another added sorrow. Ruthlessly he pushed it down.

'I am sorry Jacob,' Benjamin said, reaching out an awkward hand to his son. Jacob didn't respond. He turned his back on the empty space where once his hopes and ambitions had flourished.

'At least you and Mother are still alive,' he said before he strode off and got into the cart.

Benjamin hesitated, somehow feeling they couldn't just leave. Looking about him, he noticed, abandoned to one side, the stool he and Jacob had bought so many years before.

'What about this stool?' he called.

Jacob did not look back. 'Throw it away,' he said. 'I have no need of it now.'

Benjamin ran his hand over its smooth surface, polished by the use of so many customers. It too was faintly stained with the multiple colours of the spices. He threw it into the back of the cart and climbed up beside his son.

'I'll keep it; your mother might like it,' he said.

Jacob shrugged his shoulders. 'Do what you like, you paid for it as I recall.'

Benjamin glanced at his son's hardened face, and into his mind came a sudden image of Jacob standing laughing with the young boy who made the stool. He was surprised for he hadn't thought about it for years. It annoyed him that he couldn't remember the name of the lad. I wonder where he is now, he thought. Did he fulfil his dreams? Has his life ended up incredibly different from what he expected? Just like Jacob's? He laid the questions aside as he picked up the reins. All that mattered now was rescuing Jacob as much as he would let them.

They didn't speak as they drove away.

Jacob gathered what was left of their money, borrowed what he could and went to Jerusalem seeking the best doctor money could buy. Rebekah was too sick to travel, so the doctor came to her. He was well dressed, with eyes that missed nothing, and because he was a good man he refused to pretend. He told Jacob the truth, speaking plainly what everyone else had known for a long time. There was no cure for Rebekah.

Jacob collapsed into a chair when the doctor told him. A flood of despair washed over him. He remembered this feeling from long ago, when the High Priest had spoken to him in the temple. He wondered why it was always men from Jerusalem who shattered his hopes.

He accepted it at last. His business lost, his wife incurable, his trust in God worn to the bone, there was no way to avoid the truth. Only a miracle could save Rebekah and miracles were in short supply in Capernaum. His life lay in ruins around him. He was a broken man.

The heartbreak enveloped Rebekah like a black cloak and her health deteriorated rapidly. Gradually she came to be known as the woman with the issue of blood. She stopped going out into the streets, unable to bear the look of pity on the faces of friends and neighbours. Her house became her world, her family her only reason for living.

One day as she sat looking out of her window, she saw a man with a bird trapped in a net; on his way to market she supposed. Her attention became fixed on the bird as it fluttered its wings uselessly against the bonds of its captivity. She called out to the man, determined to buy the bird and set it free, but he didn't hear her and, in a moment, he was gone. A flood of pain and disappointment went through her. Don't be foolish her mind chided, it's just a bird! But the feeling of being trapped boiled up within her. She too was caught in a net she couldn't escape, weakened at last into submission and the acceptance of death.

Both her and the tiny bird.

Part Two

Faith

Abigail didn't go to synagogue that day because Hannah was feeling ill again, but her young sister Miriam rushed in to tell her all about it.

'Jesus came,' she said, her eyes alight with excitement.

Abigail looked up with interest. This really was news.

'How did you know it was him?' she asked.

'Oh, you could just tell.'

The mystery in Miriam's voice made Abigail smile. This youngest child in her parents' family was proving to be a bit of handful for their mother. Abigail and her other sisters had all been quiet and sedate, which Miriam definitely was not! No one quite understood where her lively nature came from, but still Abigail was always glad to see her because she brought life into the house and made Hannah laugh even on her worst days. Jairus was impatient of the young girl's flightiness and scowled at her, fearing she was a bad influence on Hannah, but nonetheless he had an unshakeable loyalty to family. Miriam was always welcome.

'I hear he has disciples now. Did you see any of them?'

Miriam nodded. 'Four! Big, burly fishermen.' She stopped and gave a little laugh. 'All except John of course. I've noticed him before. He looks a lot more sensitive than the others.'

Abigail frowned at her. 'Miriam you are too young to be taking an interest in a single man. It isn't seemly.'

Miriam giggled and danced around the room. 'I shall soon be old enough to think of marriage. Someone like John perhaps. I shall mention it to Father.'

Abigail opened her mouth and then saw that her sister was watching her keenly.

'You should not joke about such things Miriam.'

'Oh, you are all so stuffy! I want some adventure in my life. I couldn't bear to be married to someone like Jairus.'

A look of pain passed across Abigail's face. How could she expect her young sister to understand Jairus, when she wasn't sure she understood him herself? 'Tell me about Jesus,' she said.

Miriam sat down in a chair and rested her chin on her hand. 'Well, let's see,' she said. 'He taught from the scriptures.'

'There's nothing unusual in that is there?'

'No, but of course when he did that in Nazareth, they tried to throw him off a cliff, which makes it much more interesting don't you think?'

Abigail was shocked. 'Miriam, where do you hear such things?'

'It's true,' said Miriam, 'everyone knows. Sometimes I think you are locked away from the world in here Abigail; like a prisoner!'

Sighing Abigail looked towards Hannah's room.

'The world comes close enough for me,' she said.

'Anyway,' said Miriam 'that is why he's come here. They say he's left Nazareth for good.'

'Don't tell me what they say, tell me what happened,' said Abigail, exasperated. Miriam frowned as she tried to remember. 'Well, after he finished preaching…'

'Aren't you going to tell me what he said?'

'I can't do that because I wasn't really listening. You will have to ask Jairus. Anyway, the thing I came to tell you about happened afterwards.'

Resigned to her fate Abigail lent back in her chair and smiled at her sister. 'All right,' she said, 'what happened afterwards?'

'Well,' said Miriam eagerly, 'You know that strange man, I forget his name, the one with the wild eyes who talks to himself?'

Abigail nodded.

'He was in the synagogue and he was very agitated when Jesus was preaching. He got worse and worse, shouting and banging into the walls. No one took any notice of course, but Jesus did!'

'What happened?'

'The man, oh, what is his name? Anyway, he cried out, "What do you want with us Jesus of Nazareth? Have you come to destroy us? I know who you are, the Holy One of God!" It was creepy because he shouted in this really horrible voice, and there was foam all over his mouth. Ugh it was disgusting!'

'And?'

'Jesus went up to him and he was very stern, like when you tell someone off, and then the whole room became very quiet and still. Even the children on the balcony seemed to sense something was happening and stopped crying for once. Mind you, I wouldn't have wanted him speaking to me like that. I would have been frightened!'

Abigail thought she might burst with frustration. 'What did he say?'

'The strange man?'

'No, of course not! Jesus. What did Jesus say to him?'

'I forget,' said Miriam blithely, 'but the man let out a terrible shriek, honestly it didn't sound human! It sent shivers all over me. After that he lay still for a while and then Jesus helped him up. I have to say he looked quite normal, or at least the most normal I have ever seen him. It was all very dramatic. I ran straight here because I wanted to be the first person to tell you. It's odd, isn't it? I knew you would be fascinated. Nothing exciting ever happens here, but if Jesus stays for a while, that might change.' She looked across at her sister's face, 'and his disciples of course.'

Abigail didn't rise to the bait. 'Where is Jairus?' she said.

'He stayed behind talking to the other leaders. I expect he will be here soon. They say Jesus can heal people, and after what I saw in the synagogue today, I think I believe it. He certainly isn't like anyone else I have ever met. I liked him!'

Miriam had nothing else to say and she went through and sat for a while with Hannah. Abigail could hear them giggling. She wondered absently what it was her sister whispered to Hannah when no one else was near. Some mischief or other the two of them cooked up together.

Miriam left the house in time to get home before sunset. Even her indulgent parents wouldn't put up with her being late for the evening meal. Abigail waited and waited, but still Jairus did not come home. She began to wonder what was delaying him. Had it something to do with Jesus?

Eventually he came through the door with a scowl on his face. Abigail tried for a light tone.

'I heard about Jesus,' she said, placing food on the table.

Jairus washed his hands. 'Heard what?'

'That he did something unusual in the synagogue today.' Curiosity stirred in her as she watched him sit down. Something was bothering him, but she knew him well enough not to push him to speak. If she waited, he would tell her.

'Johannes was completely delivered today.' He spoke the words as if he could not believe them himself.

'Oh?'

She expected him to tell her all about it, but he only sat silent, playing with his food. There was the sound of a commotion outside and he got up at once to look out of the window. An excited group of people walked by and he grunted his annoyance.

'The whole town has gone mad! You wouldn't believe what's been happening. As soon as the sun set they began trooping past the synagogue down to the lake. To Peter's house in Bethsaida if you please! Several of us followed. We didn't know what to make of what had happened to Johannes, and now this!'

Abigail decided to leave the subject of Johannes until later.

'Peter is a disciple, isn't he?' she said.

Jairus looked furious. 'A disciple! A disciple of who exactly? We know almost nothing about this man. He turns up here, having been thrown out of his own home-town and immediately starts causing trouble. When we got to the fisherman's house it seemed the whole of Capernaum was there, at least all the demon-possessed people and everyone who is sick. It was pandemonium. It's just a poor fisherman's hut, but you would have thought it was the center of the world. Rumours were spreading like wild-fire that Jesus had just healed Peter's mother-in-law.'

'Healed her of what?'

'Some fever or another. Very convenient. Nothing anyone could prove.'

'Did she say she was healed?'

'I didn't ask her. She certainly looked fit enough to me. She was wandering around with this extraordinary look on her face. Trying to look as if she'd experienced a miracle I suppose.'

Abigail was appalled by the cynicism in his voice. Didn't he believe any of this was true? But he'd seen Johannes delivered, hadn't he? She put her hand over her eyes for a moment, hope flooding through her. What if Jesus could heal; actually heal. That was the most important thing; wasn't it?

'Did he heal the people?'

Her voice was urgent and for the first time he looked at her, his face full of anger.

'How should I know?' he said. 'I wasn't going to wait around to be in the audience when he did some cheap trick.'

Abigail was confused. 'But why didn't you stay Jairus?' she asked. 'Surely that was why you went, to see if he really can do miraculous things?'

Jairus glared at her, his mouth a thin line. How could he explain to her that as he stood outside the hut a strange panic had gripped him? He was ashamed of how he had fled, almost as though something was pursuing him.

Abigail was concerned. She loved her husband dearly, although these days she felt she hardly knew who he was. Hannah's failing health was affecting him more and more. Having waited long years for this beloved child, she knew he found it almost intolerable to watch her slow deterioration. Gradually he had grown silent, unable to share his pain. Abigail wanted so much to touch him, to hold him in her arms, to have him hold her. How was she supposed to cope with Hannah's illness and Jairus's withdrawal? His face looked harder than ever today, set in cold lines of bitterness. She hardly recognized the man she had married.

'What is it Jairus?' she asked softly, 'What is the matter?'

'He will be claiming to be the Messiah next!' Jairus almost spat the words out.

Abigail blinked. 'Has he said that?' she asked.

'No, not yet,' he said, 'but he will, just you wait and see. Another false prophet persuading all these gullible people to believe in him. It makes me sick.'

'But..' said Abigail.

Jairus put up his hand to stop her. 'No Abigail, I won't discuss this matter. Not now, not ever. Our town seems to be in the grip of some strange malady, but I won't have this charlatan disturbing the peace of my household. The subject of Jesus is closed, and it is closed for good.'

She stood with her mouth open as he slammed out of the room. Slowly she sat down in her chair and looked towards her daughter's bedroom.

'Oh Hannah,' she said, and tears began to stream down her face.

The next morning Abigail slipped out of the house early. Hannah was still asleep and Mary, Abigail's mother had come to sit with her granddaughter. Mary couldn't help but see the anguish in her daughter's eyes.

'Go out for a walk,' she said, 'Hannah will be fine, and you need some sunshine on your face. You spend too much time cooped up in here.'

'You are starting to sound like Miriam,' Abigail said, but she took her shawl down from the hook on the wall. The truth was she was grateful for the chance to escape. Ever since last night she had felt the walls of the house closing in on her and she longed for a few moments of freedom. Jairus had already left to teach school in the synagogue. There was nothing to stop her.

'I won't be long,' she said and set off down the quiet street.

She enjoyed the fresh morning breeze, walking briskly to the track that was a short-cut down to the shore. She hesitated. She could just pop down to the lake for a moment, couldn't she? Just to rest her tired eyes on the beautiful water. She had slept little last night, for Jesus had filled her thoughts. She expected the path would be busy with people making their way down to Peter's house, but there was only a small, straggling bunch of people walking up it. Not towards the lake, but away from it. One or two recognized her and murmured a greeting. She drew back a little as they passed and waited until they were out of sight before starting down the deserted path.

She wasn't really sure what she was doing there, but once she reached the shore she hardly glanced at the lake. Instead, picking up the pace, she hurried towards Bethsaida. Perhaps in the back of her mind she was hoping for a glimpse of this mysterious person called Jesus. She was already too late. In the distance a small group of men were striding off into the hills. Abigail sighed, knowing instinctively she had missed her chance. Jesus was gone.

There were a few stone buildings huddled close to the water's edge, surrounded by piles of old nets and fishermen's baskets. She wondered if Peter lived here or in one of the other fisherman's huts that dotted the shoreline. As she looked after the men regretfully, a woman came out of the house closest to her. The woman stood shading her eyes, watching the figures as they faded into the distance. One man was lagging behind and he stopped to wave in their direction. The woman gave a snort of disgust, then turning she noticed Abigail.

'If you are hoping to be healed, you're too late,' she said with a rough edge to her voice. She jerked her head in the direction of the hills. 'They took off half an hour ago.'

'I didn't come for a healing, at least not for myself.'

The woman looked at her more closely. 'You're the synagogue ruler's wife, aren't you? I'm surprised to see you here!'

'Why?'

'My Peter says Jesus is already in trouble with the religious lot, and your Jairus is one of them, isn't he?'

'Yes.' There seemed little point in denying it. Maybe it was the look on her face which touched the other woman's heart, Abigail could never be sure, but anyway she pushed open the door to her house and said,

'My name is Tamar. Would you like to come in and rest for a while?'

Abigail's natural reserve made her hesitate. She had never met this woman before, yet something prompted her to accept this unexpected invitation.

'You are kind,' she said.

Tamar led the way into the house. She seemed oddly ill at ease in her own body, clumsily slopping water into a pot before she put it on the fire. Abigail noticed her sharp movements and her strong hands. She could picture Tamar working alongside her husband, sleeves rolled up, gutting fish. There was an awkward silence and Abigail wondered if the fisherman's wife was regretting her invitation. She sat a little nervously on the seat Tamar had offered and looked around at a home as neat and clean as her own, though poorer and much simpler.

'Has your husband gone with Jesus?' she asked, hoping to initiate a conversation.

'Yes, like a fool.'

Abigail cleared her throat for another try. 'You don't approve?'

Tamar crashed about with more pots and pans. 'Approve? He has no idea where he is going, or for how long. He just rushed down the hill and told everyone Jesus was leaving, then he ran in here, tied up a bundle of clothes and was off. Just like the head-strong idiot he is! Who will fish to support us, that's what I want to know? There'll be a lot of empty mouths around here before long. Andrew and James and John have gone as well, you notice. The whole waterfront is stripped of its best fishermen. That Jesus has got a lot to answer for!'

A softer voice spoke from the door-way. 'Forgive my daughter for her harsh words. She has never handled change well.' The older woman moved into the room. 'We have a great many reasons to be grateful to Jesus, don't we Tamar?' Tamar didn't answer, but Abigail thought she saw her brush away a tear. Tamar's mother sat down and smiled at Abigail.

'Jesus healed me yesterday,' she said.

'And stole my husband today!' declared Tamar.

'No, no, Tamar,' her mother answered, 'be fair! He did that the first time Peter met him. This morning Jesus simply took full possession of his property. We both knew when Jesus moved on, Peter would go with him. Don't be so upset. One day you will see what a great privilege it is for Peter to be called as a disciple.'

Tamar sat down on a bench and began to cry openly. 'I didn't want him to leave,' she sobbed. Her mother shook her head at her.

'But my love,' she said, 'you know Peter must do what he thinks is right!'

'Not Peter,' said Tamar vehemently, 'Jesus!'

Her mother laughed and wrapping her arms around her daughter, she said,

'He will come back. I am absolutely certain they will all come back!'

Abigail stayed longer with the two women than she had intended. It was true Tamar was awkward and rude, yet Abigail found she liked her, although she couldn't have explained why. Perhaps it was inevitable her thoughts were drawn to her friendship with Rebekah as she made her way home.

She had begged Jairus to reconsider when he made the decision that she could no longer visit Jacob's household because of Rebekah's illness. Sick of heart, every footstep seemed a mile as she went that day to see Rebekah and tell her. She had wept all the way home. Later she had answered the door to Jacob's violent knocking. She had never seen Jacob angry before, never seen his lips white, or a murderous look in his eyes. Jairus hadn't been in the house and Jacob had turned away without a word. When Jairus came in at last, she asked him what had happened. He looked stricken, almost beside himself. She never found out what Jacob had said to him; Jairus would simply never speak of it, but something hard and closed settled over her husband, something even she couldn't break through. The friendship between the two men ceased, all warmth gone, with only cold looks remaining.

Jairus lost Jacob and she lost Rebekah. The agonizing separation broke Abigail's heart, and it put a distance between her and Jairus, a deep-rooted difficulty they never spoke of. She submitted to his dictate about Rebekah, although she was appalled, but she could never agree with it. Always it lay between them and imperceptibly they drew apart. Abigail wept many tears. She didn't believe the Jairus of their early marriage could have been so hard, so unfeeling, but not even Hannah's birth had managed to soften his passionate adherence to the law. Now, to add to that sorrow there was Hannah's sickness. They had never been blessed with another child, so their precious daughter had come to mean more and more to them as the years went by. Rebekah had sent a message when she found out Hannah was ill, but of course she couldn't come herself. Abigail hadn't seen her for a long time and missed her dreadfully.

Abigail smiled as she thought about Tamar, so totally different in character to Rebekah. She wondered what Jairus would make of a friendship with a family who welcomed Jesus. She was troubled by the thought, knowing he would not approve and would probably forbid such an association. Her friendships always seemed to bring her into conflict with Jairus.

The streets were full of her acquaintances and one after another they stopped her, asking after Hannah. She found it difficult to give them her full attention, her thoughts constantly occupied with Jesus. How she wished she had at least seen him! Tamar and her mother didn't speak of him as an ordinary man. They spoke with awe. Her heart beat a little faster as she hurried along. Could Jesus heal Hannah? She bit her lip to hold back the emotion which was so close to the surface. It wouldn't do to let Jairus see her crying, not when she couldn't explain it. She had never hidden anything from him, at least not up until now, but her Jairus had changed, and their relationship had changed with him.

Mary was relieved to see her. 'Where have you been for so long? I was worried about you!'

Abigail didn't answer, but went at once to place her hand on Hannah's brow. 'She has a fever,' she said in distress.

'Yes,' said her mother, 'it started a while ago.'

'I should not have left her,' said Abigail.

'Yes, you should, you must go out more Abigail.'

'I will be fine Mother, thank you for staying, you must need to be off home now.'

'I shall come again tomorrow.'

'As you wish,' Abigail said, kissing her mother good bye. 'But I shall not be leaving the house tomorrow.'

Mary opened her mouth to protest as Abigail gently ushered her out of the door. Nothing would persuade her to leave Hannah again, not for Jesus, not for anything.

Weeks went by and Abigail saw nothing of Tamar. She wondered how they were managing in Bethsaida without the fishermen to earn the money. She heard many rumours about Jesus and his band of followers: they seemed to be travelling all over the district, always moving, and often disappearing to the other side of the lake.

One day Hannah begged to be taken outside and Abigail carried her to a tree at the back of the house. Once she could hardly lift her growing daughter, but now it seemed as though only skin and bones were left. Still, it was a good sign that Hannah had energy for the outing. So, she comforted herself. They sat in the shade while Abigail told stories and sang to keep Hannah amused. After a while the child fell asleep on Abigail's lap, unaware of the tears plopping onto her exquisite coverlet as her mother looked down at her. Abigail was surprised by a voice calling to her, she looked up and saw Tamar standing in the street.

'I have some news,' she said, 'come out here and speak to me!'

Abigail shook her head and put a finger to her lips, indicating Hannah, sound asleep on her knees. Tamar looked impatient, and finally she looked both ways up the street before she came down the side of the house to where Abigail was sitting.

'It is good to see you,' said Abigail, 'I have missed you.'

Tamar flushed and looked embarrassed. 'I would have come before, but everyone says Jairus is speaking against Jesus, so I didn't dare. I didn't want to cause any trouble.'

She gazed down at Hannah's shrunken form. 'How is your little one?'

Abigail gave no answer. Strange how her iron self-control seemed to disappear around Tamar, who did nothing to provoke such a reaction. She looked up at the fisherman's wife and Tamar thought she had never seen so much agony in a face. Tamar wasn't good with people, but she knew enough to sit down beside Abigail and take her in her arms. Abigail wept and wept, drenching Tamar's shoulder with her tears. Tamar spoke softly to her, completely out of her depth. I wish Mother was here! She almost spoke the thought out loud.

When Abigail had recovered a little, she laughed through her tears.

'I am so sorry,' she said, 'How embarrassing!'

'It's all right,' said Tamar, as though such things happened to her every day. She looked at Hannah, still fast asleep in Abigail's lap. She only had boys who fought and argued, growing up as pig-headed as their father. She reached out a tentative hand and brushed a strand of Hannah's hair away from her cheek. Her skin was as white as alabaster. Tamar had never seen anything so fragile. Her heart was filled with pity.

'Why have you come to find me?' Abigail asked.

Tamar pulled her thoughts away from Hannah and back to Abigail. 'I came to tell you Peter has sent me a message. They are returning to Capernaum tomorrow. Jesus is coming back!' The excitement in her voice made Abigail wonder what exactly Jesus had done to win this woman's heart; for win it he certainly had.

'They are going to stay in our house, although where I am supposed to find enough floor space for them all to sleep, I don't know. Mother is cooking already, and cleaning, as if any of them will notice. It's just like Peter to descend on us like this without any warning!'

Abigail protested, 'But I thought he had sent you a message and given you some warning: a day at least.'

Tamar got to her feet. 'Somebody must have reminded him. John, I shouldn't wonder. It would never have occurred to Peter on his own. I know him!'

Abigail looked up at her friend and reached out a hand to catch hold of her skirt. She was unsure how to broach this subject and finally said in a rush,

'Do you need some money to buy food? I know things must have been hard for all of you with the men gone.' Tamar turned vermilion and would have pulled away if Abigail hadn't strengthened her grip on her gown.

'Don't be offended,' Abigail begged, 'it would be my pleasure to help you.'

'Do you really think Jairus would be happy to spend his money on feeding Jesus?' Tamar asked incredulously.

'No,' said Abigail after a moment, and she let her hand drop.

'Anyway, there is no need,' said Tamar. 'Ever since Peter and the others left, there has always been enough money to keep us fed.'

Abigail looked surprised. 'But where is it coming from?'

'I don't know.' Tamar spread out her hands and shrugged her shoulders. She seemed mystified herself. 'Sometimes someone will come with some money they owe Peter, other times the food just seems to stretch and stretch. We have never gone hungry. I don't understand it.' She pulled a wry face. 'Mother says it is a miracle.'

'I can imagine she does. She really believes in those doesn't she?'

'Well, I have to say it does seem strange. Anyway, there is no need for you to worry. James and John's father landed a huge catch this morning and sent us along a big basket of fish. There will be no shortage of food for tomorrow.' She shifted her weight from one foot to another.

'Thank you for your kind offer though,' she said.

Abigail shook her head. Tamar had spoken like a child who has been laboriously taught its manners. Abigail thought sometimes this friend seemed no older than Hannah.

The child began to stir in Abigail's lap and Tamar at once began to speak, before Abigail's attention was totally distracted.

'I wanted to invite you to come and meet Jesus; at my house,' she said.

Abigail blinked as she looked up at her. Meet Jesus? It seemed impossible. Whatever would Jairus say?

Tamar saw her hesitation and spoke earnestly, trying to persuade her. 'Mother says he could heal Hannah.'

'Mother says?' queried Abigail.

Tamar pulled a face. 'All right, I say! He could, he really could. You can't let Jairus stand in the way of that, can you?'

Abigail was silent and Tamar looked at her impatiently. She would never let Peter get in the way of the well-being of her children. Woe-betide him if he tried! Surely Abigail felt the same? Tamar had seen the stern faced Jairus. She had no time for him at all. Why would Abigail hesitate? She wanted to shake her! Nothing could be allowed to stand in the way of this precious child's healing; absolutely nothing! Tamar felt like picking Hannah up and taking her to Jesus herself. She had no clue about the terrible tussle going on inside the other woman.

Abigail's loyalty to Jairus pulled her one way, her love for Hannah another. She looked at Tamar without seeing her. She saw only the closed look on Jairus's face when he had forbidden her ever to speak about Jesus again. What was she supposed to do? Hannah stirred again in her lap, and something broke inside her. Hannah came first, Hannah had to come first! For the first time she admitted it to herself. Hannah was dying. Her breath caught in her throat. She would give everything she had to save Hannah; everything! Still, she had to be certain before she disobeyed Jairus so fully. Completely certain Jesus could really heal her sick child.

In the end she spoke almost to herself. 'I could arrange for Mother to sit with Hannah, and come down alone. Jairus will not be here and he wouldn't need to know. I have to see Jesus for myself, don't I?' She hesitated for one more moment. Then she spoke in a determined voice.

'Yes,' she said, 'I will come tomorrow.'

'Good,' said Tamar and strode off before Abigail could change her mind.

As Hannah lifted her head, she caught a glimpse of Tamar disappearing around the corner.

'Who was that?' she asked.

'Just a friend,' Abigail replied, 'Come, it is time for you to go back into the house.'

Hannah looked surprised as her mother picked her up. 'Why are your eyes so red Mother?'

'It is nothing,' Abigail said, trying to hide the deadness in her voice. 'Did you have a nice sleep?'

'Oh yes, the best ever. I had a wonderful dream, but I can't remember all of it, except I know I was well and playing with the other children in the street. I liked it.'

Abigail turned her face away. 'Yes, my darling,' she said, 'Mother would like that too.'

The next morning Mary came to look after Hannah. She was surprised Abigail had asked her because she really thought her daughter would never leave Hannah's side again. Abigail had indeed made that decision, but the desire to see Jesus was very strong and she had promised Tamar.

'I will be gone just a little while,' she promised her mother and she hurried off down the path to Bethsaida.

She didn't really know what she had expected; a quiet private interview; an opportunity to explain about Hannah? Nothing like that was possible. The whole of Capernaum and Bethsaida had got wind of Jesus' coming and Tamar's house was being mobbed.

Abigail nearly turned back when she saw the crowd. There were men, women and children milling around the door and a big burly man was standing there trying to keep them out. Abigail guessed it must be Peter. He looked extremely annoyed. A wave of hopelessness washed over her as she hovered at the back of the crowd. She hated masses of people; and spending so much time with Hannah had meant she had hardly seen anyone for weeks. So much noisy humanity in one place assaulted her senses and she was about to give up all hope of seeing Jesus when she felt a hand on her arm.

A young man was standing close to her and he spoke quietly in her ear.

'My name is John. Tamar asked me to keep watch for you. You are Abigail, aren't you?'

'Yes, but how could you possibly know me in all this crush?'

'I have seen you once or twice before from a distance. Tamar is waiting for you in the house.'

'But how on earth will we get in there?'

'We will go round the back and slip in quietly while Peter is busy making a fuss at the front.'

Abigail followed him obediently. 'Peter looks very angry,' she said as they passed close to the door.

He chuckled. 'Peter is very angry. He never expected a reception like this. The house is absolutely jammed to the doors, so be prepared for even more people inside.'

He looked into her face, 'Several of the leaders from the synagogue are here. Pull your shawl forward if you do not want to be recognized.'

She thought how right Miriam was; John was a sensitive soul, understanding without her saying Jairus must not know she had been here.

'Jairus?' she asked.

'No,' he said.

She nodded and taking his advice, she adjusted her shawl so no-one could see her face. Her cheeks flushed as she did so. What was she doing hiding her actions from Jairus? What was she doing?

Tamar was in the kitchen apparently waiting for her. She hugged Abigail and whispered,

'It's a mad-house here. Peter can't work out how everyone found out they'd come home. The people started arriving almost as soon as they did and there was no way to keep them out. Jesus is teaching now. Come and listen. There was never anyone like him.'

Abigail wondered at the sparkling look in Tamar's eyes. John opened the door and they squeezed into the packed room beyond. Abigail stood behind him hoping no one would notice her. She needn't have worried, every eye in the room was focused on Jesus who sat in the midst looking very relaxed.

Abigail stared at him for a long time. The things he was saying made almost no impression on her at all, she couldn't have repeated a word, but he held her spellbound, nevertheless. Afterwards Abigail could only say she had never understood what goodness was until she saw Jesus. She was a sensible, level-headed woman, but still she found his face, his very presence, had a profound effect on her. She trusted him implicitly from the first moment, believing in him utterly for the rest of her life.

After a while she dragged her eyes from him to look around the room. Every age and every level of local society had somehow managed to cram themselves into that small space. There were fishermen and merchants, old women and children who held onto their mother's skirts. Jesus held all their attention without apparent effort. In one corner sat a group of men with whom she was very familiar, Jairus's friends and colleagues, the men from the synagogue. They sat watching with solemn faces that didn't smile. A shiver went over her as she looked at them. Had they come to criticize and pull Jesus' teaching apart? What would they report back to Jairus? She knew they were all sticklers for the law, but then so was Jairus. That wasn't a bad thing, was it? They must surely approve of this wonderful man. How could they help themselves?

As she stood watching them a strange noise began above their heads. Jesus stopped speaking and looked upwards where dust and debris began to fall from the ceiling onto the indignant Pharisees. A moment later a hole appeared above them and an anxious face looked down through it. A furious bellow suddenly exploded from the area of the door and Peter pushed his way none too gently through the mass of people.

'Hey!' he shouted, 'That's my roof you're demolishing!'

The face disappeared at once, but only to reappear again as the hole got considerably bigger. Peter looked upwards in frustration and then cast around him for some way to get to whoever it was who was destroying his home.

Jesus stood up laughing and placed a restraining hand on his shoulder. 'Peace, Peter, peace,' he said. 'Let's see what they want before you throw them off your roof.'

'They?' said Peter, even more incensed, and it seemed Jesus was right, for another face came into view and then another. The hole grew larger and larger until to everyone's amazement a stretcher was lowered through it. Four men on the roof held the ropes and slowly, gently let down a fifth man who was strapped to the stretcher. He landed just in front of the Pharisees who moved their feet in disgust and drew their cloaks around them so not even the fringes of their garments would come into contact with him.

Jesus watched their behaviour and he ceased to smile. There was a buzz of surprised chatter as people recognized the man on the stretcher. Most of them knew who he was and had watched his slow deterioration into the condition where he could no longer walk. Jesus, however, was not looking at him, but at the four earnest faces gazing down at him through the hole in the roof. Not one of them spoke, but Jesus looked into each face very carefully, as though examining why they had brought this man to him.

He gripped Peter's arm and said quietly, 'Look Peter - faith!'

Peter glanced upwards but saw only a huge hole in his ceiling. The fisherman ground his teeth.

Jesus had turned his attention to the man on the stretcher and he looked him full in the face, holding his gaze, although the man obviously wanted to look away. The room became quiet, everyone silenced by the tension of what was taking place. Slowly the sickly pallor of the man's skin changed as he flushed a fiery red. Abigail had never seen shame written so clearly on a man's face and her heart was wrung with pity for him. What would Jesus say to him?

'Son, your sins are forgiven.'

The words rang around the room, causing an immediate stir among the Pharisees.

Abigail watched the man on the stretcher. He pulled himself up on one elbow and stared at Jesus as though he was finding it hard to believe what he had heard. Gradually the colour faded from his face and his whole body seemed to relax. Then he simply lay back down and covered his face with his blanket. Abigail thought she could hear the sound of muffled weeping.

The Pharisees were muttering amongst themselves, clearly scandalized, yet they kept glancing around at the people who surrounded them. Abigail could see they wanted to say something, but were frightened of the crowd. It wasn't hard for her to guess what they were thinking, for the audacity of it had made her draw in a breath herself. She was well versed in the law and knew only God could forgive sins. What Jesus had spoken was blasphemy!

Jesus also knew what they were thinking. He looked at them directly and said, 'Why are you thinking such things? Which is easier: to say to the paralytic, "Your sins are forgiven," or to say, "Get up, take your mat and walk?" But that you may know that the Son of Man has authority on earth to forgive sins....' He turned his attention back to the man on the stretcher who had lowered the blanket and was hanging on Jesus' every word. Once more Jesus looked steadily at him, and this time the paralytic returned his gaze eagerly.

To Abigail the sick man looked better already, some of the drawn desperation gone from his eyes. The silence in the room was so complete Abigail thought she could hear the sound of the waves pounding on the shore outside. She had the strangest feeling she was caught up in history, that whatever happened in the next few moments would somehow be known right across the world. Such a strange thought for a woman who lived in a quiet backwater on the edge of Roman civilization; yet it was clear to her who Jesus was could not be hidden in their provincial town. He was destined for great things.

When he spoke, there was a quiet authority in his voice.

'I tell you, get up, take your mat and go home.'

The man threw back the blanket and there was a shocked murmur as people caught sight of his legs. They were emaciated and pale, twisted like deformed branches from a tree. He looked at them himself, and then back at Jesus, a doubtful look on his face.

Jesus nodded encouragingly as he tentatively swung his legs off the stretcher and onto the floor. Abigail never took her eyes off them for a moment. She was convinced a miracle was about to take place, and if it was, then the man's legs were going to be healed. She watched them unblinkingly. Nothing happened for a few moments and the crowd began to look at each other, and then at Jesus. Abigail was not distracted. Perhaps she and Jesus were the only ones watching when it happened, she never knew, but she narrowed her eyes so she could be sure she wasn't imagining it. The man's legs began to untwist, all by themselves. Her gasp of amazement drew everyone's attention back to the stretcher, and they watched incredulously as Jesus bent down and offering his hand, pulled the man up from the floor. He stood like a newly born foal, unsteady on legs which seemed too thin to support him. But standing he was, and Abigail had never seen anything like the look of wonder on his face.

He grasped Jesus by the arm, too shocked to speak, and Jesus beamed, apparently as pleased as he was. The man bent down and picked up his mat where it lay on the stretcher. Abigail wondered how many years he had lain on that thin mattress, how many long hours of despair and hopelessness he had endured as life passed him by. He rolled it up and tucked it under his arm, obedient to what Jesus had said. Then he walked through the crowd to the door.

The people parted to let him through, a reverent hush falling on them as they watched him pass between them. He turned in the doorway and made a grand gesture of farewell, before stepping outside. A moment later there was the loudest shout of praise and thanksgiving Abigail had ever heard, followed by many others. She looked up to the ceiling. The four faces of his friends were gone.

The hut was filled with pandemonium. The spell which had held everyone quiet was suddenly broken, and the noise became deafening as men pounded each other on the back, and women talked excitedly, while no one listened. Even the Pharisees seemed genuinely impressed. They couldn't refute the healing, having seen it with their own eyes. They obviously didn't know what to think, but Abigail did.

She pulled gently on Tamar's sleeve.

'I am leaving now, Tamar, I have stayed too long. If you can, come and see me tomorrow. Jairus won't be there. I need to talk to you.'

Tamar nodded, hardly able to give her any attention as Peter began the long process of getting rid of everyone from his house. After all, he had a roof to mend before it rained, and someone had to think of practical things, healing or no healing.

Abigail lay awake for a long time that night. Jairus had come home suspecting nothing and she hadn't lied, she just hadn't mentioned what she had done during the day. She couldn't believe she was deceiving him, but what choice did she have? In one encounter she had become a believer in Jesus, and she knew without a doubt the teacher could heal their daughter. If only Jairus would agree.

She tossed from side to side, rising often to look in on Hannah. As she lay in the darkness she thought about Jesus and the sudden decision she had made that he could be trusted. How did she know that? It was inexplicable, yet it helped her to understand why someone like Peter would leave everything and follow him. How could you not? She wondered why Jairus was so against Jesus. Why hadn't he seen for himself the man's integrity and kindness? Jairus was such a good judge of character. It made no sense to her, and then she remembered the odd comment Jairus had made right back at the beginning,

"He will be claiming to be the Messiah next!"

Was that the problem? But why should it be a problem? They had all been taught to believe the Messiah was coming, indeed Jairus could quote every prophet who had spoken of him! Why was it impossible for Jesus to be the one they were looking for? He was a fine man, people loved him, and he could do miracles. Why couldn't Jairus accept that? What was he afraid of?

The endless questions robbed her of sleep for hours and she got up in the morning anxious and uncertain. Should she speak to Jairus? Try to explain who Jesus really was? She had no idea what to do; so, in the end she did nothing.

Jairus went out as she knew he would and she waited impatiently for Tamar. It seemed unlikely Jesus would sit in the house all day, and Abigail devoutly hoped Tamar would be able to slip away to see her.

Mid-morning the door flew open and Miriam danced in.

Abigail frowned. 'What are you doing here?'

If Miriam noticed the unwelcoming tone in her sister's voice, she chose to ignore it. She was big with news.

'I came to keep you up to date with what is happening, Jesus is back and he did a healing in Peter's hut yesterday.'

Abigail found she was blushing and picked up her sewing to hide her cheeks from Miriam's needle-sharp eyes.

'Really?' she said, nonchalantly. She was sure she couldn't fool Miriam and hated having to try.

'Yes, really! Aren't you at least a little bit curious? It's all over town.'

'You know I don't listen to gossip Miriam.'

Miriam pretended to be shocked, 'This isn't gossip, it's… information,' she concluded triumphantly.

Her older sister bit her lip, unable to think of a way to stop the flow of Miriam's chatter once it had started.

'Anyway, that was yesterday's news, today Jesus called Levi to follow him.'

Abigail sat with her mouth open.

'Levi? The tax collector? That can't be right!'

'See,' said Miriam, 'I knew you would be interested!' but her voice trailed away as she looked at Abigail's face. Why had this piece of news produced a horrified, stricken look? Miriam was always trying to lighten her sister's mood, make her laugh, draw her out of herself. The calling of Levi was just that, something diverting, something to draw Abigail's mind away from worrying about Hannah. Miriam never intended to make Abigail look more worried than ever. Her brows knit together as she tried to grasp why Abigail was reacting like this, but she could make nothing of it.

'What is the matter, Abigail?' she asked, and sat down beside her sister reaching for her hand.

'Jairus hates Levi,' Abigail said, as though that explained everything, but when Miriam pressed her, she would say no more.

Miriam knew the people in Capernaum had begun to hate Levi from the first day he had started working for the Romans, and it didn't help that he cheated everyone who had to pay their taxes to him. Now Jesus had taken him into his band, told him to follow, and Levi had simply obeyed. Not that Miriam had seen it of course, but she had heard all about this strange event and was looking forward to sharing it with Abigail.

She was a little offended by her sister's odd reaction and had just decided to leave when there came a gentle knock on the door. To her amazement Abigail gave a guilty start and looked at the door and then at her. Miriam was intrigued and before Abigail could move, she had leapt to her feet and answered it.

A complete stranger stood on the doorstep, a woman dressed in poor clothes, who seemed as surprised to see Miriam as the young girl was to see her.

'Yes?' said Miriam coldly.

The woman ignored her, looking past her to Abigail who had come up behind. 'I'll come back some other time,' she said.

'No,' said Abigail, and reached out a hand to draw her in. 'My sister was just leaving.'

'I was not,' said Miriam, indignantly.

'Yes, you are,' whispered Abigail. 'I want you to go away and forget you ever met this lady.'

'I will not,' said Miriam furiously. 'Who is she anyway?'

Abigail looked perfectly harassed. The woman had gone to stand in the middle of the room. She looked extremely uncomfortable and awkward, not at all the sort of person Abigail usually had in her home. Miriam disapproved of her.

'I can't tell you now,' said Abigail, 'but I promise I will explain it all to you when I can. Please do this one thing for me Miriam and say nothing even to Mother.'

Miriam looked slightly mollified.

'I can keep a secret you know,' she said in a superior voice.

Abigail doubted it, but felt she had no choice but to trust her. 'Then keep this one, as you love me!'

Miriam looked into her sister's face. She thought of all Abigail's goodness and how little joy there was in her life. Her sister lived out her whole existence here, in these four walls, with a sick daughter and a pompous husband. Miriam felt a sudden surge of affection for her and hugged her convulsively.

'Of course, I won't say anything. You can trust me!'

She looked over Abigail's shoulder and pulled a face at Tamar, trying to communicate she still didn't approve of her. Tamar lifted her eyebrows and pulled a face right back. Miriam blinked in surprise, secretly revising her opinion a little. Anyone who could give as good as they got went up in her estimation.

Eventually Abigail managed to get rid of her, though for how long she wasn't sure. As soon as the door closed, she turned to her visitor.

'She's quite a handful,' said Tamar.

'Yes, but let's forget about her. I hear Jesus has invited Levi to become a disciple.'

Tamar sat down, 'Yes,' she said, 'Peter is livid, he hates Levi.'

'Well at least our husbands agree on one thing.' said Abigail.

'There is a big party at the tax collector's house tonight. The disciples are all invited. You should hear Peter on the subject. He's been complaining ever since Jesus called Levi.'

'Will he go?'

Tamar shrugged her shoulders. 'Jesus doesn't take any notice of their likes and dislikes. I've told Peter he'd better get used to it. If he wants to follow Jesus, he will have to rub shoulders with all sorts of different people, won't he? Just like you and me!'

Abigail flushed. 'Don't you think we would have met if it hadn't been for Jesus?'

Tamar gave a scornful laugh. 'I know we wouldn't, but Jesus changes everything.' She leant forward in her seat eagerly. 'What did you think of him Abigail? Did you like him?'

Abigail sat looking at her hands. 'Like him?' she said, as though such a thought hadn't occurred to her. 'I love him!'

Tamar nodded her head with satisfaction. 'I knew you'd understand once you'd seen him. He asked about you.'

The look of stunned amazement Abigail turned on her made Tamar laugh.

'Did you think he wouldn't notice?'

'But there were so many people there, how could he possibly notice me?'

'Perhaps it was because you were doing such a bad job of hiding. Jonathan saw you too.'

Abigail frowned. Jonathan was a young man of outstanding promise Jairus had been training for years. Jairus had high hopes for him and saw him as his successor in the synagogue.

'I was afraid he'd recognize me,' she said.

'Don't worry, he won't tell Jairus. He was talking to John after you left. I think he intends to travel with Jesus for a while.'

A shy look came over Abigail's face. 'What did Jesus say about me?'

'He asked what the trouble was you carried in your eyes. I told him about Hannah, and Jairus. I hope you don't mind. I know he can help her Abigail, you must bring her to see him.'

Abigail could just imagine what Tamar had said about Jairus. She felt as though her heart was breaking within her. How could she take Hannah to Jesus without Jairus's permission? He would never forgive her. Yet if she didn't Hannah would die. The arguments chased themselves around in her head endlessly. Yesterday it had all seemed clear to her. Jesus would heal Hannah, Jairus would be grateful and all would be well. Now the terrible consequences of flouting Jairus's authority seemed to outweigh all the faith she had felt as she looked at Jesus. Perhaps if Jesus hadn't added Jairus's sworn enemy to his list of disciples she could have risked talking to Jairus; tried to persuade him. It was all going from bad to worse. What should she do? Her head dropped in despair. There seemed to be no hope.

Tamar sat watching her friend. She was trying hard to understand the conflict she saw in Abigail's face. Jesus was full of compassion and she wanted to be like him, to care for people, to be kinder and just plain nicer. Peter didn't think he was cut out to be a disciple and he was absolutely positive Levi wasn't, but Tamar didn't think she was either. She was too scratchy and impatient. Abigail on the other hand was sweet and lovely, yet she seemed to be struggling more than all of them. Tamar found it confusing.

At last, she broke into Abigail's silence.

'Can I ask you a question?' Abigail looked at her in surprise. Something about Tamar's tone told her this might be a difficult question.

'Yes,' she said cautiously, 'You can ask me, but that does not necessarily mean I will answer.'

'Well, I've been thinking about it for ages and I just can't fathom it. Honestly I don't mean to be rude, but..'

'But what?'

At last Tamar blurted out. 'Why did you marry Jairus? I mean you're so good, and he - well he doesn't seem your type at all!'

Abigail's head dropped so Tamar couldn't see her expression, then after a moment she said,

'But I didn't marry this Jairus. I married someone really different. We have been through some horrible things and they began to change him. I wish you could have known him right back at the beginning. I think you would have liked him.'

She looked into Tamar's face. 'I wasn't in the least bit surprised when he asked for me you know.'

'You weren't?'

'No, not at all. My father was delighted of course because everyone thought Jairus was a fine man who would run the synagogue one day.'

'Don't tell me you married him for his position in the synagogue,' Tamar snorted. 'I don't know you very well, but I know you better than that!'

'No, of course not, although of course it meant a lot to my parents. No, it wasn't that. The truth is I had been waiting, hoping he would speak to my father. It wasn't an unwelcome surprise. It was a joyful relief. We had seen each other one day, almost by accident, and somehow we both knew.'

She laughed at the memory. 'Actually, I had known for some time before that, but of course I couldn't say anything. I just had to wait, and he took a long time to decide, even though he felt certain I was the one.'

'Was he mad? Why did he take a long time? Any man would be proud to have a wife like you; you are beautiful and intelligent and kind. Why did he wait?'

'I can't explain it to you, because he has never really been able to explain it to me, but I do know it was about who he was, not who I was.'

Tamar frowned. 'That's all a bit too deep for me! But you never doubted you should say yes?'

Abigail laughed. 'Never. I remember the day my mother told me. I thought I would burst with happiness it was so perfectly right.'

She looked at Tamar with her head on one side. 'Can you understand?' she asked.

'No,' said Tamar baldly. 'But then I don't understand why I married Peter either, so you can't expect me to make much sense of it.'

Tamar rubbed her hands briskly down her skirt. Abigail had noticed this gesture before and knew it meant Tamar was experiencing an unwelcome emotion. Abigail looked at her fondly. Almost every emotion seemed to be un-welcome to Tamar.

'You're the one who asked the question,' she reproved gently.

'I know' said Tamar and she seemed angry at herself.

Abigail waited.

Tamar had never been good at friendship, but ever since the first time she met Abigail she'd wanted to get close to this remarkable woman. She admired Abigail for her courage and her goodness, even her unswerving loyalty to Jairus, and she wanted to be a friend to her. Someone Abigail could talk to.

'So Jairus was different back then?' she queried; and Abigail smiled, for it was obvious Tamar didn't really believe it.

'Jairus was like a treasure, tightly wrapped and hidden in a wooden box. Everyone else had always seen the hard exterior, but for a while, for just a short time, I was privileged to see the precious man inside. I was hopelessly in love with him.'

Tamar's eyes grew round with wonder. 'What was he like?' she said.

Abigail blushed. 'His mother said Jairus had been waiting patiently for the love of his life, so he could finally become himself. I suppose that was true, but of course I didn't know him very well before. When we got married, he was a man full of joy. He would sing around the house and he was always making me laugh; we laughed and laughed.'

Abigail looked transformed, her face radiant, but it only lasted a moment.

'What happened?'

'I couldn't carry a child,' said Abigail and the weariness in her voice appalled Tamar.

'I'm sorry, I didn't mean to …'

'No, no, don't worry, that was long ago, but it affected Jairus terribly, perhaps worse than me.' Abigail wiped away a tear. 'Please don't judge him too harshly Tamar, he has suffered so much and all the grief has changed him. Little by little he withdrew from me. I longed to reach out to him, to comfort him, but he was slipping away, becoming unreachable. It seemed the happy man I married was gone forever. That was when he turned more and more to the rituals, and the exact fulfilment of the law. I think he came to rely on them as the only stable things in his life.'

'But what about you? It sounds as if it was very lonely for you.'

Abigail sighed. 'I had Rebekah.'

'Rebekah?'

'Yes, my dear friend Rebekah. She couldn't conceive and I lost one baby after another. We understood each other. She was always there for me.'

'And she isn't now?'

'No,' said Abigail sadly. 'It is me who isn't there for Rebekah!'

Abigail fell silent.

It was obvious even to the fisherman's wife something awful had happened. Tamar wondered why on earth she had got into this conversation. What did you say to someone whose heart was broken?

'You don't have to talk about it you know,' she said, and she reached out to take hold of Abigail's hand.

Abigail placed her other hand on top of Tamar's. 'It is a relief to talk about it. No one mentions Rebekah to me these days. Everyone here knows what happened, but I suppose in Bethsaida it is old news now. Well, we had a child eventually, our darling Hannah. Jacob and Rebekah had two children as well, Sarah and Benjamin. Benjamin was born just before Hannah. Those months when both Rebekah and I were pregnant were amazingly happy. Jairus seemed to hold his breath the whole time, and when Hannah was born, oh my, the rejoicing! I really thought I had my old Jairus back. But it didn't last.'

Abigail drew in her breath. 'Rebekah grew sick, and Jairus forbade me to go and see her ever again.'

'What!'

'I know, I couldn't believe it myself. It was the law you see. Rebekah had become unclean, and Jairus couldn't risk defilement.'

Tamar sat in shocked silence gazing into Abigail's face. She was wondering what she would have done in such a situation. Would she have disobeyed her husband? Would she have gone to see her friend anyway? Tamar thought she probably would have. She wasn't the quiet, submissive type. Still, she could see what a hopeless situation Abigail had been in. Disobey your husband when he is synagogue ruler? What would that have done to Abigail's marriage? And now the situation was happening again.

'Has Jairus forbidden you to take Hannah to Jesus?' she asked.

'I haven't asked him,' Abigail replied.

Tamar understood, or thought she did. She shrugged her shoulders. People's lives were complicated; too complicated for her!

'I should go soon,' she said, 'why did you want to speak to me?'

Abigail sighed, 'I don't really know. I think I felt you would understand what an effect Jesus has had on me. You felt it too, didn't you? Of course you did, that is why you invited me! I wish I wasn't so confused. I don't know what to think now.'

Tamar knelt in front of her and took hold of her hands. 'Jesus is teaching us to trust that God is our father and that he will take care of us. I can see how hard all this is for you, but I know Jesus will sort it all out. Be patient, and keep on believing. Jesus will never let us down!'

This speech surprised Tamar almost as much as it did Abigail. She got up quickly and made her way to the door. Abigail thought she had never seen her look so self-conscious. Red-faced she seemed hardly to know how to say goodbye, but murmured something before pulling the door almost off its hinges in her haste to leave.

Abigail laughed despite herself. She had certainly found an unusual friend.

From Law to Grace

Jairus heard from the other Pharisees that Jesus was going to a party at Levi's house. They discussed it amongst themselves and decided to go along to this notorious sinner's home to observe Jesus mixing with the dregs of society. Jairus didn't think through very clearly what it was he was expecting Jesus to do, something outrageous that broke the law he supposed. The Pharisees had told him about the healing at Peter's home and their confusion made him angry. Wasn't it obvious this man was dangerous? How could they be fooled by a spurious miracle? He was in no mood to listen when they assured him they had seen it with their own eyes. He simply refused to believe it.

They could hear the music even when they were some distance away. No pious gathering this, for the sound of laughter and merry-making spilled out onto the street and Jairus's face set in a grim mask of disapproval. He wouldn't enter the building of course, not with tax-collectors and other riff-raff inside, so he and the other religious leaders gathered around the door. They looked on in disgust as those inside ignored their presence and gave themselves fully to enjoying themselves.

Jesus was reclining at a table on the far side of the room. Jairus couldn't see his face in the flickering light of the lamps, but he could see all the people gathered around him. Jesus' popularity offended him almost as much as his fake miracles.

'Imposter!' he muttered under his breath.

He had never even spoken to Jesus, and he couldn't have explained to anyone why all his frustration and pain had become focused on this man, but anger seethed inside him pushing inexorably against the rigid bounds of his self-control. He pulled at his beard repeatedly.

Levi came close to the door and raised his cup in Jairus's direction, gloating it seemed in the obvious discomfiture of the religious leader who had been most vocal in condemning him. He made his way through the room and sat close to Jesus, still unable to believe the miracle-worker was really here in his home.

Jairus stood outside, somehow feeling excluded, even though he didn't want to enter. He was appalled to see that Jesus was actually eating with these people, the worst in Capernaum. Anyone with an understanding of the law would have distanced himself from these unclean people. He felt more justified than ever in his judgement of Jesus as a fraud. A godly man wouldn't associate with sinners, not for a moment.

As he watched, one of the disciples who had been with Jesus in the synagogue brushed past him. He caught hold of the man's arm.

'Why does he eat with tax collectors and sinners?'

The fisherman looked around the room in disgust. 'I'll ask him!' he said, and made his way to where Jesus lay laughing and talking.

Jairus watched as the man said something to Jesus and pointed to the door. Jesus sat up and looked over. For some reason Jairus instinctively drew back, so one of the other Pharisees was left standing there, as though he had asked the question. Jesus had a remarkable voice, it lifted across the room and somehow entered Jairus's heart. There was nothing he could do to prevent it.

'It is not the healthy who need a doctor, but the sick. I have not come to call the righteous, but sinners.'

Then Jesus lay back down again, giving his undivided attention to the sinners all around him.

"It is not the healthy who need a doctor, but the sick, not the righteous, but sinners."

The words echoed in Jairus's brain, bouncing off the walls of his thinking endlessly. What did they mean? He was righteous, wasn't he? He had spent his whole life perfecting his righteousness. Yet this man dismissed all his effort in a moment, as though it meant nothing. He wanted to be angry, but he couldn't. He just felt lost. He stepped further back into the darkness and after a moment he slipped away from the back of the crowd. No one noticed him leave. His footsteps made a hollow sound in the night air and his thoughts seemed hollow too, echoing inside his head.

"Not the righteous. Not the righteous!"

How could these three words have had such an impact on him? He was a leading member of the community, respected, admired even. How dare Jesus drain away all his sense of worth and identity in a single moment? He felt empty and exposed. He'd spent years convincing himself, convincing others, building a reputation, becoming a man of stature. I'm a good man, he thought to himself, everyone in Capernaum says so. He couldn't comprehend why the weight of everyone's opinion held no power to smother what Jesus had said. He was angry with himself for having listened to the man in the first place. I'll ignore it, he thought to himself. It should be easy to forget all about it.

"Not the righteous, not the righteous,"

His hands curled into fists in the folds of his garment as he made his way home.

The next Sabbath, Jairus was at home with Hannah when Jonathan appeared suddenly in the doorway. Jairus was pleased to see this young Rabbi of outstanding promise, he loved

Jonathan, and had high hopes for him, although lately it seemed he had been avoiding him.

'Good to see you,' he said and smiled.

He watched as Abigail appeared from Hannah's room. Her eyes flew momentarily to Jonathan's face and then she turned away, murmuring a greeting. Jairus frowned. Something strange was going on. He could feel it. Abigail was not her normal self, even quieter than usual and disinclined to enter into conversation. He had put it down to Hannah's illness, but now as he saw the silent interchange between her and Jonathan a horrible suspicion entered his mind. Had Abigail's endless patience run out at last? Was she looking elsewhere for comfort in the hopeless situation they were in? He knew he was being hard and cold, but he couldn't help it. Had his beloved wife found a place in her heart for Jonathan, this remarkable young man? Jairus had never doubted her integrity before, but now suddenly several odd little things began to fall into place for him, her unexplained absences, the tight look about her mouth, the way she would not meet his eye.

A cold shiver ran over him. He knew she would never leave, not Hannah, not him, but what did it matter that her body was here in the house if her heart had flown away into the hand of another? He cursed his stupidity and looked with smouldering eyes at Jonathan.

That was the first time it occurred to Jairus that Jonathan was just like Jacob, utterly unable to hide his feelings, looking both hopelessly guilty and embarrassed.

Jairus crossed the room and sat down heavily in a seat. Years and years fell onto his shoulders.

Jonathan looked over at Abigail. He hadn't come to speak to Jairus about her, but about Jesus. In his youthful ignorance he couldn't understand the look Jairus had given him, so he stumbled into speech, not knowing what else to do.

'I came to ask you a question,' he said,

'Yes,' said Jairus without apparent interest.

'Jesus and his disciples were walking through the corn-fields last Sabbath, and his disciples were picking the grain and eating it.'

Jairus raised his head. 'That's against the law,' he said.

'Yes, so the other Pharisees said, and they challenged him on it, but then he said David had eaten the consecrated bread in the house of God and given some to his companions, just because he was hungry. He said the Sabbath was made for man, not man for the Sabbath, and that the Son of Man was Lord even of the Sabbath.'

'Did he now! Well that just goes to prove the man is completely demented, doesn't it? Does he think he is this Son of Man? I am amazed anyone follows him at all; but then you can't expect the common folk to have any clear idea of good behaviour. That is for us who know the law, isn't it Jonathan?'

Jonathan looked at him in distress. He was confused by Jairus's venomous tone. He liked Jesus, admired his teaching, as well as the incredible things he did. The trouble was, he cared about Jairus too. How was he supposed to tell his mentor he was thinking of following Jesus; in fact, the decision had almost been made. He had hoped talking to Jairus about the interesting things Jesus said would make Jairus change his mind. Now, in some indefinable way, he seemed to have made things worse. He decided the best thing to do was leave, which he did, as quickly as he could. The strained atmosphere between Jairus and Abigail was a mystery to him.

If Abigail hadn't had a secret of her own, she probably would have noticed the silence that descended on her husband, but as it was, what with Hannah and Jesus on her mind constantly, the fact Jairus said nothing was simply a relief.

The worst week of their life went by, with no opportunity for Abigail to see Tamar or Jesus, and Jairus hardly speaking to anyone. In fact, he only left the house when he had to and Abigail began to wonder if he was watching her.

Jairus was tormented by his belief he had lost Abigail and it was all his own fault. He didn't sleep, as the old feelings of self-hatred returned and thoughts of Jacob and Rebekah intermingled with the words of Jesus in the long hours of the night. Rebekah had been ill for so long, and Hannah was ill too, both desperately needing a doctor, but he was righteous, the most righteous man in town and the most lonely. His thoughts were chaotic and recriminations went around in his head, as though a persuasive accuser was inside it. He wondered how someone who had made every effort to keep the law could be so filled with self-loathing.

He went out to synagogue of course. Abigail didn't go with him. He saw Jonathan only briefly and avoided speaking to him. He sat as he always did, surrounded by the hard liners of the synagogue, but in some indefinable way he felt uncomfortable and out of place. He had come longing for the familiar rituals to soothe the turmoil inside, but for the first time the service was empty of meaning for him. A strange coldness was invading his soul. He wondered if Jesus would come, but there was no sign of him. People spoke to him, but he found he had nothing to say. He looked terrible.

Another week went by. Jairus still wasn't sleeping, but he had his thoughts more under control. He was determined not to allow this preacher to influence him. Abigail was still hardly speaking. He tried not to think about it.

On the second Sabbath he went to synagogue as usual. As he entered the building, he was surprised to see a whole group of Pharisees who were unfamiliar to him. A friend whispered that they had recently arrived from Jerusalem where news of the local prophet had reached the temple. Jairus felt resentful of their presence, though he wasn't quite sure why. He looked into their venerable faces, wondering what they would make of Jesus, or even if he would appear. No one ever knew where he would turn up next, but as it happened on that day, he came to synagogue with his straggling retinue of followers. Jairus sneered at what a strange bunch they were, not the most likely candidates for a prophet's companions! He looked long and hard at Jesus in the daylight. He wasn't remarkable, a strong face, clear eyes, nothing to make him stand out in a crowd. Jairus couldn't understand what all the fuss was about.

There was one thing that perplexed him though. Along with the unknown Pharisees, a man Jairus had never seen before was sitting in the front row. Nothing unusual in that perhaps, but he kept glancing across at the Pharisees from Jerusalem, as though he knew them. Jairus wondered what he was doing here and where he had come from.

As Jesus came further into the room there was a buzz of excitement. Jairus tapped his foot impatiently. He didn't want his synagogue to become a place of entertainment. God was to be honoured here. He noticed the Pharisees talking amongst themselves and watching Jesus. He had the strangest feeling they were planning something, and a moment later he understood it, for the man in the front row pulled out his right hand from the folds of his garments. It was shrivelled, bent in on itself like a claw.

So that was it. The Pharisees had brought someone who was crippled to synagogue to see if Jesus would heal on the Sabbath.

He had to admire their strategy, for such a healing would clearly be against the law, and would give them ammunition if they wanted to mount an accusation against him.

He looked across at Jesus. He in turn was staring at the Pharisees who were leaning forward in their seats, eager to see what he would do. Jairus knew Jesus understood it all. Whatever he was, he was no fool. He wondered if the carpenter's son would turn the moment aside, ignore the challenge and do nothing. There was a tense moment and Jairus found he was hoping Jesus would escape this trap. How dare they appear in his synagogue playing games as though they owned it?

A moment later Jesus rose calmly to his feet and said to the man with the shrivelled hand,

'Stand up in front of everyone.'

The Pharisees looked at each other with satisfaction. Jesus was going to do something! If he did a miracle, they would accuse him of Sabbath breaking. If he tried and failed, he would be disgraced before the people. They couldn't lose!

Jesus walked over and stood in front of them. They became silent and leaned back in their chairs. He looked into every face, one by one, as he asked them a simple question,

'Which is lawful on the Sabbath: to do good or to do evil, to save life or to kill?'

Jairus put his hand over his mouth. Now he had them! There could be only one answer and they knew it. They looked at each other and then down at the ground. Not one of them spoke.

Jesus gazed at them with great intensity and there was unmistakable anger in his eyes, then turning on his heel, he walked over to the man with the shrivelled hand.

Jairus sat close by, riveted to the expression on Jesus' face. He knew if he had been placed in the same situation, he would probably have been angry with the man, but Jesus was not. Jesus looked at the hand and such compassion was in his eyes that Jairus felt it assault him, almost like a hammer blow falling on his own hardness of heart. Any thought that this was a public demonstration of power vanished instantly from his mind. One thing was clear to Jairus, if Jesus did heal this man, it would be a simple act of kindness.

'Stretch out your hand,' Jesus said.

The man looked down at his hand and began to try to move it. There was a sound, like a bone cracking, that reverberated round the room; then another and another. The hand moved and straightened, flesh appearing on the withered fingers. Within moments it was as normal as the other, the miracle complete.

Jairus sat calmly in his seat while the synagogue exploded around him. Jesus and his disciples had simply walked away, and he was left watching intently the faces of the Pharisees from Jerusalem. None of the excitement or noise entered his conscious mind, he just sat staring, gripped by the look on their stony faces. He had never seen such cold hatred before. It shocked him. The miracle was undeniable, they had seen it themselves. Yet not one of them smiled.

He sat and looked at them, almost in wonder. How could they be so heartless? The angry hatred in their eyes, even as they looked at the man who was healed, held Jairus's attention, and he found he could not look away. He sat and stared and stared. Slowly a thought began to form in his weary brain. A very unwelcome thought. Painfully he acknowledged the truth of it. He was looking at himself! Here they were before him, representatives of the very center of his nation's faith, the best of the men who claimed to serve God, yet their hearts were like pieces of rock. They didn't care for people or show any compassion. All they loved was the law! So what if Jesus could heal: that meant nothing to them. The only thing that mattered was adherence to the traditions of their fathers; and how passionately they cared about that!

He saw the light on the face of the man who was healed; the awe, the joy; and he saw the deadness of the Pharisees; their echoing emptiness. It almost frightened him. Into his mind came a vivid recollection of how he'd felt as he walked home from Levi's house. Just like them he had felt empty and dead. Those words described him. He shivered as though a cold hand had touched him and he moved as quickly as he could out into the sunshine. He didn't speak to anyone and hurried around the corner out of sight, wanting to be alone. He stood in the shade of the synagogue trying to compose himself before he went home. He lent his head against the solid wall of the building he loved, as everything within him shifted and moved and changed. Jesus had done a miracle, a real miracle, and he had seen it.

He realized he had been avoiding this moment ever since his first encounter with Jesus in the synagogue. He hadn't wanted to witness a miracle because he didn't want to believe in them. But now he had to face it. Jesus could heal. Jesus who flouted the law and seemed to live by his own set of rules. He could heal. How many times had Jairus prayed for Hannah, redoubling his efforts at piety in order to earn a touch, a brief respite, anything which would bring relief to her fragile body. Now this man had simply spoken a word and a life was changed forever.

The man with the withered hand had gone from one to the other in the synagogue, repeating over and over again, 'I don't deserve it. I don't deserve it.'

Jairus didn't doubt the truth of that statement, but then Jesus hadn't healed him because he deserved it. Jairus knew that for certain. The moment of the healing came vividly into his mind, especially the expression in Jesus' eyes. His face crumpled as he was impacted again by that look of love, that graciousness.

'He has come for the sinners,' he repeated, wrapping his arms around himself as though to hold himself together.

He wondered where the self-righteous stood in Jesus' estimation.

As soon as he entered the house he went and sat by Hannah's bed.

Hannah. His precious Hannah, their only child, who had won his heart from the moment of her birth.

He had fully expected a boy, but then he had never been very good at predicting the sex of children. After all their disappointments he had no thought of a girl, but when they had put her in his arms, his surprise had turned to delight. As she lay there like a sweet token of heaven, something stiff and cold within him began to melt away. Everyone saw the change in him and smiled knowingly as he turned into a doting father. He didn't care. Her first smile, her first tooth, her first steps were an enchantment to him. She comforted him in the sadness of losing the friendship of Jacob and Rebekah. She made him smile.

Her eyelids fluttered open and she moved slightly in the bed. He bent over her, lifting her so she could drink, speaking softly to her. He saw her grimace with pain. He thought the frustration of being able to do nothing would choke him.

'I love you Father,' she said in a voice no louder than a whisper, and he felt old as he looked at her.

"It isn't the healthy who need a doctor, but the sick."

Jesus' voice sounded clearly in the silent room. He sat for a long time looking at his daughter's face, unable to decide which one of them was sickest, Hannah or her righteous father.

Abigail heard from Miriam Jesus had done another miracle and this time Jairus had seen the whole thing. She wondered whether to speak to him; ask him what had happened; what he thought of Jesus. Questions tumbled over themselves in her mind, but she didn't know how to begin. She longed to talk to him about Jesus, about Hannah, about Tamar. Silence was burning a hole in her faithful soul. She hated secrecy, needing to be open and honest, to share everything with her husband, but it seemed those days were long gone. In the end she could stand it no longer. Hannah was getting worse, Jairus had taken refuge in silence and Jesus had turned her world upside down before leaving town. She had no idea when he would return.

One evening she came into the room to light the lamps. She wasn't aware of Jairus looking longingly at her, moved, as he always was, by the sheer fact she had married him. She had loved him back then, he was sure of it. Evil thoughts tormented him. Did she love Jonathan? When had he lost her? When had the distance between them grown to the place where she could no longer bridge it? When had she ceased to try?

He turned to gaze at the fire and the light fell on his face. He looked old and worn, aged by anxiety. Her heart went out to him and she put her arms around him from behind as he sat at the table. Let him shrug her off if he must. To her amazement he gripped her hands and drew her to where he could see her. Her eyes scanned his face. He looked wretched, fresh lines on his forehead, weariness in his eyes. She knew him well enough to know something was eating away at him. She felt sure she knew what it was.

'I have to talk to you Abigail,' he said.

She felt her heart skip a beat. He had found out she had been to see Jesus! She was determined not to lie about it, after all he had seen Jesus himself now; but still she hung her head.

He lifted her chin so he could look into her eyes. 'I know about Jonathan.'

She held his gaze. 'I was afraid he would tell you, or one of the other Pharisees would.'

'One of the other Pharisees?' his confusion was obvious.

'Yes, about seeing me in Peter's house.'

'What!'

She looked earnestly into his face. 'Jairus what are you talking about?'

'I thought I was talking about you and Jonathan.'

'Me and Jonathan?' Her amazement was so total Jairus blinked.

'What about us?' she asked, bewildered.

Jairus found he didn't know what to say. At last, he stammered, 'I thought, I mean, you seemed, well, you and Jonathan looked so guilty!'

Abigail let out a peal of laughter, the first genuine sound of joy in the house for a long time. 'Oh Jairus,' she said, leaning forward to kiss his furrowed brow. 'I'm not in the least bit interested in a boy like Jonathan.'

Jairus felt his heart lighten, but he frowned. 'So, what were you guilty about and what were you doing in Peter's house?'

Abigail sat on the floor beside him. 'I have been wanting to speak to you about this for weeks.'

Jairus felt a stab of pain. 'Am I so hard to talk to?'

'Yes, my darling, you are,' she looked up into his face and smiled, 'on this subject anyway.'

She was silent for a moment as though gathering together her courage, then she spoke all in a rush.

'I went to see Jesus, down at Peter's house, and I saw him do a miracle, and I really do believe he could heal Hannah, and I'm sorry I disobeyed you, but he is wonderful Jairus, just wonderful, and Jonathan saw me there and I wondered if he would tell you, but he didn't, and I have become friends with Tamar, Peter's wife, although I know you won't approve, but I miss Rebekah so much, and I needed someone to talk to!'

Jairus sat looking at her with his mouth open. It was the first time he had ever seen a likeness between Miriam and his reserved Abigail. He knew she must have been thinking about these things endlessly. His darling Abigail. She had needed someone to talk to. He knew it should have been him.

Later Jairus sat at the table his hand resting on a parchment. Although his whole world lay in ruins around him, still he held doggedly to this one thing: the law. Jesus was a miracle-worker, that much was undeniable, but Jairus could not, would not throw all his faith in tradition away just because a man could do miracles. No matter what his wife said!

His reconciliation with Abigail had been unbelievably sweet, yet still his heart was hard and unyielding. Abigail had begged him to allow Jesus to see Hannah. He shook his head at the thought of it. Each encounter he'd had with Jesus challenged him, called him to be different, to change the way he saw the world. He felt torn in two, his stubborn nature refusing to give in. He would not believe Jesus was the Messiah, not even in the face of these astounding miracles.

Jesus had left Capernaum and taken Jonathan with him.

Jairus shifted his weight in the chair. How dare this man steal his best pupil away on some mad journey around the countryside? It was outrageous.

His thoughts gave him no comfort, asking him repeatedly, if you were given the choice to follow Jairus, or Jesus, which would you choose?

He shut his eyes and sighed wearily. The whole world had gone after Jesus. Jonathan, Abigail, probably Jacob too. He felt incredibly alone.

Jairus was at home when there was an urgent knocking on the door. It was Jonathan unexpectedly returned to Capernaum. They were genuinely pleased to see him of course; the weeks he had been away fading Jairus's difficulty with him so only their friendship remained. Jonathan was overflowing with news of all he had seen and heard on his travels with Jesus, but he quickly saw concern for Hannah was uppermost in their minds.

'She is very ill now,' said Jairus. 'But come, we are about to eat. Please stay and share a meal with us.'

Jonathan listened as Jairus talked about their mutual acquaintances and the small affairs of the town, but afterwards, when at last they were alone, the young man turned the conversation to Jesus. Jairus was uncomfortable, finding himself resisting everything Jonathan said. Oh, he didn't doubt Jonathan was speaking the truth, he had seen the amazing things this man could do for himself. Still one question was foremost in his mind.

He asked, almost casually, 'Who does he claim to be?'

Jonathan shrugged his shoulders. 'I told you before, he calls himself the Son of Man.'

Jairus frowned. Jonathan looked at him keenly. He was no fool and he understood the significance of the question. He took a breath, intending to declare his conviction that Jesus was the Messiah, but as he looked into Jairus's closed face he thought better of it and turning the matter aside he spoke instead of the man himself.

'He is an incredible teacher, Jairus, and he presents God in a way I have never heard before, as though we could actually know Him.'

Jairus shut his eyes; hearing again as though it were yesterday, Jacob's endless questioning. Someone who taught that man can have a relationship with God? Now he would be Jacob's kind of a teacher! He pushed the thought firmly aside.

'And he isn't just talk, he has a way with children, and a compassion towards sinners that makes you feel....'

'Humbled!'

Jonathan chose to ignore the edge on his Rabbi's voice. 'Yes, humbled. I am beginning to think he can do almost anything. I have seen him open blind eyes, and deaf ears. They were healed, it's as simple as that. I was there when they lowered the man through the ceiling on his mat; that was down by the shore, before I left. I saw his legs straighten, right in front of me.'

Jairus looked at the excitement in his friend's face. He had never been good at understanding people, but even he could see that behind Jonathan's eyes there was a whole storehouse of amazing stories just waiting to be told. Waiting for what? Waiting for him to be prepared to listen? Well, he wasn't. Jesus, Jesus, Jesus. No one seemed capable of thinking about anything else. He looked away from Jonathan and saw Abigail standing in the doorway, her eyes sunken with exhaustion.

'She is worse Jairus,' she said. She looked from her husband's face, white and almost angry, to Jonathan's, alight with hope.

'I know Jesus can heal her,' she said and left without another word.

Jonathan nodded emphatically; he knew it too!

'They say he is coming to this side of the lake tomorrow. I came on ahead as quickly as I could to tell you. Will you ask him to touch her? Believe me Jairus, a touch is all it takes!'

Jairus felt trapped by the thoughts that flew through his head. Hannah, Jesus, the law, compassion, the Messiah, faith and miracles, was there no escape from their insistent demands for his attention? His aching brain seemed unable to rest on any one thing.

Eventually he said, 'He may not come.'

'But if he does?' insisted Jonathan, pressing him.

'I don't know,' said Jairus as though he were in torment. He was silent and then he asked the oddest question.

'How old do you think he is?'

Jonathan threw up his hands in despair. 'How should I know?' he declared, completely at a loss. 'Early thirties?' Younger than you I should say. Why do you ask?'

Jairus didn't answer.

He lay awake for a long time, turning over and over again in his mind the things Jonathan had told him about Jesus and the one statement which lay unspoken between them. He punched the mattress in his frustration. How was he supposed to work out who Jesus was? No one could help him because they were all convinced already! When the night was at its darkest, he faced the possibility head-on. Was this the Messiah? The one Levi had spoken of all those years ago? How could he be?

He remembered vividly the day he and Jacob had stood watching as Levi clambered into the cart which was to take him back home. He even recalled how determined he had been to be strong and grown-up, and how Jacob had fidgeted endlessly beside him.

Levi had looked at them both fondly.

'Remember these two things,' he'd said, leaning down so he could speak more softly, 'you two must remain as brothers!' They'd looked at each other and shrugged their shoulders. Nothing was ever going to change that, was it?

'The second thing is even more important. Always remember what I told you. He is here! Watch carefully for him, as I shall. You will not forget?'

Forget? How could he forget, with Jacob in on the secret? He tried to banish the image of Jacob from his mind, but it lingered persistently. He was sure Jacob would be watching this Jesus with interest, remembering Levi's words, just as he did. Jacob would surely accept Jesus as the Messiah without hesitation. He had always been hopelessly impulsive!

I cannot afford to be gullible, a man in my position, he thought to himself disdainfully, but then a sob escaped him. A man in his position. A man with a daughter lying in the next room dying! He turned his face to the wall, trying to control his thinking and somehow ease the constant thumping in his head.

He slept for a short time, but thoughts of the Messiah never left him. The words "he is here, he is here!" ran ceaselessly through his troubled sleep, and he woke sweating and disorientated when Abigail called to him softly in the darkness.

It was his turn to be with Hannah, and he sat close, watching her shallow breathing and mopping her brow. Others of the family had offered to sit with her, but he and Abigail always took the night watches in case she awoke and needed them.

His thoughts remained muddled and confused, the only thing that was clear to him was that Jesus wasn't the Messiah. He couldn't deny the miracles, but accept him as the Saviour of all Israel? That was different. A good man, perhaps even a great man, but nothing more. No matter what Levi said.

In the beginning, respect for his teacher had made him half believe the story of Simeon; but not now. He had known for years Levi had been mistaken about the birth of the Messiah, and just as the old man had been wrong about him and Jacob remaining as brothers. No, it was obvious Levi had believed a wild story and Jairus was convinced he had been wise to dismiss it.

So, his logical mind assured him, but as he looked at his beloved daughter his heart turned over within him at the thought of losing her. He saw again Jonathan's pleading eyes, could almost hear the urgency in his voice. After all, did it matter whether Jesus was the Messiah or not? There was no doubt he could heal the sick and that meant there was hope for Hannah.

One last hope.

A battle raged within him, the like of which he had only known once before.

Did everyone think it had cost him nothing when Rebekah had become unclean? Night after night he had paced the floor, agonizing over the choice before him. Should he distance himself from Rebekah, or abandon the strict dictates of the law? He had made the right decision, hadn't he? That assurance was the only thing that had comforted him in the dark days when he had lost Jacob's friendship and had watched as something died in Abigail. An ugly grimace passed across his face as he remembered it. He knew how he had appeared to them all; like some marble statue! He could hardly believe he was faced with the same decision again. Another impossible choice! Should he stick with the rigid traditions of his faith, or seek a miracle for his darling daughter? Why did everything within him resist the endless knocking of this preacher on the hardness of his heart?

He sat by the bed, dropping his weary head into his hands. A painful thought began to nag at him. Had he been wrong about Rebekah after all? Was this actually a second chance?

The faces of the temple Pharisees came up before him, hanging like spectres in the black darkness of his soul's agony. Was he like them? Is that why he had shut Rebekah out of his heart? The look in their eyes mocked him, and he groaned as he remembered who Jesus was: kindness and compassion personified. Indeed, his face became so clear it was almost as though he stood in the room.

Jairus shook his head to get rid of the unwelcome image. What was it the man had said? "The sick need a cure."

Well, Hannah was sick, that much was certain. And him? Still the question hounded him. What about him?

He didn't bother going to call Abigail, he just let her sleep, knowing she was close to exhaustion. He sat gazing at Hannah's face in the glow of the lamp. All these weeks she had amazed him, never complaining even as her strength vanished and the flesh shrank from her bones. As the long days passed it seemed the pureness of her young life had begun to shine out of the transparency of her face and the hugeness of her eyes. His heart was breaking and he longed to gather her into his arms.

Hannah, his precious Hannah. How could he bear to lose her?

The darkness was fading before he made his decision. He would swallow his pride and approach the miracle worker simply because he must. Hannah came first. A deep sigh of relief escaped him and in the soft light of dawn at last he knew a measure of peace, although he muttered to himself,

'But nothing will induce me to follow him!'

Resting his head on the bed he slept for one brief hour, holding Hannah's hand.

Transformation

On the other side of town Jacob was getting ready for the long, weary journey which lay ahead of him. He didn't want to go. He stood looking down at Rebekah, adoring her as he always had. Her face was in shadow, but her hand where it lay on the blanket, was thin and prematurely aged. He wanted to reach down and tuck it under the cover, but he held himself back. It always distressed her if he made himself unclean by touching her.

He went into the kitchen and found Sarah already up and about. He hugged her without speaking. What was there he could say? Sarah would take care of everything until he got back. He relied on her. He ate some bread and pulled his cloak off the peg, unable to delay, for he had to travel far away along the shore of the lake. There was no escaping this journey no matter how ill Rebekah was and he would not disturb her to say goodbye. Hurrying out of the door he determined to do the trip as quickly as he could and then return to his troubled household.

The sun was just above the horizon, promising a blistering day to come, as he started out. He wished he could afford a donkey, but those days were gone forever, and he resigned himself to the tedium of putting one foot in front of the other. At first, he walked with swift purpose and long strides which ate up first one mile and then another, but slowly, unconsciously, his pace slackened as his thoughts dwelt upon his wife.

Rebekah. He chose his memories carefully, the carefree days of their youth, her laughter and the glow of her skin; and in his mind she danced, as she had at their wedding. He smiled unconsciously.

Rebekah, his whole heart and soul!

As he left the last straggling houses behind him, the happy thoughts, reaching back into their childhood, faded. Somehow in the busyness of life he managed to keep himself from dwelling on their pain, but in the solitude of the wilderness when his mind was free, there was nowhere to hide. Like a cart unexpectedly emptied on the market floor the reality of their situation tumbled out upon him and it was useless to try to hold it back. The constant disappointment and hopelessness swept over him. Rebekah was still unclean. After twelve long years she was no better, and she was now so frail he felt a breath of wind could blow her over.

Rebekah, the love of his life.

A tear trickled down his lined face, washing the dust into his dark beard. He wiped it from his cheek impatiently. What use was it to cry? Biting his lip, he willed himself to stop, but it was impossible. Now he was alone he found his self-control began to crumble away and a sob escaped him, then another. Stumbling off the road he threw himself down in the shade of a huge rock. Hidden from view he gave himself over to a torrent of weeping, as when a swollen river rushes suddenly through a dry gully, sweeping all before it. All he could think of was Rebekah, how his lovely vibrant wife had faded away before his very eyes. His heart broke for her. He admired her courage, her refusal to surrender completely and take to her bed. He wept from a deep well of emotion, the tears he hid from her, for she hated every expression of sympathy. Only when the weakness was at its height would she allow him to see her despair and afterwards they never spoke of it. Sometimes he was sure only her love for him and the children kept her alive.

He gulped as the sobs seemed to redouble. Now he had begun, he was afraid he might never stop. As if it mattered! Nothing had mattered for years. Kneeling down he laid his forehead on the ground, pulling his cloak over his head as he became lost in the violence of his grief.

He had no idea how long he knelt there, but at last the fury of his weeping grew less, and wiping his face he thought again of his journey and Rebekah left alone in Sarah's care. Sitting up and leaning on the rock, he tried to muster enough strength to rise and continue as before. He shut his eyes for an instant and then he struggled to his feet.

Was it his imagination, or had he heard someone call his name? His first thought was of Rebekah. Had someone followed him from the town to bring him back? Was Rebekah worse? He scanned the road in both directions. It was completely empty. Had he heard the cry of a bird? He was certain he had heard something.

Only slowly did he realize the atmosphere around him was changing. He sat down again pushing his back hard against the rock. His eyes darted here and there seeking for some clue as to why the skin on his arms was prickling and his breathing had become shallow, as though he feared to draw the air into his lungs. There was nothing to be seen, only the haze of heat over the scrub land and a solitary bush growing nearby. Yet for all its emptiness, the atmosphere was full, charged as when an electric storm was in the air.

Cautiously he knelt down again. Even movement felt irreverent. God was in this place. Everything was full of him, the sky, the hard ground, even the stillness all around him. He stared in fascination at the bush just a few feet away. So extraordinary was the moment he wondered if it would burst into flames before him.

He thought of how Jairus would have sneered at him for his presumption.

'You're no Moses!' he would have said.

'But God is still God, isn't He?' Jacob whispered, almost like his old self, and slipping off his shoes he bowed his head towards the ground, lost in reverence. He knew without doubt the hand of God was upon him and initially he felt only wonder and awe.

'Rebekah,' he whispered, for it seemed the most natural thing in the world to bring before God the desire of his heart.

'Rebekah,' he repeated, and found he could say no more. His mind flew at once to his only other experience of the presence of God; the night God had told him he would marry Rebekah. That had been as gentle and fleeting as a caress, but this was different, more intense, and as time passed, more frightening.

The fear of God took hold of him. He began to relive again the days in his bedroom all those years before, yet he hardly recognized the person he had been back then. He had vowed undying gratitude to God, but instead his heart had grown hard; to God and to men. He was still grateful for Rebekah, of course he was, but the pain of her uncleanness had seared his soul. He knew he had become a different man. Other memories came before him. There seemed no way to keep them out. Remorselessly his life came under review. First there was Jairus. His anger towards him had never died away. It burned as fiercely as ever. Next came his parents. He saw the anguish in his father's face when he had refused Benjamin's offer to go back and partner with him when Micah died. How he had clung to his pride. He remembered clearly how he had felt. So, his business was gone, so what? He would make his own way! Ruthlessly he had shut out of his mind how he was hurting his father. He didn't care! In the market place, as he began to work for another merchant, men observed his hardness and the harsh edge to his voice. His ability to strike a bargain became ruthless. He was no longer well-liked and he knew it. It meant nothing to him. Rebekah and the children were all that mattered. If they rejected his beloved, then they rejected him, and his love for his community slowly died until there was nothing left.

Gradually over the endless years of Rebekah's illness, Jacob had begun to shut out even those who loved them. Rebekah had been powerless to stop him. Only faithful Jocabed ignored whatever his pain dished out to her. She would not be separated from her daughter. She loved Rebekah as much as he did, she declared vehemently to Jacob, and he came to be grateful for a will as stubborn as his own. Jocabed cleaned and cooked and cared for the children, but now she was sick herself and Sarah had shouldered responsibility for the household.

As he knelt behind the rock, he knew God's eye was upon him and nothing could be hidden. He looked long and hard at who he had become and saw with horror that this pain too had been added to Rebekah's burden. He hated facing it. Anger boiled up inside him. What did God want from him? Did God expect him to pray? He had prayed, Rebekah had prayed, and the children had never stopped. Slowly the sound of his own promise began to deafen him. How easy it had been in the days of sweetness to rejoice and thank God for Rebekah. But now, when she could no longer leave the house, when his heart broke at every sight of her, when people whispered about her in the street; now his heart was empty of thanksgiving. He loved her more than ever, but speak to God about her? This God who never answered their prayers?

He saw he had turned his back on God in anger and resentment. A shiver went over him. What was acceptable back in Capernaum looked very different out here. God was God, here, there, everywhere. In every season of life His name was to be honoured. The searing breath of the Holy God was upon him and stripped of every excuse he felt naked and exposed. He knew he had to speak, but what could he say? How could he ask for the only thing that mattered? How dare he? What could he offer God in exchange for Rebekah's healing? Once, long ago he had offered gratitude, yet he had been unable to give even that out of his meager resources.

There seemed only one thing to say. 'Have mercy on me, a sinner. Heal my wife, not because I have anything to give, but because you are good to the poor, and your love endures forever.'

This time there was no whispered reply. The silence held him captive. He dared not move. He felt a pressure growing inside him, as though he was being compelled. Compelled to do what; to give what? Mystified, he could think of only one thing to say.

'I will give anything you require of me.' The presence grew more powerful and he sensed something momentous had just happened. A cold hand of fear clutched his heart. What had he said? What would God ask of him? He focused his mind on Rebekah and the fear passed. She was worth it, whatever it was!

He took a deep breath. 'Anything,' he reiterated, and immediately his mind flew to a chance meeting which had happened some months before.

He had travelled to the other side of the lake on business. It was always bitter/sweet to visit Gennesaret, for it was impossible not to remember the time he had spent there with Micah. The familiar streets reminded him of when he did business there for himself, although now of course he had been sent by his employer. As he had walked through the market it had grieved him to see Micah's stall standing empty. It stirred great sadness, both for himself and the fine merchant Micah had been, all gone now; long gone.

He completed the main part of his business and was satisfied with the bargain he had struck. He knew his employer would be pleased. Leaving the market, he rounded a corner and was surprised to bump into Simon. Somehow, he hadn't expected to see him. Simon had grown into a slight youth, about the same age Jacob had been when he married Rebekah. Jacob suddenly understood his own father's reluctance to grant permission when he looked at him. He is simply a boy, he thought to himself. It seemed strange to think all the wealth of his father's house now belonged to someone so young.

Simon was handsome, dressed in the finest fabric, rich beyond anything Jacob had ever known, yet it had always seemed to Jacob he was purposeless, raised in the lap of luxury, protected from any need. Jacob had seen him now and again and his overriding memory was of Micah's great pride in his son. Simon had always seemed happy-go-lucky, enjoying life to the full without a care in the world, but now as Jacob looked at him, he thought him subtly changed. They greeted each other warmly, but there was a weariness upon Simon and his eyes were dark. Jacob frowned, wondering if he was still grieving over his father's death.

'Are you well?' he asked, and Simon nodded absently, his thoughts obviously elsewhere. Jacob was at a loss what to say and had decided to move on from this awkward encounter when suddenly Simon said,

'Would you come and share some refreshment with me?'

Jacob looked into his face, and although he had things left to do, he agreed to go. Afterwards, when he asked himself why he accepted, he was honest enough to admit he had wanted to relax in someone else's home. He didn't do that in Capernaum any more. Simon still lived in his father's house, and Jacob knew how rich and opulent a mansion it was. A servant greeted them at the door and washed the dust from their feet and hands. The cool water was delicious on Jacob's skin, for it had been a long journey, and he was grateful to step inside out of the sun's remorseless heat. He looked around at all the luxurious furnishings, the fine furniture and wonderful hangings that would have taken Rebekah's breath away. She had created a simple home from what little they had left, but this was another world.

The servant brought them cool drinks and a dish of the dates that Jacob loved. Jacob smiled with pleasure. Simon used to serve the dates himself when he was a child. It was a sweet courtesy he always remembered.

They sat together and Simon was unusually silent. He asked after Rebekah and the children, but didn't seem to be listening to Jacob's reply. Jacob looked across at him. What was the matter with him today? Eventually he felt he could no longer endure the difficult silence.

'Is everything all right Simon?' he asked, 'has something happened?'

Simon had been sitting studying the rings on his hands, twisting them ceaselessly, transferring them from one finger to another, never still. Now he looked up and Jacob thought he looked haunted. 'Jesus has been here,' he said.

Jacob looked around him in surprise. 'Here in your home?' he asked.

'No,' said Simon, 'I wish I had brought him here, although perhaps in some ways that would have been worse.'

Jacob frowned. 'I don't really understand what it is you are saying. Jesus is often in Capernaum and I have heard a little about him. Did you meet him?'

Simon sighed as though the weight of the world was on his shoulders. Then he began to speak, gesturing with his hands, his voice full of some pent-up emotion.

'He was here in the town, and I followed him. In fact, I followed him for days. I wanted to be close to him and see the miracles and hear him teaching. It was incredible Jacob! You should have seen him.' The scene with Jesus and the centurion flashed into Jacob's mind. He pushed it away ruthlessly.

Unconsciously Simon rose and began to walk about, unable, it seemed, to sit still any longer with his guest. Restlessly he picked up and put down one object after another from the tables scattered around the room.

'What happened?' asked Jacob.

'I listened and I watched and gradually one great question began to occupy my mind. I kept expecting him to address it in something he said, and often I thought he was going to, but then he would talk about something else. It was very frustrating.'

He hesitated for a moment and then he looked at Jacob directly. 'You see there are things which have bothered me my whole life.'

Jacob was amazed. 'What things?'

'Well, I have never had to work for anything, ever. You know I inherited all this from my father, and I am rich, and comfortable and safe. But there is something nagging inside me, and it never lets me rest.'

'What sort of thing?'

'Something which insists there must be more to life than just money and position. I mean, there just has to be, doesn't there?'

Jacob nodded, but he turned his face away. Simon didn't notice.

'I had always wanted to talk to my father about spiritual things; about God, and why he put us here on earth. It couldn't be just for our pleasure, could it? But Father would brush my questions aside, as though such thoughts belittled his success and his wealth. He said those matters belong to priests and teachers, not to ordinary men like us. He seemed to want me to be content just enjoying his generosity, and having a great time with my friends, and of course I did. Then Father died, and one day I happened to get caught up in the crowd around Jesus. All my questions came rushing back at once. He fascinated me because he only spoke about spiritual things, absolutely nothing else! That is odd, isn't it? I didn't grasp very much of what he said, but it drew me back to him again and again.'

Jacob didn't know what to say. Simon had never spoken in such terms to him before and he had never guessed the young man had such hidden depths. Jacob's head dropped into his hands. He remembered his own childhood, full of unanswered questions, but he never spoke of these things now, dismissing every thought of them. Once, long ago he would have rushed to hear Jesus speak, but those days were gone, buried under the mountain of pain he and Rebekah had endured together.

Slowly Simon continued. 'I planned to ask him a question. The thought of it consumed me. I knew I would only get one chance, so the question had to be perfect, something which would really find out what I wanted to know.'

Jacob lifted his head, enthralled by the young man's intensity. 'What did you ask him?' he said, drawn into this quest for truth despite himself.

Simon came and sat down once more. 'He was walking along the road and I got closer to him than I ever had, and the opportunity was just there, so I decided to ask him this one thing, this one important question. I ran up to him and fell on my knees before him and I said to him, "Good teacher, what must I do to inherit eternal life?"'

Jacob drew in a sharp breath. 'That is an amazing question,' he said, and there was awe in his voice.

'Yes,' said Simon eagerly. 'It's a good question, isn't it? I thought it was a good question. I thought if anyone was going to inherit eternal life it was me. I mean I have always kept the law, and I am generous with my money, and I truly desire to understand these things. Don't you think I am a good candidate, Jacob? I must be a good candidate for eternal life!'

Jacob looked at him with sympathy. 'I would have thought so,' he agreed. 'What did Jesus say?'

Simon let out a long slow breath. 'Well, first he asked me why I called him good. He said only God is good. But then he spoke to me about the commandments; do not murder, do not commit adultery, do not steal, do not give false testimony, do not defraud, honour your father and mother, as if I didn't know them all off by heart.' He stopped speaking and looked away, apparently lost in thought.

'Was that all?' asked Jacob, deeply disappointed. How right he had been to dismiss this preacher. Anyone in Israel could quote the commandments!

Simon looked back at him and shook his head. 'Oh no, that was not all. If only it had been! But I assured him I had kept all these commandments since I was a boy, and I have, I really have!'

'I believe you. What happened next?'

'I don't think he had really seen me up until then, but when he focused his attention on me, it was almost frightening. It was the most penetrating gaze I have ever felt. His eyes pierced me, as though my fine robes could not hide who I am'. Simon trembled at the memory and his voice became a whisper. 'He looked right into my eyes, no not even that, but deeper still, and I knew he could see inside me. Really, really see me. I will never forget it. No one has ever looked at me in that way before. I wasn't sure I could hold his gaze, and I blushed fiery red, though I had no idea why.'

Tension filled the room, and Jacob waited quietly, lost in thought.

Simon sat for a few moments considering again the look Jesus had given him and the words he couldn't shake off. At last, he turned to Jacob.

'He said, "One thing you lack. Go, sell everything you have and give to the poor, and you will have treasure in heaven. Then come, follow me"'.

The silence was profound. Jacob had no idea how to respond. He glanced around at Simon's possessions. 'Sell everything you have - everything?' Jacob thought it an impossible thing to ask of anyone, outrageous in fact, and only slowly did the truth dawn on him. Wasn't that just what he had done? Hadn't he stripped his home, his business, his whole life of everything that could be sold in order to buy a cure for Rebekah? Yet he had never found one.

'That is a huge demand,' was all he could find to say.

Simon nodded and looked at him with anguished eyes. 'I found it hard to believe he had suggested such a thing. I think I went into shock. He said sell everything, and follow him. I mean, how could anybody do that?'

Jacob said simply, 'Only if you truly love someone is it possible to do it. Only then.'

Simon looked surprised. 'Love?' he said, as though he hadn't considered such a concept before.

'What did you say in reply?' Jacob asked, wanting to move the conversation on.

'I didn't say anything, I don't know there was anything I could say. I just turned away. I couldn't have done it; I just couldn't have done it. Everything my father worked for all his life! Just to give it away? Impossible, simply impossible! He can't have understood what it would cost me, could he? Otherwise he wouldn't have asked!'

Jacob could only shake his head.

Simon sighed. 'He can't have understood,' he repeated quietly, and Jacob looked at him with sympathy.

'Did he say anything else?'

Simon nodded, 'Oh yes, but not to me. I glanced back as I was leaving. He was standing watching me and I heard his voice as he spoke to those around him. "How hard it is for the rich to enter the kingdom of God," and his face was full of such love Jacob, such love for me and such sadness. It was as though I was breaking his heart.'

'What happened next?'

'Nothing! I really thought he would come after me and say, "I know that may seem a bit harsh. Sell half; that would be enough!" But he didn't come, or even call out after me. He simply left me to walk away.'

Simon paused and gestured around the room. 'I came home and looked at all my things. You know I don't think I had really seen any of them for years. I examined every treasure, one by one, and then I went into Father's secret room, where not even the servants are allowed, and I counted all my money.'

He shut his eyes. 'Sell everything and give it to the poor!' he whispered and he shook his head, as though trying to rid his mind of the words.

Sighing he focussed his gaze on Jacob again. 'I can't sleep, I can't eat, I don't think I will enjoy anything I own ever again. It's all dead to me. Dead!'

'So, what will you do?' Jacob asked, his heart wrung with pity for the distress in the young man's face.

'That's it,' said Simon, 'I'm still not sure. Can I really give it all up? Can I really sell it all? I mean if I got to the end of my days and I was rich, but I didn't have eternal life, what use would that be to me?'

'No use at all,' said Jacob quietly. 'You cannot take your wealth beyond the grave. Your father could not and neither can you.'

Jacob's mind was consumed with one burning question. Almost against his better judgment he asked it. 'Do you really think Jesus can offer eternal life?' Unconsciously he held his breath.

'If you had heard him as I have, you would not doubt it.' Simon's face was suddenly alight with memory.

'I have seen miracles, Jacob, watched in wonder as the cripples walk, as the deaf hear and the mute speak. But healing is still only a temporal matter, isn't it? We cannot take even that with us when we die. Jesus offers something else, something which reaches beyond this life into what lies beyond death. I believe he offers eternal life. I am absolutely certain of it.'

Jacob went cold. Just for a moment he had been caught up in Simon's story, but now reality grasped hold of him again. Healing was just a temporal matter, a blessing bound to the short span of man's life on the earth. Jesus offered more than that, for those who believed! Jacob shook his head. He no longer desired that which reached beyond the world, into the knowledge of God. Not anymore. Jesus had come too late for him. All hope was dead. He no longer believed Rebekah would be healed. He would not seek out this Jesus, not for healing and not for eternal life. He had no faith left for either.

Simon sat with his head bowed and Jacob determined not to let his own unbelief damage this precious young man.

'What will you do Simon?' he asked again.

Simon looked up and to Jacob's amazement there was a radiant look on his face.

'I will sell all I have, give it to the poor, and follow him.' he beamed. 'Talking to you has really helped me, especially what you said about loving someone. I see it clearly now. I do love him, you see, and I must follow him. My life has no meaning outside of that. Father's whole life was given to making money so he could prevent me from suffering the hardships he knew as a child. That was his aim, his purpose, and how well he achieved it. But money is not enough for me, it will never be enough for me.'

He stood up in his excitement, 'But following Jesus,' he exclaimed, 'now that would be a life worth living! Wouldn't it? If only you'd seen him, seen the things he does, the look in his face. Of course, I have to follow him. What have I been thinking of?'

Jacob looked at him with wonder, envying the light which had come into his eyes as he spoke of Jesus. 'Do you think he is the Messiah, Simon?' he asked, almost despite himself.

'Yes,' said Simon without hesitation. 'I believe it, and I must go with him wherever he leads me.'

Youthful impetuosity, Jacob thought, and he sighed, feeling a hundred years old and tired, so very tired. He rose to his feet and Simon embraced him.

'Thank you, Jacob,' he said. 'I was destined to meet you in the street today. Of all my father's friends you are the only one I could have trusted to discuss such a subject.' The hardness on Jacob's face softened a little and he smiled uncertainly.

'I am honoured,' he said, 'but I am not sure I understand why that should be.'

Simon laughed. 'Because you love spiritual matters too,' he said.

Jacob took a step back. Why did such a simple statement make him feel almost as though Simon had struck him?

'Are you all right?' Simon asked. Jacob pulled himself together. 'Of course, I am just interested in all you have said.'

'Jesus isn't just interesting, he is fascinating!' Simon said, and putting his hand on Jacob's shoulder he led him to the door.

Jacob rubbed his hands together. Sometimes they still hurt where he had hit them against the wall.

'Next time you come to town I fear I shall not be here.' Simon's eyes were filled with excitement.

Jacob turned in the doorway. 'I am delighted for you Simon. I hope you find all you are looking for.'

Simon embraced him warmly. 'Don't worry,' he said. 'I've found him already!'

Jacob could only smile. He had never found what he was looking for, and now he had no will left to try. He devoutly hoped Simon would do better and that giving all his money away would miraculously meet the need in his heart. Jacob was unconvinced.

Now he sat in the desert, wondering why that encounter with Simon was running ceaselessly through his brain. He tried to ignore it, but it was insistent, demanding he give it his full attention. It was obvious he could not sell everything he had and give it to the poor. Apart from anything else there was almost nothing left! So why was that conversation haunting him? What was God trying to say? Was there something as precious to him as wealth was to Simon? Something he was holding on to despite the years of sacrifice? What could it be? He felt certain God required something of him, but he had no idea what it was.

He shut his eyes and the face of Jairus appeared with astonishing clarity in his mind, as plain as if the synagogue ruler were standing before him. He opened his eyes at once and looked all around. Of course, there was no one to be seen. Why had Jairus suddenly intruded into his thoughts? He shook his head and decided to think about Rebekah. That was the most important thing - to think about Rebekah! He shut his eyes again and there was Jairus, looking at him, face to face. His mouth twisted as the hatred he felt for his old friend ran through his body. Just as he had not been able to stifle his tears, so now he could not control his anger. His fists clenched and he snarled at the image in his head, murder in his heart.

Jairus, the town's spiritual leader, the best friend he had ever had. Jairus, too devoted to the law, too holy to even enter their house once it was clear Rebekah was unclean. Jairus, who had betrayed their love and trust, rejecting them in their time of need.

Jairus!

'I will never forgive him!' he snarled into the still air.

There was no voice. Jacob had no need of one. He knew what was required of him, knew it without it being spoken, had known it for years, but had refused to acknowledge it, even to himself. He tried to think of something else, anything else to defend his conscious mind from the thought pounding away in the background, demanding to be heard. In the end he allowed it to come to the forefront of his thinking, and with it came Rebekah's voice, pleading with him.

"You must forgive Jairus, you must Jacob, or your own heart will grow cold!"

That was the only conversation he had ever allowed on the matter. He had refused to listen then, and he was determined not to listen now. Jairus did not deserve forgiveness, God must surely see that! The man would get off completely free! He knew it wasn't true, even as he thought it. How many times had he rejoiced to see he was hurting Jairus as he refused to speak to him? Did he really believe he and Rebekah had been the only ones to suffer; that Jairus had felt nothing?

His body was contorted with pain. So many years had passed, yet still the agony of it made him want to cry out, like a wound he could not bear to be touched. The sense of betrayal remained a constant agony. If Jairus had rejected him perhaps he could have borne it, but to reject Rebekah! How could he forgive that? How could anyone be expected to forgive that? Yet he knew Rebekah had forgiven it freely, had assured Jacob she understood. Her graciousness had simply made him more determined than ever Jairus should be made to pay. He had lain awake at night planning evil, vengeful things, and the fact he had never carried any of them out only made him angry at himself. How dare Jairus hurt Rebekah? The man had no heart!

'And what of your heart?' He could not escape the voice inside even if he wanted to.

His heart? He hardly dared to look.

Scene after scene came up before his eyes; the tears on his mother's face as he turned away from her; the way the children flinched at his tone; the unexpected flashes of anger which surprised even him. For the first time Jacob allowed himself to see how bitterness was affecting him. He had criticized Jairus for coldness, yet now he was cold himself, growing more distant even with the children. What would it cost him if he didn't forgive, refusing to let the offence go at last? Who would he become?

Simon's voice echoed in his ears. 'If I got to the end of my days and I was rich, but I didn't have eternal life, what use would that be to me?'

The voice spoke again. Was it his conscience?

'If you got to the end of your days and all you had was bitterness and hatred, what use would that be to you?' The truth of it was undeniable. But forgive Jairus? Simon had faced just such a challenge and declared what Jacob felt deep inside. It was impossible; simply impossible! Yet this rich young ruler had come to it in the end, had sold all for love, holding nothing back.

Now it was his turn.

In the same way in which Simon had carefully counted all his wealth, so Jacob did the same, picking up and examining every offence and every unforgivable thing Jairus had done. It almost choked him. Slowly he tallied the most painful memories like treasures and even he couldn't fathom why it seemed impossible to let them go. He knew he had failed to understand the measure of Simon's sacrifice until that moment. Not until he counted the cost himself.

In the end he just had to choose. He had promised "anything," and now had come the moment to fulfil his vow. It was inescapable. He lay prostrate on the ground his fists clenched into agonizing knots with whitened knuckles and fingernails biting into his palms. From some deep place he groaned his conflict into the dirt. It surprised him how stubbornly resentment refused to die.

Like a soft whisper from the past, he heard Levi's voice, 'You two must stay as brothers.'

It was the final blow. One last groan escaped him as something broke inside and lifting his head he shouted,

'All right, all right, I forgive him!'

Instantly he felt the change. Slowly his fingers uncurled. He knew he was letting Jairus go.

He looked down at his bloodied palms, amazed at their emptiness. At last, he understood. God did not require him to forgive Jairus because he was demanding the most costly sacrifice, but because this intractable bitterness was like a chain. It meant he could never be free. He had to forgive for his own sake. It was God's goodness to him. He wondered if it was the same for Simon, had his money been preventing him from being the person he was meant to be?

He could hardly believe it. After all these years had he actually done it? Was it as simple as that to forgive? Could he really bear to look Jairus in the face? Would he feel no hatred? He shut his eyes and focused on where the seething, molten anger had always been. There was only a dead pile of ashes. Then he knew for sure. Jairus was free and so was he.

He lay his face once more in the desert sand and felt a peace he had long forgotten flow into his soul. A gentle, cleansing stream ran through him.

'Thank you, thank you,' he whispered, overwhelmed with gratitude, and then, with a sigh, he slept.

A Miracle

Jairus awoke with a start as Abigail came to replace him at Hannah's bedside.

'Where is Jonathan?' he asked. His friend appeared at once in the doorway. Jairus wondered if he had stayed awake all night.

'What is it Jairus?'

Jairus spoke without hesitation. 'Go at once to the lake, if Jesus comes, run back and tell me!' Jonathan needed no second bidding and was gone in a moment.

The morning passed slowly. Jairus split his time between Hannah's room and standing in the road, watching for his friend. Impatience and fear were eating a hole in him. He knew if Jesus didn't come today, it would be too late. The pity of those who surrounded the door washed over him and he ignored them, holding his emotions in check with an iron will. At noon he was still outside, waiting for news, straining his eyes as he looked down towards the sea. Inside Abigail would not move from Hannah's bedside. The child's face was white against the coverlet and she had not spoken for hours. They both knew she was slipping away.

'I should be with her,' Jairus fretted frantically, but suddenly his heart lifted as Jonathan ran towards him up the dusty street.

'He is here, Jairus, he is here!' he panted, trying to catch his breath. 'He has just landed at the fish dock.' He looked with anxiety into the Rabbi's face. 'How is she?' he asked.

Jairus could not bear to speak the words, he simply shook his head.

'Come then,' said Jonathan urgently, 'or should I bring him to you?'

'No,' said Jairus, 'stay here with Abigail, and if there is any change come at once to tell me. I have to go and ask him for myself. Hannah is my child.'

Jonathan looked into the anguish in his eyes and simply nodded.

Jairus's mind was in turmoil as he hurried towards the lake. Would Jesus come? Would he perform a miracle for a man who didn't believe in him? He could not imagine it, after all he had been so vocal in his criticism, declaring to the whole town the man was a charlatan. Why should he come? Because I will beg him to, determined Jairus, almost beside himself. He tried to think of something he had done which might earn him Jesus' favour, but it was hopeless. There was nothing. How could you earn a miracle?

'I don't deserve it,' he thought, his memory refusing to tell him where he had heard the words before.

A gentle voice spoke in his mind. 'No one deserves it. That's what mercy is all about.'

A cry escaped him and throwing dignity aside he ran as fast as he could towards the shore.

Jairus had forgotten how unpretentious and ordinary Jesus looked. Dressed in white, he was standing laughing with a group of men, relaxed and happy. Jairus couldn't bear it. How dare he be happy when Hannah was dying? How could anyone be happy? He pushed his way into the crowd, his face set.

'Jesus,' he said loudly and the man turned at once, the smile vanishing as he caught sight of Jairus's face.

'What is it my friend?' he asked, and reached out to grip Jairus's shoulders, as though they had known each other for years. Jairus swallowed hard. Gazing into those eyes unnerved him. He had not expected to feel the overwhelming need to lay his head on this stranger and let out all the pain bottled up in his soul. What was he thinking of? He searched Jesus' face, trying to comprehend why so many had left everything to follow him, and as he gazed, to his own amazement it all became clear to him. He saw this was no ordinary man, but someone full of searing reality. There was no pretence in his eyes, nothing false, indeed the very depths of him were on display, and those depths were challenging and loving, and holy. Light came to him. This was a man who knew God! I wish Jacob was here, he thought as hope flooded through him and he didn't hesitate but threw himself down at Jesus' feet.

'It is my little girl,' he said. 'She is about to die, please come and place your hands on her; heal her so she can live.'

Jesus agreed to come at once, but people were appearing from nowhere and it was a large crowd that decided to follow them. Jairus's face took on a stern, angry expression. Inside he wanted to scream with frustration. They needed to run, to run like the wind, to get to Hannah as fast as they could. He pushed and shoved, trying to clear a path for Jesus, but the mass of people impeded their progress until they were traveling painfully slowly. The whole road was clogged with people. He didn't see Jacob's children, Sarah and Benjamin at the edge of the crowd. His whole being was focused on one overwhelming certainty. He knew they were going to be too late.

Rebekah wasn't aware anything momentous was happening down at the shore. She was sitting in her chair gazing out of the window, as she had a hundred, a thousand times before. She was alone, for Sarah had gone out to the market and Benjamin had run off down to the lake again. He was always a handful when Jacob was away. The hope someone would visit her had died long ago. Jocabed was too ill to come, and Jacob had alienated both his parents. She knew Abigail still thought of her. How could it be otherwise? Her faithful friend had trouble enough of her own with Hannah getting worse and worse. No one would come. Loneliness just had to be endured along with everything else.

This day was no different from any other, except if anything she was more impatient and restless than usual. Her sickness irked her. All around were household tasks screaming for her attention, but she had no energy even to rise from the chair, so she was compelled to leave them to Sarah. Poor Sarah was responsible for shopping and cooking and drawing the water, but Rebekah had never got used to being unable to do these things. This was her house and she longed to sweep and clean and make it sparkle.

She sighed, wishing at least there was Jacob's homecoming to look forward to. He had set out before sunrise on business. She could guess how reluctant he would have been to leave her, especially since only the day before he had found her collapsed in a heap on the floor. The anxiety in his eyes had cut her to the heart, and when he made her promise to rest, she vowed she would. She laughed at the thought of it. Rest! She never did anything else.

A dark shadow of fear touched her as it always did when he was away. She pushed it from her mind. They needed the money and he had to go; that was an end of it. Resting her head on the back of the chair she sighed again, regretting not being able to get up early and see him off. She hated the fact she always slept late and she knew he would not return until long after exhaustion had closed her eyes. She would have to be content with seeing him tomorrow.

At least his hands were healed now. When he had come home with them swathed in bandages, she had known without being told this was no accident in the market. He hadn't tried to explain and she didn't press him. Had he fought someone who spoke disparagingly of her? Had his frustration boiled over at last? She guessed she would never know. There was so much they didn't speak of now. This was just another secret pain.

Her eyelids dropped as she began to doze. Strange muddled dreams made her mutter in her sleep. She saw Jacob pick her up and twirl her off her feet. Throwing back her head she laughed, but then the dream changed as his face became dark and angry. In fear she called out for her beloved Jacob to come back to her, but she hardly recognised him as he dumped her on the ground and turned away. In her distress she reached out a hand to him, but he shrugged it off, and she awoke whimpering. Shudders ran through her emaciated body. Though he tried to hide it, her sweet, kind Jacob had changed and it was all her fault. Rebekah didn't need a dream to tell her that.

The morning wore away as she sat looking out of the window onto the alleyway and gradually her foot began to tap with impatience. Where was Sarah? What was taking her so long at the market? She bit her lip and took several deep breaths trying to calm herself. She didn't want to lose her temper. She knew she was changing too, becoming irritable and easily angered. Frequently now she took out her frustrations on Sarah and Benjamin. Jacob did the same. What was becoming of the family they had yearned for, and what were she and Jacob doing to the children?

Suddenly she heard the sound of hurrying feet in the alleyway. She fixed her eyes on the door expectantly and a moment later Sarah rushed in, her eyes alight with news. Rebekah's bad mood vanished in an instant. Sarah was her window on the world, recounting all the local gossip.

'What is it, Sarah?' she asked. 'What has happened?'

'It's Jesus,' Sarah said breathlessly. 'He's down at the shore.'

Rebekah stared at her daughter, trying to collect her thoughts. The name Jesus had been on everyone's lips for weeks as he travelled around the district. He could do miracles they said, heal the sick, even cleanse leprosy. Jacob was silent on the whole matter, leaving the room when Sarah spoke about Jesus, which was often. She was fascinated by the stories about him. Right from the start she had believed without question Rebekah could be healed. Her young face, alight with hope, had made her mother's heart ache. Rebekah had declared she believed it too, but there had always been a lump in her throat as they spoke about it, a reticence she couldn't share. Did she believe she could be healed? She wasn't sure, but one thing she knew without a doubt, the simple, child-like faith on Sarah's face was far too precious to destroy.

Her heart beat fast within her chest. She couldn't bear Sarah to be disappointed and she couldn't bear to be disappointed herself, but she had no idea how to prevent it from happening. How could she prepare Sarah for the possibility nothing would change? The child was ecstatic, and unaware of her mother's anxiety, a torrent of words simply poured out of her.

'He is going to pray for Hannah and that means he has to pass along the main street, just at the end of our alleyway. Oh, it's so close Mother! I know I can persuade him to stop for a few moments and come here to pray for you. You could be healed!'

Excitement and expectation were written all over her face, but Rebekah was still silent. Did she believe she could be healed? After all the years of disappointment, how could she? Yet this man's reputation was growing and growing. Was it possible he could do a miracle? Was there hope even for an incurable illness like hers?

Eventually she whispered, 'I wish Jacob was here,' and she looked into Sarah's face as though searching for inspiration.

Sarah's hands fluttered before her, just as they had when she was excited as a child. It seemed to Rebekah her calm and responsible daughter had vanished without trace. She was hopping from one foot to the other and looking eagerly at Rebekah obviously waiting to see if she would say anything else. Rebekah just gazed back at her blankly and after a moment Sarah's impatience got the better of her. She bent down to kiss her mother's cheek.

'Healed!' she breathed as though it had happened already and then she hurtled out of the door leaving it wide open.

Rebekah lifted a hand and called after her, 'Sarah!'

But Sarah didn't turn back, she was already far down the alley, racing to find Jesus.

Rebekah sat, trying to collect her thoughts. It had all happened so fast. Was Jesus really in their neighbourhood? Was he going to walk up the road just a short distance away? Was there the faintest chance he would turn aside and come to her house?

Her mind began to race, faster than Sarah's flying feet. It's all very well, she told herself, convincing Sarah you believe in miracles when Jesus is at a safe distance, but what about when he is here in your town, striding down your streets, talking to people you know? What if he were to walk through that open door and stand right in front of you? What then?

She was confused, unsure if she would be glad if he came, or relieved if he didn't. Eventually only one thought was clear to her.

He won't come, she thought bitterly, he won't set foot in the house of an unclean woman; no Rabbi would, not Jairus and not him. The anguish of her life boiled constantly just below the surface of her rigid self-control. She would never let anyone see it of course, but as she thought about the possibility of being rejected again, something broke inside her and she found it impossible to subdue it any longer. Tears began to pour down her face, tears of anger and frustration and endless pain. For years she had prayed, believed, tried to be brave and never give up hope, but suddenly and overwhelmingly she began to tell God exactly how she really felt.

'I hate my life,' she said through gritted teeth.

'I hate what my illness has done to Jacob and the children, to his parents and mine. I hate being trapped inside this stupid lump of a body, inside this house, inside these walls. I wish I could burst out and escape. But there is no escape.'

She trembled as anger coursed through her. 'I hate this chair, this view, this affliction. I hate the fact I am too sick even to shout and scream and pound my fists on the walls. I hate my weakness and my loneliness and my desperation, and most of all I hate the fact you never answer, not even when the children beg you to heal me.'

Her lips quivered with exhaustion as the passion drained away. Almost in a whisper she said, 'And I am afraid; so afraid! I'm afraid of who Jacob has become, and I'm afraid of who I have become. Will eventually even his incredible patience wear out? Will he stop loving me? I'm afraid of the future that stretches out endlessly before me. The emptiness frightens me. Could I endure another twelve years like this? Do I even want to?'

She sat silent for a moment looking into the depths of her despair and then she said softly, 'I think Jacob is afraid I might die, but my fear is quite different.'

She paused and shut her eyes. 'I'm afraid I might live.'

As she spoke the words, never before acknowledged, her own need burned within her and she cried out passionately, 'I hate being unclean, I hate being unclean!'

The walls rang with the words. Her heightened colour began to drain away as weakness once more laid hold of her. Racked with sobs she lifted her shawl to cover her face as every last shred of her self-control was swept away. Her mind was hopelessly confused and she began to fear for her own reason. Her thoughts were a jumble of disjointed half sentences and painful memories, while powerful emotions tossed her about as though she were in a storm at sea. She had always been afraid of this moment, fearing that if ever she let go, she would never be able to regain control again. Now it was upon her and where would it lead her? Would Jacob return to a wreck of a wife? Would Sarah bring Jesus to a mother she didn't recognise? Rebekah struggled to pull herself together. It was all to no avail. She had no resources left and thoughts she had kept at bay for years flooded in on her, horrible, ugly thoughts which seemed incredibly real; almost inevitable. She shuddered, and in her desperation, she spoke out the first thing that came to her.

'Jesus,' she cried, 'help me!'

There was a moment of silence, not just in the room, but in her mind. In utter amazement she lowered her shawl, wiping the tears from her eyes. She put her head on one side as though listening, but the silence continued, every evil thought swept away and her raging emotions calm, stilled into unaccountable peace. Blinking, she turned to where the sunlight blazed in through the open door. Perhaps she was half expecting to see Jesus standing framed in the doorway, but it was empty, the door swinging lazily in the breeze. No one was there.

She sat very still, unable to take it all in and then she realised something strange was happening. She had often experienced that when her weakness was at its worst the whole room would swim about her and darkness would close in. She thought it was happening again; that the expenditure of emotional energy had pushed her to the edge of fainting. She gripped the arms of her chair, willing herself to stay conscious, but then she began to look around in wonder. It wasn't that she was feeling faint, it was something else, something outside of her altogether, something she had never experienced before.

The room seemed to shimmer and change and there, on the wall by the window, a picture appeared. It was so clear and sharp she passed her hand over her eyes in puzzlement. What was she seeing? She leant forward, utterly dumbfounded, for the picture began to move, showing one scene after another. It was just as though the wall had melted away and she was watching... what? There was no way of understanding it.

At first Rebekah didn't recognise the figure who moved miraculously across her wall. There was certainly something familiar about her, but she couldn't place what it was until the woman turned her face towards her and then she felt a cold shiver go over her. The woman was the image of Sarah, yet thin and worn like some pale shadow of her vibrant daughter. Was she seeing Sarah in years to come? She shivered again, frightened and fascinated. Only slowly did the truth begin to dawn on her. The woman on the wall was wearing the same robe she was. Confused she stared down at it and touched it gently. Then she looked back at the wall. No wonder the woman looked like Sarah. She gave a stifled cry. She was watching herself! Every detail of her haggard appearance shocked her to the bone. It was years since she had looked into the burnished surface of a mirror because Jacob had removed every one of them from the house. Now she could see why. It seemed unbelievable. She looked so old; old, and worn and painfully thin. What a sad creature I am, she thought, as she gazed at the wall through her tears.

The moving picture still held her attention and she watched as her slight form became enveloped by a pushing, shoving, noisy crowd. Although she was immediately carried along by the sheer volume of people, still she seemed purposeful, moving always in a certain direction, concentration written on her face. Rebekah hardly drew breath as she watched herself, so insignificant, lost in the midst of that heaving mass of humanity. She wondered where she was going with such determination, spending her strength as though she had enough and to spare. Slowly the figure edged her way forward in the crush, slipping under an arm here, sidestepping a big man there and all at once Rebekah realised what she was doing. She was gradually making her way towards the man in white.

Dressed in a simple robe he was walking in the very centre of the crowd, surrounded by a group of men who kept very close to him. They looked about them anxiously, obviously trying to keep the crowd from jostling him. What an impossible task! Rebekah couldn't see his face, but his hair shone in the sunlight, and his robe made him stand out clearly from those who surrounded him. But that wasn't the thing which fixed her attention on him. It was something much more extraordinary than that.

All around him there was a light and its glow somehow outshone the sun blazing down on him. His body was like a lamp, with some kind of flame burning inside, sending out a glorious radiance to every part of his being. It was odd that no one around him seemed even slightly aware of it. They pushed against him, apparently unable to see anything, but she watched entranced as it glowed and flowed over him, even down to the hem of his white garment. She became captivated by him; almost forgetting she was just watching a picture.

Completely focused on him, she lost sight of herself, but suddenly there she was, almost on the ground behind him. She drew a sharp breath. Surely she would be trampled in the crush, lost under so many heedless feet? She wanted to cry out a warning, but then she understood and sat with her hand over her mouth, rigid with tension. Just for a moment the crowd forced him to a standstill. Now was her opportunity. Now or never! Rebekah couldn't take her eyes off the thin, claw-like hand stretching unnoticed through a tiny gap and reaching, reaching, finally touched him, grasping for a second just the very edge of his radiant robe.

She cried out in amazement, for instantly the light transferred from his garment onto that outstretched hand. The light hadn't touched anyone else, why was it touching her? She was drawn to the edge of her seat as she watched it move swiftly up her arm until it encompassed her whole body. The crowd began to move forward again and miraculously it parted around her motionless figure. No one even noticed she was there. She was left sitting on the ground, bathed in light. Healed. It was obvious. She had been totally healed!

As the picture faded from the wall; she grasped the arms of the chair and stood up. Hope was coursing through her veins. Without a second thought she left the house, almost expecting her strength to have returned already. It only took a few steps to convince her she was still desperately sick, but she didn't care. She knew without doubt God had spoken to her and her healing lay just down the alleyway, around the next corner. It was so clear. This was not the time to be waiting for him to come to her. She had to go to him!

She did her best to hurry. How much time had passed since Sarah had come rushing into the house? What if it was already too late? Jesus was walking to Jairus's house and he had to pass this way. Had they gone by already? She stood leaning against the wall in the alleyway straining her ears. She could hear the crowd clearly enough. Was it coming towards her or moving away? For a second the drumming of her heart deafened her and then she was certain. It was coming towards her. She waited for the feeling of nausea to pass and then pushed herself forward and around the corner into the street.

Almost at once the crowd was upon her and she had no time to think or recover her breath. She caught a faint glimpse of white off to the left and began at once to make her way towards it. It was a miracle she stayed upright in the throng. Her breath came in laboured gasps but still she kept repeating to herself, 'I will be healed, I will be healed,' over and over again.

She gave every ounce of her strength to working her way forward, edging closer and closer. Even though he was walking so slowly she knew she would only have one chance as he passed by. She could see him more clearly now. There was no light shining from him, which surprised her, but his face was wonderful.

She knew he could heal her.

One last push and she was just behind him. Mustering her courage, she threw herself down in the midst of the hot, seething crowd. Fear almost overcame her. What if he didn't stop? She knew she didn't have the strength to get up and follow him again. The robes of the men surrounding him brushed against her face and her vision wavered. Was she going to faint and lie unconscious on the ground, trampled in the crush?

She prayed without thinking. 'Help me Lord!'

A sudden spurt of strength came from nowhere and her eyesight cleared. There before her she could see the hem of his robe, unmistakably white though dirtied by the road. It was just out of reach. She pushed forward stretching through the gap just as she had seen in the vision. Her heart seemed to stop beating and time stood still. No second thoughts came to hinder her. This was her moment and she wouldn't let it slip out of her hand.

'If I can just touch the edge of his garment,' she whispered, as with a superhuman effort she reached out and touched him. Just for one fleeting second, she felt the cloth of his robe between her fingers and then the next instant it was gone.

The pressure of the people moved him forward and she was left behind, unnoticed. The crowd surged around her, but she was oblivious to all of them. There was a tingling in her fingers where she could still feel the sensation of having touched his robe. Unconsciously she rubbed them gently together as warmth began to flow through her hand and then steadily up her arm. She sat on the ground staring at her hand, turning it this way and that. She was looking for some physical sign of the wonder going on inside her, but there was nothing to see. Her hand and arm were as thin as before, but she still stared at them stupidly, as though expecting to see the light shining out of them. When the sensation of warmth reached her shoulder, it spread through the rest of her body like liquid fire and touching the very centre of her sickness it burned with a fearsome blaze. Rebekah wondered what was happening. She gripped her stomach, panting, half with agony, half with ecstasy. Then it was gone, the work of a moment.

Enough healing for a lifetime.

The miracle took only a minute and Rebekah sat on the road lost in the wonder of what God had done for her. The crowd had stopped and were jostling roughly around her. She didn't feel very safe and as she struggled to her feet, she heard a gruff, impatient voice beside her.

'He says someone touched his clothes and that power has gone out from him, whatever that means!'

Rebekah felt the blood rush to her cheeks and she pushed her way forward in time to hear one of Jesus' companions speaking in tones of complete exasperation:

'But master, you see the people crowding against you and yet you can ask, "Who touched me?"' There was a murmur of assent from those who stood closest, but Jesus stood perfectly still, scanning the crowd; determined to find her. She hesitated for a moment, hiding her guilty face behind the tall man in front of her. This she had not seen in her vision! He knew. She shut her eyes and swallowed hard. He was a Holy Man and a miracle worker, of course, he knew! Even the slightest contact with an unclean woman would defile him and he had felt it as her touch had besmirched his purity. Her body began to tremble. This was why she had been so sure he wouldn't come and lay his hands on her. Not even if Sarah begged him.

She chided herself for her stupidity in thinking she could hide in the crowd and steal her healing, unseen and without his knowledge. Shame washed over her. It had all become clear to her. She hadn't cared what she did to him as long as she obtained her healing. Swept along in the moment, she had suppressed the thought it was wrong to touch him, but now she realised that in the days to come she would live to regret it. How could her conscience ever be at rest again? To make a Holy Man unclean, deliberately, secretly, just to gain your healing, was an incredibly selfish thing to do and there was no excuse for it; not even the years of waiting for a cure. She would never have done it to Jairus, and she shouldn't have done it to Jesus either.

Gulping back the tears she knew she had no choice but to slip out from her hiding place and face the inevitable wrath which was about to fall upon her. Better that, she thought, than to live a life of regret where eventually even her healing would have become bitter to her.

Jairus had been doing everything in his power to keep Jesus moving, yet with all his effort they still kept grinding to a halt.

He was straining to push ahead when suddenly he realized Jesus was no longer at his side. He turned and saw the Rabbi had stopped a few paces behind.

What now? he thought frantically. Doesn't he know we must get there quickly? He ran a shaking hand over his sweaty brow.

'Oh God, spare Hannah,' he prayed.

A moment later he listened incredulously as Jesus declared that someone had touched him. He was interested in spite of himself. How could this man know that power had gone out from him? What power? Why was it that everything surrounding Jesus was always full of questions? He used his elbows and shoved men out of the way until he stood once more beside Jesus. Was another miracle about to happen?

Jairus's mouth dropped open as Rebekah pushed her way forward through the crowd. He was stunned it was her - Jacob's Rebekah! He hadn't seen her for a long time, not even in the street and her appearance shocked him. Her face was as pale as Hannah's and so thin he hardly recognized her. His pleasure at seeing her lasted only a moment. Instinctively he moved back a step, surprised Jesus hadn't done the same. A Rabbi could not afford to be defiled, could he? Anyone could see Rebekah was a sick woman. Yet Jesus did not draw away but stood in the blistering sun as Rebekah came and knelt at his feet. It seemed to Jairus the Rabbi was actually waiting for her and he moved forward a little, straining his ears to hear every word. Instinctively he knew this interaction had significance for him as well as for Rebekah. In the back of his mind, he wondered where Jacob was.

At first Rebekah didn't even notice Jairus was there. Her heart was beating wildly, and she wanted to tell Jesus how sorry she was she had touched him and transferred her uncleanness onto him. She knew it was unforgivable. As she sank to her knees she could still feel inside the warm glow of that touch. The wonder of it confused her. There was no doubt she was healed, but what would Jesus say? Would he condemn her? Would this life-giving healing be withdrawn? The very thought of it crushed her, but determined to hide nothing she bowed her head and blurted out the truth.

Jairus looked at her in amazement and then he fixed his eyes on Jesus. How would he respond? Would he be angry, or offended? Obviously, he would have to rebuke her! After all, she knew the law, knew she was not supposed to touch him. Another rejection for Rebekah. He wondered where that thought came from. Guilt ran over his face, but he pushed it down, just as he had all those years before. Rebekah was the one at fault he assured himself. How dare she do such a thing? You couldn't just ignore the law because it suited you. If anyone knew that, he did. The law was his whole life. You had to keep the law!

Afterwards Rebekah wished she had had the courage to look up into Jesus' face, but instead she concentrated her gaze on the fine linen hem of his robe. She longed to grasp it in her hand, to cling to it and beg for mercy, but she disciplined herself not to touch him. She had done enough damage already.

Jesus looked first at Jairus and then at her. When at last he spoke, it wasn't what she expected at all, or what Jairus expected either for that matter.

'Daughter,' he said, 'your faith has healed you. Go in peace and be freed from your suffering.'

His words flowed down over Rebekah like the healing balm which soothed her hurts when she was a child. Unconsciously she had been holding her body rigid, waiting for his rebuke, but now everything in her relaxed. He had called her daughter and commended her faith! How was that possible? She knew only sweet release as he bade her go in peace and be free.

Jairus was unable to believe his ears. He wanted to correct Jesus - re-educate him - something. But as he looked at the simple goodness in the man's face, unexpected light burst upon him and he understood who it was who needed re-education. He saw who he was and he saw who Jesus was. He saw the harshness of the law and he saw the power of grace and he knew he would never be the same. It was a life changing revelation, but he had almost no time to take it in; the crowd parted to let Jonathan through and he knew his worst fears were realized.

'Hannah is dead,' Jonathan said hopelessly. 'Why bother the teacher anymore?'

Everything around Jairus turned black and he staggered momentarily. Jesus immediately put out a hand, but he shrugged it off. He did not want sympathy. If Jesus had come quicker, hadn't delayed to talk to Rebekah, perhaps Hannah would still be alive. Jesus reached out again gripping him by the arm, compelling him to look into his eyes.

'Don't be afraid,' he said, 'just believe!' Jairus withdrew his eyes from the urgency in Jesus' face to gaze at Rebekah who was still kneeling on the ground behind him. She smiled up at him and he stood transfixed, his eyes dilating with shock. Rebekah was radiant. Her pinched face, old long before its time, was transfigured, full of youth and vitality, just as Jairus remembered her on the day of her wedding. He looked back at Jesus in amazement. Who exactly was this man who could do miracles and who asked him to have faith even in the face of death? He looked down at Rebekah again. How could he not believe with her glowing eyes fixed upon him, declaring her healing? Somewhere inside a voice cried out, 'everything is happening too fast!' But he silenced it ruthlessly. Today was not the day for measured thinking. No! No! Today was the day for abandoned believing!

Swallowing hard he looked Jesus full in the face and gave one single nod of his head. Jesus hugged him as though he were relieved and immediately, they were once more swept up in swift events. Jesus spoke a word to his disciples and then he moved quickly up the road with Jairus towards his house. Only three disciples came with them. Jairus never worked out how they got rid of the crowd. That seemed like a miracle too.

Rebekah was still kneeling on the road when the children found her.

Sarah had run down towards the shore, only to find a slow-moving mass of people and Benjamin, sticking to the outside of the mob, hungry for excitement. Sarah grabbed him by the hand and tried to get to Jesus, but it was impossible and they were caught up and swept along with everyone else, past the entrance to the alley. Eventually they were crushed against a building on the other side of the road and watched helplessly as Jesus passed by in the middle of the street. The people were like an impenetrable wall. There was no way through as the crowd stopped and started erratically. Sarah pulled Benjamin into a narrow space between the houses and they managed to catch their breath. Jesus was some way ahead now and Sarah knew he couldn't make his way back to the alley. Her dreams for her mother's healing were shattered; and feeling utterly defeated, she hung her head. At first, she ignored Benjamin's attempts to speak to her, but eventually, when he pinched her arm, she turned to look at him.

'What?' she said indignantly.

'Look! Over there! On the other side of road! I think I just saw Mother!'

Sarah caught her breath, and began searching for some glimpse of Rebekah's familiar figure, but there was no sign of her. She shook her head, certain her sick Mother could not have come down the alleyway alone. Trust Benjamin to be seeing things!

All around, the crowd had begun to disperse and suddenly Benjamin grabbed her arm again, pointing to a gap appearing just where Jesus had been standing. They both gasped. There on the ground they could clearly see Rebekah kneeling in the dirt amongst all the people's feet. Instantly they began to fight their way through to her. Sarah was beside herself with worry, afraid she would be trampled in the crush. She knew Rebekah was weak, with no strength to get up and walk away and the people were still pushing and shoving all around her. When they finally reached her, they couldn't tell whether she had been hurt or not. She was still kneeling, leaning forward on her hands, with a dark patch appearing on the ground between them. The dusty road was soaking up her tears.

Sarah knelt beside her crying out in alarm, 'Mother, are you all right?'

Benjamin stood with his arms folded, uncomfortable because so many people were lingering close by and pointing at his mother. He felt anger stir inside him. What did they think they were looking at? He wished he was a man and could drive them all away, but he was just a boy, so he had to content himself with glaring at everyone belligerently. He did his best to shield Rebekah from their curious stares.

Sarah put her arm around her mother's thin shoulders and said again, 'Mother, are you all right?'

Rebekah lifted her head, and for a moment Sarah and Benjamin's faces both wore exactly the same expression. Their eyes grew wide and their mouths hung open in shock.

Benjamin stammered, 'Mmmother?' for he hardly recognized her. Never in his life had he seen his mother with colour in her cheeks, or with such a glorious smile. Her eyes were overflowing with tears, but still she looked young and happy, her face full of some extraordinary glow, as if a light had been lit inside her. It beamed out through every pore of her skin.

Sarah spoke the first thought which came into her head. 'Mother, you are beautiful!'

Rebekah laughed and hugged her. 'So are you, my darling!' she said, and then she turned to her son.

'Close your mouth Benjamin and come down here and embrace me.'

Benjamin shook himself as though he were waking from a dream. He knew it was his mother from her voice, but he still was finding it hard to believe what he was seeing. Rebekah and Sarah looked up at him together and he thought they looked like sisters, except Mother was more beautiful.

'Your face is full of light Mother. You look just like an angel,' he said, and Rebekah, looking from one face to the other, laughed delightedly. Benjamin threw himself down next to her and hugged her so violently Sarah protested.

'Be careful, Benjamin, you know Mother is ill.'

Rebekah pulled her daughter close with her free arm. 'Your brother is wiser than you are my sweet. I am no longer ill.'

Then in the midst of this scene of great joy Rebekah suddenly looked up and said, 'Jesus went to Jairus's house, didn't he?'

Benjamin shrugged his shoulders. 'We were stuck in the crowd and couldn't see.'

Rebekah looked at Benjamin without seeing him.

'Of course; he has gone to pray for Hannah.'

Her eyes sparkled, and she grabbed Benjamin by the hand. He was surprised at how strong her grip was.

'Run Benjamin to Jairus's house. Run and see what is happening.'

Benjamin struggled to his feet. 'Why?' he asked, not unwilling, but slightly confused.

'Go and see what happens, catch up with them if you can.' The urgency in her voice bewildered him.

'But,' he said,

'Run,' she insisted, 'run, run, run!'

New Life

Jairus stumbled as the sound of wailing floated down to him from the house. Jesus steadied him with a hand on his arm. There was a huge commotion with people all around the door, both those who loved his family, and those whose curiosity brought them to the home of the bereaved. The people parted as Abigail almost fell down the steps into his arms.

'Oh Jairus,' she whispered, broken hearted. Jairus held her tightly. Jesus walked calmly past them and into the house. Jairus quickly drew Abigail up the steps again, away from the stares of those outside.

The house was full of their family, aunts and uncles and cousins, all sobbing loudly and holding onto each other. It was the saddest scene. Jesus looked around him impatiently.

'Why all this commotion and wailing? The child is not dead but asleep,' he declared confidently.

There was a shocked silence and then several of the men laughed at him, while the women looked at each other indignantly. Did he think they didn't know the difference between death and sleeping? They felt insulted. Besides he hadn't even seen the child, so how would he know? They looked expectantly at Jairus who was speaking quietly to Abigail. He seemed unperturbed despite the fact he had brought a madman into the house. In fact, a great calm had fallen upon Jairus. He had seen the light in Rebekah's face and it was enough for him. Abigail fixed her eyes on Jesus and he smiled as though to reassure her. She smiled herself, more certain than ever she could trust him.

Jesus put everyone else out of the house, firmly, if not very politely. Jairus was amazed because he knew what his relatives were like, but inexplicably they all just did as they were told, with the disciples ushering them out onto the road and closing the door behind them. Taking a deep breath Jairus led Jesus and the disciples into the room where Hannah lay. Abigail hesitated by the door, unable to bear the sight of the small body lying motionless in the bed, but Jairus went immediately to the bedside and gazed down at his daughter in perplexity.

Where was Hannah? He shook his head, hardly recognizing the empty shell which lay before him. At first, he couldn't take it in, but after a few moments the truth dawned on him. Hannah was gone. Only her body had been left behind. His beloved Hannah was dead. He realized he hadn't really believed it up until then, had stupidly hoped there had been some mistake. He didn't move. He couldn't think, he couldn't breathe. The airless room closed in on him.

'Too late,' he murmured at last. 'Just too late.'

Jesus came to the other side of the bed and took hold of Hannah's cold, dead hand. Jairus wondered what he was going to do, but Jesus seemed unaware of him as he looked intently into the child's face. Then he spoke very clearly, 'Talitha koum!' (which means, "Little girl, I say to you, get up!").

Jairus had never heard such a tone before. It had an authority that seemed to reach far outside the confines of that familiar room, into some realm he had never been aware of. There was a silence, filled with tension, as though a struggle was being played out in the air all around them, and for a split second, although he could see nothing, he thought he felt something rising from the bed in front of him. Something indescribable. Like a dark breath it touched him fleetingly as it passed, and although everything appeared just as before, the hair on the back of his neck was standing up and a cold wave of disgust passed over him. He looked at Jesus in astonishment, his mind full of questions, but a second later he knew he should never have taken his eyes off Hannah, for there was a slight movement in the bed and then the sweet sound of a sigh.

He stood transfixed, distantly aware of Abigail's gasp behind him and Jesus helping Hannah up and leading her around the room by the hand. None of it was real to him. Stepping back from the bed, Jairus watched as Abigail enveloped Hannah in her embrace and then he looked up, opening his arms, abandoning himself to the wonder which flooded into the room as Hannah returned to life.

Later, when Jonathan asked him to describe what happened, he found it impossible. All he could say was it seemed heaven came and touched the earth and he was caught up in it. He laughed softly, for he was inundated with love, every breath full of it, every heartbeat thrilled with it. To Jairus if felt as if the love of parent for child, and lover for beloved, and friend for closest friend, had been distilled into its purest form and was filling the room with its fragrance. He could feel it in his veins! He was intoxicated. Putting his hand over his heart he knew the last traces of deadness were fading away and then his knees gently buckled as he fell to the floor in an ecstatic heap.

'Jacob,' he whispered, grinning, 'you should be here! You were right my friend. May God have mercy on me! You have always been right!'

Abigail and Hannah came to help him up. He hugged and hugged Hannah as though he would never let her go, then he sat on the bed one arm wrapped around her and Abigail standing beside him. Gently he ran his hand over Hannah's hair; overwhelmed with gratitude. The wonder of the miracle never left him.

He looked around the room. What had just happened here? Would he ever be able to explain it? Would anyone ever believe it?

He gazed at Jesus for a long time and felt understanding had come to him at last; revelation. No one needed to persuade him or cajole him into believing. Now he knew for himself. Jesus was the Messiah; the one long looked for! To him it was almost unbearably obvious. He knew without a doubt this was the baby Simeon had held in his arms, and that Levi, Jonathan, Abigail, all of them had seen much more clearly than he. He shook his head at his own blindness. Not only was Jesus the Messiah, but what a Messiah!

Jesus had raised his child from the dead and it wasn't because he was a righteous synagogue ruler. No, it had nothing to do with that at all. In fact, all his years of hard work had earned him nothing, because in the end the thing he needed most in life had turned out to be a free gift. Here in this room at last it all made sense to him. God's heart was a heart of love, Jesus had come to reveal that love, and Hannah was alive because of love. He laughed with wonder and Jesus looking down at him, laughed too.

Jesus sat on a chair and called Hannah to him. He took her onto his lap and putting his mouth near her ear he whispered to her. She looked very earnestly into his face and nodded enthusiastically. Then she threw her arms around his neck and kissed him. Jesus was obviously enjoying himself hugely and he laughed again when he saw the bemused faces before him. Peter, James and John looked as bewildered as Jairus felt, and only Abigail seemed able to cope, her hands clasped before her mouth, her eyes shining. Then a more serious look crossed Jesus' face.

'It is important you don't tell anyone about this,' he insisted.

Abigail stood up, looking at him in disbelief. 'How are we supposed to do that?' she queried. 'Half our relatives saw her dead body and the whole town knows you came here. What exactly are we supposed to say?'

Jesus shrugged his shoulders. 'Just do your best,' he said. 'We will slip away now. Wait a little while before you bring her out. He tipped Hannah's chin up and looked into her dancing eyes. 'And give her something to eat. You're starving, aren't you?'

Hannah nodded vigorously as Jesus gently put her off his lap.

Jairus came and stood before him, humbled, chastened, completely transformed. 'Can you forgive me?' he asked.

Jesus stood up and hugged him. 'I did not come to abolish the law, but to fulfil it Jairus, and God forgives anyone who asks him. Mercy triumphs over judgment! Always remember!'

'I will never forget,' Jairus promised solemnly and he never did.

Jesus beckoned to the disciples and made his way to the door. Peter stuck his head outside to make sure no one was around, but Jesus looked back at Hannah standing close to her mother. With a huge smile she lifted her hand to wave at him. His face alight with joy he beamed back at her, and then in a moment he was gone.

Benjamin picked up his heels and ran as fast as he could. He was confused and excited, all at the same time. What had happened to Mother? Where had the light come from that shone so brightly from her face? And why was it so important to find out what was happening at Jairus's house?

He arrived hot and panting, just in time to see Jesus and his disciples disappear with Jairus up the steps. He waited outside, gradually recovering his breath, wondering what it was he was watching for. He whiled away the time kicking a stone up and down the road. A large group of adults were standing around and they all frowned at him, as though he was being irreverent. He wondered if they were waiting for the same thing he was; whatever that was.

Suddenly, the door opened and a whole mass of indignant people poured out into the street. They were talking very loudly, although none of them seemed to be listening to each other, and the people outside buzzed around them like bees round the honeycomb. He went closer and heard their complaints that Jesus was a madman, had calmly declared the girl was not dead but asleep and then insisted they all leave. He thought it was all very confusing. Hannah couldn't really be dead, could she? Hannah was his age. Much too young to die! None of it made any sense to him. In the end he went to sit under a tree.

He hadn't been there very long when he noticed a woman watching him. She stared at him for a moment and then seeming to make up her mind she came and sat down next to him in the shade.

'I'm Tamar,' she said. 'You're Benjamin, aren't you? Rebekah and Jacob's boy?'

He nodded. 'How do you know that?' he asked. 'I don't know you, do I?'

She smiled. 'No, but someone mentioned your family to me and I have been looking out for you and your sister in the fish market.'

'Oh,' he said, losing interest.

'How is your mother?' she asked awkwardly.

'Well,' he said, 'I don't know really.' He scratched his head as he thought about it. 'Sarah and I found her kneeling on the road and her face was all sparkling or something, and then she sent me here, but I haven't got a clue what for.' He stopped for a moment and then he said, 'I think she might be better. I mean she hasn't been out in the street for ages and Jesus was in the street too, and hundreds of people, but something definitely happened to Mother.' He frowned and nodded his head. 'Yes, something definitely happened.'

'Jesus was there?'

'Yes, but he's here now, in Jairus's house. Didn't you see him go in?'

'No, I've only just got here. I came because someone told me Hannah was very ill, but no one bothered to tell me Jesus was arriving today!' Benjamin wondered who had made her angry.

'He hasn't been here long,' he said. 'Jairus came down to the lake and fetched him as soon as he got off the boat.'

'Jairus did?'

'Yes! Some people say Hannah has died, but Jesus said she is only asleep.'

'Only asleep!' the woman repeated, and she stared towards the closed door of the house.

Benjamin yawned. He found this conversation very boring. Why shouldn't Jairus go and get Jesus if Hannah was ill? He knew Father would go if it was Sarah. He was glad Tamar had stopped talking and wondered how long he was supposed to hang about in the noonday heat. He was hungry and thirsty and had just decided to go home and tell Mother nothing at all was happening, when he saw a movement out of the corner of his eye. Tamar saw it too and they both turned and looked down the side of the house. Benjamin watched with interest as a head appeared cautiously out of a doorway. It was one of the men who had been with Jesus. Tamar drew in a sharp breath and the man looked surprised to see her. Quickly he put his finger to his lips and shook his head as she started to get up. She sat down again, but Benjamin thought she looked more angry than ever.

'What is that idiot up to now!' she muttered under her breath.

They sat and watched as Jesus and two other men came cautiously out of the door and strode away towards the back of the house. As they turned the corner Benjamin knew they must be heading for the path which led down to the shore. He wondered if they were avoiding all the people on the road, and of course the path was much quicker! When they were out of sight the first man beckoned to Tamar, but she looked again towards the front door of the house and shook her head, saying under her breath, 'Abigail may need me.'

The man shrugged his shoulders and with one last backward glance he rushed off after Jesus. Benjamin shrugged his shoulders too; nothing seemed normal today.

After a while he began to doze and then there was another commotion which woke him up again. The woman sprang up as Jairus appeared in the doorway, holding up his hand to still the loud questions bombarding him.

'Hannah is better,' he said simply and then his solemn face split into a huge grin as though he couldn't contain himself. Unexpectedly, out of the door came the sound of Abigail singing and everyone turned to listen. In the sudden silence they heard the sweet music of Hannah's laughter. Jairus looked over his shoulder in wonder, and when he turned back the crowd saw his face was wet with tears. No one had ever seen that before. A man strode up and hugged him, clapping him on the back repeatedly.

'Praise God, praise God,' he said, while others pushed forward to embrace Jairus, their faces alight with joy. Everyone began to talk excitedly amongst themselves, until someone shouted out, 'But what happened, and where is Jesus?'

Ignoring the first question Jairus aimed at the truth for the second.

'I don't know,' he said.

Benjamin got to his feet, delighted to be able to tell everyone he knew exactly where Jesus was. He opened his mouth just as Tamar grabbed hold of his tunic, a warning look on her face. She needn't have worried, for Benjamin had already changed his mind. He shut his lips tight and said nothing. Tamar got up and stood beside him. Benjamin saw the relief on her face and he smiled to himself.

Leaning towards her he whispered, 'My mother says I am wiser than my sister Sarah. She will be pleased I kept Jesus' secret, won't she?' Tamar nodded, grinning at him and then to his unending embarrassment she reached out and hugged him! He didn't like that at all and she looked as surprised as he was.

Benjamin couldn't decide what to do next. Some of the people disappeared inside with Jairus, and Tamar watched them, rubbing her hands on her skirt, unsure whether to go over to the house or not. Just then a young girl came out of the door. She hesitated, scanning the crowd, and after slowly coming down the steps she walked towards them. Benjamin watched as she approached. He wondered what she wanted.

'Hello Tamar,' the girl said in a faint voice.

'Hello Miriam'

Tamar looked into her face and instinctively reached out a hand. 'Are you well Miriam? You look very pale.'

The girl shuddered and pulled her shawl up over her head. 'I was inside earlier with the family, before Jesus arrived. We came to support Abigail. Jairus wasn't there and she needed us.'

She was silent for a moment, biting her lip and then she said in a rush. 'Hannah was dead. Really dead! I saw her. She was cold and white, different even from how she's been over the last few days. Her body was empty or something. I've never seen a dead body before. It was horrible!'

Tamar nodded, remembering the tiny stillborn child her mother had laid in her arms all those years before. 'I know,' she said. 'But Hannah is…' she hesitated, unsure how to express it, 'she is alive now, isn't she?'

Miriam passed her hand across her eyes. 'Yes, yes. I've been inside and seen her. She is eating a meal and laughing, but how can she be? She was dead, and seeing her full of life again is almost more frightening than…. Oh! I can't explain it.'

Tamar hesitated for a moment and then she took the girl into her arms. 'It's all right, you are allowed to be shocked,' she said. 'You have seen a miracle and they can be hard to cope with!'

Miriam began to weep. 'I thought we had lost her forever.' she sobbed. Tamar patted her gently.

'I know, I know,' she whispered. After a while Miriam dried her eyes on the edge of her shawl and smiled at Tamar.

'You weren't here earlier, were you? I was looking for you.'

'Me? Why?'

Miriam's face was full of pain. 'None of us could be of any help to Abigail. We could only stand and watch as Hannah faded away. It was terrible. Everything in me went cold, as though I was dying too. But Abigail never gave up hope. She kept saying, "It will be all right when Jesus comes," over and over again, and she asked for you.'

'For me?'

'Yes, I think she needed someone who believed as much as she did. You do, don't you?'

'Believe in Jesus? Oh yes, I do! But raising the dead? That's incredible!'

Miriam shut her eyes and sighed. 'Yes, it was. After Hannah died, Mother and the other women started wailing. I thought Abigail was going to hit them. I don't know what would have happened if Jairus and Jesus hadn't arrived. Jesus made us all leave. I was glad to go, but Mother was furious. We were sitting outside and I was trying to calm her down. She was beside herself. She loved…. I mean loves, Hannah so much. She was absolutely livid when Jesus said Hannah was only asleep. She felt insulted, as if she couldn't tell the difference, and now Jairus has forbidden the whole family to tell anyone Hannah was dead, so we are all going to look like fools. Of course, that's not important. Mother is inside now, almost dancing with joy, and Hannah is alive. That is the important thing. But somehow, I want someone to know what a miracle it was. What Jesus did. You believe me don't you Tamar? You know it is true!'

'Oh yes, I know it's true. It's all true. Heal the sick, cast out demons, raise the dead. I think Jesus can do just about anything.'

Miriam laughed uncertainly. 'Thank goodness!' she said, and Tamar laughed too and hugged her as if they were old friends.

Benjamin looked on. He'd only been interested in what Miriam had to say about the dead body. He'd seen a dead goat once. It was horrible and smelly. He was sure Hannah couldn't have looked anything like that and anyway even though she'd been dead, now apparently, she was alive again. Except no one was supposed to know! No wonder this girl was confused. He was confused himself.

Suddenly it dawned on him. This must be the thing Mother had sent him to find out about. Mother had guessed Jesus was going to do another miracle and she'd been right! He stamped his foot at the thought that two miracles had happened and he hadn't seen either of them. It was just not fair!

He left the two women standing in the street. He was determined, even if it was a secret that Hannah had been raised from the dead, he was still going to tell Mother, and that he had kept Jesus' other secret as well! He thought one thing was especially important. Hannah was eating!

His own hunger drove him home.

Sarah supported her mother as they walked slowly towards the alley. Rebekah felt wonderful, but her legs were still thin and she was trembling from head to toe. It took them some time to reach the house.

'Tell me what happened,' begged Sarah as she helped her into her chair.

'Not yet. I need time. Could you fetch me a drink and some food? No wait I will go and see your grandmother first. Oh dear, I can't think straight.'

She laughed uncertainly and then she sat staring out of the window for a moment. When her eyes focused back into the room she said in wonder, 'I am healed!' and she reached out and grasped Sarah by the hand. 'You were right, absolutely right, Jesus was able to heal me. Even a poor unclean woman like me! It's a miracle!'

And then she laughed and cried, unable to speak while Sarah, as attentive as ever, fetched bread and cheese and the honeyed drink Rebekah loved. When she had eaten, she sat for a long time with her eyes shut while Sarah sat at her feet and just watched her. The light wasn't fading from her face and huge tears ran down Sarah's as she gazed and gazed at her own personal miracle. Then quite unexpectedly Rebekah's eyes opened, and they were sparkling with such life and vitality Sarah blinked in surprise.

'Come on Sarah, let's clean the house!'

Sarah blinked again. 'Clean?' she queried.

'Yes,' said Rebekah joyfully. 'I've been waiting for years for this!'

So, they cleaned, as Rebekah sang and danced around the room. It seemed the more she cleaned the stronger she got, and Sarah marvelled at where her energy was coming from. While they were in the midst of sweeping, Benjamin returned. His mother pounced on him,

'What happened Benjamin? Tell me everything!'

He grinned from ear to ear. 'Well,' he said, 'there is a lot to tell, but I need food or I may faint from hunger and not be able to remember anything.'

'Feed him at once,' commanded Rebekah laughing, and they sat around the table while Benjamin crammed his mouth with food and garbled the whole story at the same time. Sarah grew impatient, but Rebekah only laughed all the more. Once she had heard Hannah was healed, nothing else really mattered.

At the end Benjamin said, 'But the best thing of all Mother, is I kept Jesus' secret. He slipped away down an alley and this lady and I were the only ones to see him, but we didn't say anything about it, and then later on everyone was asking where he was, and she thought I was going to tell them, which I could have done, but I didn't, and she was very pleased with me, and I knew you would be too!'

Rebekah kissed him. 'Of course, I am pleased with you. I have the best son and daughter in the whole world, and now I must go and see my mother.'

Jacob returned late into the night. His long delay in the desert had meant his business had taken much longer than expected. He was worried about Rebekah. He knew she would be asleep by now, but how had Sarah managed being left alone for so long? He wished Jocabed was well enough to care for the family as once she had. He sat wearily in a chair. He tried to remember what he had done after he had finally resumed his journey, but the whole day was a blur to him. He had almost turned for home, but his sense of responsibility held him to his original purpose. Presumably he had conducted his business and struck a good bargain. He had no idea.

He shook his head as he tried to recall the long walk home. Jairus had been at the center of his thoughts as hour after hour he had been thinking and forgiving, weeping and being healed. He knew he was different, and life was bubbling up from some forgotten place. He wondered how Hannah was, how Abigail was, and how he was going to explain to Jairus why, after all these years, he had forgiven him. Would Jairus even care?

Carrying a light into the children's room he looked at them lovingly; his precious children. Sarah shouldering the responsibility that was too old for her and Benjamin, loving the lake, always trying to evade his share. What had they been doing today? He sighed and turned away.

He entered the bedroom as quietly as possible although he knew it would make no difference. Rebekah slept deeply and long, worn out by her illness. The room was dark, but he knew his way around it, recognizing the dim shape of Rebekah's bed and beyond it his own. Despite his fatigue he guessed he wouldn't sleep. This had been the most momentous day, he could hardly explain it to himself; he needed to think how he would share it with Rebekah.

Rebekah's voice, though hushed to a whisper, made him jump. 'Jacob!'

He frowned with surprise. Not only was Rebekah never awake, but her voice held some quality he didn't recognize. His heart missed a beat. Was she worse? He hurried to her side and knelt upon the floor.

'Are you ill?' he asked foolishly.

She chuckled in the darkness and to his utter amazement reached out a hand to touch his face.

'Not now, my darling, not now.'

They both knew the marriage bed law, the days of waiting after a woman's period finished, the ceremonial bath, where every part of her body was immersed to ensure complete cleansing, and then the thrill of coming together again. They hadn't been through that ritual for twelve long years, for in all that time Rebekah's flow had never stopped. Wonder flooded over Jacob as Rebekah cast the tradition aside. She drew him into her arms, silencing his protest with her kisses, murmuring constantly, 'Jesus healed me, Jesus healed me, I am clean, completely clean.'

At first, he held himself back, years of self-control restraining him, but then, quite suddenly every barrier collapsed and he began to smother her with kisses. He couldn't speak, he didn't want to speak as the glory of touching her overwhelmed his soul, only he repeated her name again and again, as though he would never tire of the sound of it.

Later, as she lay in the darkness, Rebekah placed a hand upon her stomach. She had forgotten what feeling well was like! Life was coursing through her veins and she wondered if she might be pregnant, one miracle following hard upon another. Waves of joy made her skin tingle, she and Jacob were one again, in love again, thrilling to each other's touch. Not even the tiniest hint of doubt came to trouble her. Although no words could explain it, she knew she was healed, head to toe and inside out. It was as though the years of bitterness had never been and she was whole again.

Hearing a strange sound beside her she reached out a hand to Jacob. For years he had trained himself to weep silently, but now he turned and burying his face in her hair he released the grief he had always hidden from her. Rebekah soothed him, kissing his hands again and again.

'It's over darling,' she whispered. 'I'm healed, I am truly healed! Jesus has set me completely free.'

Later, as he lay quietly in her arms, she began to tell him the whole story. It was as if she were recounting a dream, so improbable it seemed, yet, caught up as he was in his own miracle, he never doubted the truth of it.

The only question he asked was, 'What time were you healed?' It didn't surprise him to learn it was at exactly the same hour when he had been lying on the desert floor, yielding to God; Jairus's face before him. He spoke reverently into the darkness, 'Thank you. Thank you for saving us.'

Shutting her eyes, Rebekah murmured a heartfelt, 'Amen.'

Jacob wondered if he would ever sleep again. The presence of God was very near, he drew it in with every breath and he knew he also had been healed. Deep inside he could feel his love for God springing up, renewed like a withered desert plant at the first hint of rain. Rebekah listened to the prayers pouring out of him and felt herself the sense of presence in the darkness. It was as though heaven had come down and filled their bedroom, and this husband she loved was met at last in the fullness of its reality. The years of emptiness melted away. She did not know what tomorrow might bring, but this she was sure of - Jacob would find Jesus and follow him. Perhaps tonight was all she would have of him. She bit her lip. How could she bear to lose him? In the midst of all this joy, must another sorrow be faced? She brushed the tears away. Jesus deserved everything and could ask anything. They owed him so much. If her beloved husband left Capernaum to be with Jesus; so be it. As Jacob had done, only hours before, she yielded to her maker, gratitude overwhelming sacrifice. Like the many millions who followed after her, she began to understand the cost of following the Christ.

As the first glimmers of morning light fell upon Rebekah's face, Jacob stared at her, mesmerized by the beauty of her skin, the radiance of her smile. Then he leapt out of bed with a great whoop of delight and began to sing at the top of his voice. Rebekah sat up in bed.

'Jacob, you will disturb the whole neighbourhood,' she remonstrated.

Jacob ran to the window and shouted, 'Rebekah is healed, Rebekah is healed!'

The children ran in and he embraced them, beside himself with joy, and Sarah gasped with amazement as he pulled Rebekah from the bed and spun her off her feet. Just for a moment his face changed, for she weighed no more than a child, but seconds later the stomach-churning fear was gone, swept away by her laughter.

They were a family again.

Jacob hurried up the road. The need to speak to Jairus filled his thoughts.

After their early awakening Rebekah had baked bread, taking such pleasure in this simple task he could hardly take his eyes off her. As they ate, he began to share with her what had happened in the desert, but there was no time for detail for before they had finished their meal, family, friends and the downright curious were knocking on the door, demanding to see her.

He wanted to stay, but she whispered to him, 'Slip away and see Jairus. Go now while you can still get out of the door!'

Although there were many things for him to talk to Rebekah about and decisions which had to be made, he knew there would be no opportunity in such a crowd. He pushed his way out into the alley and to his amazement there was Benjamin striding towards him, holding a stool in his hand.

'Father!' Jacob cried and ran towards him.

Benjamin dropped the stool and flung his arms around his son.

'I came to see Rebekah! The news is all over town! Your mother is on her way, but I ran on ahead because I had to speak to you.'

'No, Father, it is I who must speak to you. I am so sorry for the hard-hearted idiot I have been! Can you forgive me?'

Benjamin looked into his face. 'What happened to you? Why this change of heart? Is this the result of Rebekah's healing?'

'No, it is the result of me making my peace with God!'

Benjamin nodded with satisfaction. 'Well, it's about time!' he said, and he slapped Jacob on the back.

'I will explain it all to you later, but now I have to go and find Jairus.'

'Very good,' said Benjamin, 'but you can't run off until I tell you what I came for.'

'Quickly then Father, I am in a hurry.'

'Don't rush an old man!' Benjamin bent down and picked up the stool he had been carrying.

'Do you recognize this?'

Jacob looked confused. 'Of course, it is my stool from the spice-stall. Didn't you throw it away?'

'No, I kept it, and what a good job I did! I have been sitting on it for years and every so often I would try to remember the name of the boy who made it. It seemed important somehow! Do you remember Jacob?'

Jacob tried to keep his impatience out of his voice. 'No, I don't. Is this really important now?'

Benjamin gripped him by the arm. 'Think, Jacob, think! You must remember. It came to me this morning. We bought it in Nazareth! Nazareth!'

Jacob looked at him blankly and then down at the stool in his hand. Slowly a look of wonder came onto his face and reaching out he took the stool and ran his hand over the surface.

'Jesus!' he said.

Benjamin looked triumphant. 'Exactly!' he said.

Jacob's face was alight. 'All these years we had something he had made, and I never knew how important he was.'

Benjamin nodded his head. 'His father said he had a destiny beyond carpentry. We should have believed him!'

Jacob looked lovingly at the stool. 'I have been so wrong about him,' he said.

'Well frankly Jacob you have been wrong about a lot of things, Jairus included. But today is a new beginning. I'll take the stool into the house. I expect Rebekah needs it. Hurry along now and find Jairus, and don't stop and waste time chatting with anyone!'

'Yes Father,' Jacob said submissively, but there was laughter in his voice.

The alley was jammed with people on their way to his house, but no one took the slightest notice of him as he walked away. Everyone had come to see Rebekah. He looked around him, knowing he was retracing Rebekah's steps from the day before. Everything looked the same, yet nothing was, or ever could be again. In the main road he hesitated at the spot she had described. How he wished he had seen her healed. He knew it had happened, right here, but still he found it hard to believe! He was convinced the very moment he forgave Jairus was the moment of her healing. He would never know for certain of course, yet he was certain the two things were linked. He gave another prayer of thanksgiving and as he looked up, he saw

Jairus coming towards him. He wasn't really surprised. Jairus had experienced the power of Jesus too. It was time for them to talk.

Jairus quickened his pace as he caught sight of Jacob and reaching him, he stepped aside into a quiet corner hidden from the road. Jacob followed him without a word. They needed privacy.

'Jairus,' Jacob started, but Jairus held up his hand to silence him. The synagogue ruler seemed different and Jacob looked enquiringly into his face. Was he really holding back emotion; self-controlled Jairus?

'I was coming to see you Jacob to ask you to forgive me!' Jacob's eyebrows flew up in surprise. 'I should never have treated Rebekah as I did,' Jairus rushed on. He stood for a moment looking at the ground, too ashamed to lift his head. When he looked up, he gazed intently into Jacob's face, as though willing him to understand.

'It was the law you see. The law was all I had! I wasn't like you, always looking deeper, always searching. For me it was very clear and simple. I had to stick to the law and the traditions of the elders. They were solid and dependable. God had to be pleased because I was working hard at doing my best. That's what I thought. But I was wrong, so horribly wrong!'

He stopped for a moment as though remembering. 'Oh Jacob, if you could have seen Jesus with Rebekah! He just loved her. I was rooted to the spot. There I was, her friend for years, and I had completely rejected her. But Jesus received her. He was not angry or distant; not like me. She was healed, Jacob, not just of the sickness, but all the anguish she has suffered as an unclean woman. I saw it in her face. She was radiant, simply radiant.'

Jacob chuckled to himself. 'You should see her this morning,' he said.

Jairus reached out a hand to his friend. 'You must forgive me Jacob, you and Rebekah.'

Jacob looked inside to the place where all his bitterness had been. There was nothing left except gratitude for the goodness of God. He smiled and looked almost as radiant as his wife. 'If you had asked me this time yesterday, I would certainly have hit you,' he said. 'But today everything is different. Rebekah is coming to see Abigail and Hannah later and as for me….'

Jairus searched his face, looking for mercy.

'I forgave you yesterday, old friend. All is forgiven and forgotten. Jesus has changed everything for both of us. I need your forgiveness too. I have held anger and resentment, even hatred, in my heart towards you.'

Now it was his turn to look intently into the face of the other. 'Forgive me Jairus,' he said. Jairus didn't answer, he just took Jacob in his arms and hugged him until Jacob thought his bones would break. When at last he released him, Jairus beamed at him.

'So now we begin again,' he said, and Jacob thought he had never seen his friend look so happy.

'Jairus,' he said, 'you must tell me about Hannah. Benjamin brought home some garbled story about her having died. But that's not true, is it? Jesus healed her, didn't he?'

Jairus leaned his back against the wall and shook his head. 'No, he didn't heal her.' he said. 'We came too late.'

Jacob's face grew pale as he saw a look almost of fear in Jairus's eyes.

'Oh Jacob, my friend,' he whispered, 'I wish you had been there. He didn't heal her; he raised her from the dead!' The words seemed to hang in the air. What impossible words, Jacob thought, as impossible as, "Rebekah is healed." Jairus's face crumpled and Jacob stepped forward and took him in his arms.

Long shuddering sobs wracked Jairus's body as though he had held himself together for years, waiting for his friend to be there to comfort him. Jacob spoke gently to him as if he were a child, 'It's all right Jairus,' he said. 'Everything is all right now.'

Eventually Jairus stood with his head on Jacob's shoulder. Jacob could hardly imagine what depths of despair his friend had experienced, what strength and fortitude he must have displayed for Abigail's sake. Raised from the dead? Jacob still struggled to believe it, yet he knew this man of solid integrity would never lie or exaggerate. It must be the simple truth. Jairus lifted his head and grinned sheepishly.

'I have wept more in the last day than I have in a lifetime.' he said ruefully.

Jacob laughed. 'I could never be the one to criticize you for that, could I?'

They stood together for a while, Jacob longing for more information, but unwilling to push Jairus until he was ready.

'You and Rebekah will come and share a meal with us, then we will tell you all about it. It will be an honour to entertain you in our home.'

'It must be very soon,' said Jacob, 'for I plan to leave almost immediately.'

'Leave?' said Jairus. 'So soon after Rebekah's healing?'

'Yes,' said Jacob, 'I cannot afford to wait. I must follow soon or I will lose sight of him.'

Jairus's brows twitched together in a sudden frown. 'You will become a disciple?'

'Of course,' said Jacob. 'I promised God that if he healed Rebekah, I would give him my whole life. Such as it is! Years ago, Levi spoke of this day. I know you remember. I cannot let personal considerations delay me.'

'But Rebekah?' said Jairus.

Jacob nodded his agreement. 'It will be hard, but she is encouraging me to go. She wants me to meet Jesus for myself.'

'But doesn't he have his band of hand-picked disciples already?'

'Yes, that is true,' said Jacob, 'but there are many others who follow him. I will join them, learn his teachings, serve him in any way I can. I wasn't born to be a merchant Jairus, I have always known that. After all that has happened, I am sure he is the Messiah. I will follow him. I must.'

'He is certainly the Messiah,' said Jairus and then he put back his head and laughed. 'Do you know the first thing Jonathan said to me when Jesus landed on the shore? He ran up to me and said, "He is here! He is here!" It was just as though Levi had reached out a hand to touch me from the past. You have to see him Jacob, such grace and peace is upon him. It is remarkable.'

'He sounds like Levi,' said Jacob.

'Yes, Levi was like that too, but on Jesus it is intensified as though his goodness could burn a hole in you and reach inside to your very soul. His love is so great I found I didn't want to keep him out. He has changed me forever.'

Jacob looked at him in amazement. 'So, you have become a believer too!'

Jairus nodded absently, but he looked troubled. 'How can I follow him? There is the synagogue to consider and Abigail and Hannah.'

Jacob shook his head. 'You must stay here and teach the people to love him Jairus. At least for as long as they will let you! I foresee there will be problems ahead for both of us. Levi spoke of that also, didn't he?'

'Of course, of course,' said Jairus, brushing such an irrelevance aside. 'Do you really think I can follow him here, without leaving my family?'

'Of course, of course,' Jacob mimicked. 'Come Jairus, we should both return home. We will talk more, eat together. I remember Abigail's cooking very well.'

'It shall be a feast of celebration,' said Jairus. 'Bring the children. Our families have been separated for far too long, and who knows what may happen between your Benjamin and Hannah!'

Jacob laughed. 'I remember where that thought comes from, but I was joking all those years ago when they were babies. We cannot scheme Jairus. They must decide for themselves.'

'That is not our tradition,' said Jairus in a serious voice, but Jacob only laughed again and linked his arm into his friend's. They walked back out into the road, and people eyed them with interest, these two men at the center of the most astounding events. Jacob and Jairus ignored the stares and the whispered comments, standing facing each other in the morning light. Without a word being spoken they both knew another, less spectacular miracle had just occurred. A miracle of reconciliation.

'It was Levi's desire we should be brothers,' Jairus said. Jacob met him eye to eye.

'I believe all followers of Jesus will one day be called brothers. May we be the first!'

'Amen!' said Jairus devoutly and they embraced once more.

Levi's spiritual sons. Joined at last in the Messiah.

Epilogue

The two men hammered urgently on the door. Levi's eldest son answered it as quickly as he could. Levi was seated in his favourite chair; shrunken almost to skin and bone, an extremely old man.

They begged to be allowed to speak to him.

'We have just come from Jerusalem.'

'It is late and he is very tired, you must return in the morning.'

The shorter of the two shook his head. 'We have to go back to Jerusalem immediately, but we couldn't leave without speaking to him.'

The sound of Levi's frail voice surprised them all. 'Let them in. I know that accent.'

His son clicked his tongue impatiently. 'Now you have woken him up,' he said.

The taller man looked positively distracted. 'We must speak to him,' he insisted.

Their air of scarcely suppressed excitement finally convinced him. 'Oh, very well, but only for a few minutes. No catching up on years of news, not that the news from Jerusalem isn't enough to keep us all talking for hours. Come in, come in.'

The men walked softly over to Levi's chair. He peered at them in the gloom for the lamps had not yet been lit.

'Jacob? Jairus?' he queried. 'Is it really you?' They knelt down in front of him and kissed his hands.

'Yes, dear Rabbi, it is us your two Galilean sons,' said Jairus; and Levi chuckled as they embraced him.

'I knew I would see you both again, but you have been a long time coming. How are things in Capernaum? And what have you two been up to? Have you been in Jerusalem? Have you brought news? Are you following him as I told you? I have heard about him; such incredible tales. What has been going on in the city? He is there I know.'

He waved a hand at his son who had brought chairs and drinks for the travellers.

'I told the family he is the Messiah, but they don't believe me. They think I am just a fanciful old man. Well, I hate being old, but I have simply refused to die until his day had dawned.'

'Don't agitate yourself father, or I shall have to ask your guests to leave.'

Levi whispered, 'Don't grow old, your children start to control your life!'

Jairus looked up at Levi's son who stood close by. 'Have you heard nothing of Jesus over the past few days?' A warning look came over the man's face and he shook his head. Levi looked from one to the other.

'They are keeping something from me. They whisper in corners. Come Jairus tell me the truth, you could never lie to me. What is the news from Jerusalem?'

Jairus looked again at Levi's son who sighed resignedly. 'All right, you can tell him. I suppose he will have to know sometime.'

Jairus and Jacob exchanged glances and it was Jacob who spoke. 'Jesus was tried and convicted on false evidence. The Romans crucified him at Golgotha.'

Levi's son came and gripped his shoulder. 'I'm sorry Father,' he said.

Levi frowned, looking from Jairus's face to Jacob's and back again.

'You followed him from Galilee and after he was brutally murdered you made this journey to come and tell me?'

'Yes,' said Jacob.

Levi looked up at his son. 'Go away,' he said.

'But Father!'

'Don't "but Father" me. These men have something to say to me and I don't need you to be listening. I may not have very long to live, so surely I can be allowed one private conversation?'

His son shrugged his shoulders hopelessly and left the room.

Levi leaned forward. 'You two do not have the look of men bearing terrible news. What is it? What can't you go back to Jerusalem without telling me?'

Jacob didn't even bother to deny it. 'It's all true, the crucifixion, the burial, everything. Jairus and I couldn't bear to stay in Jerusalem so we decided to travel here to Emmaus to see you. We were devastated, but as we walked along the road a man joined us.'

'We had never met him before,' continued Jairus, 'but he was fascinating. He talked to us about Jesus and explained to us from the scriptures that he had to die! It made such sense Levi. I wish you could have heard him. His knowledge of scripture was outstanding.'

'Anyway,' said Jacob butting in, 'when we got here to the Inn, he wanted to keep on traveling, but we had planned to have a meal and then come and see you in the morning, so we invited him to stay and eat with us.'

There was a pause.

'And?' said Levi.

Jairus looked around to make sure they were really alone, and then he said,

'Now this is the part you may find it difficult to believe....'

Printed in Great Britain
by Amazon

86874787R00180